Crimson Return

Daelynn Quinn

Copyright © Erin Meredith 2013

All Rights Reserved

ISBN: 1491084731

ISBN-13: 978-1491084731

Prologue

Dear Drake,

To say I miss you is like saying the summers have gotten a little warm. The world has gone to hell and beyond since you died. A virus was developed and released by three very rich, very powerful people that they are calling the Trinity. It has destroyed nearly every living species in the animal kingdom. They blamed the southern region of Deimos where you were deployed, but it's clear now that the Deimosians had nothing to do with it. Now I find myself wondering whether the war was even legit, or if it was simply a ploy set up by the Trinity to point fingers.

Evie and I were both very fortunate and survived the fallout because we carry the genetic double mutation that gives us immunity. Mom and dad didn't make it. But if your soul still exists on some metaphysical plane you probably already know that. Evie and I were abducted and taken to live at Crimson State Penitentiary (although they call it Crimson Survivor Refuge now, as if that makes it any less of a prison). Glenn was there and he became one of them—Enforcers, they call them, the ones who side with Crimson and keep the prisoners in line. Needless to say, we are no longer engaged. But I knew something was amiss and I managed to escape and take Evie with me. We are both safe now.

Speaking of Evie, Drake I don't know how to raise her and its making me a nervous wreck. How can I go from being the fun aunt to a mother for her? I care for her and love her like a daughter, but I'm so scared I'll do something wrong and put her in danger—like I did with Lex. I could never forgive myself if anything happens to her.

On a brighter note, the virus and our captivity at Crimson brought Marcus and I together. You'd like

Marcus. He's a wonderful father figure for Evie and treats me like a goddess. We've been living at the COPS headquarters for three months now and the three of us are a happy family. I wish you were here with us, but it's probably best you're not.

If mom and dad are with you tell them I love and miss them.

Love,
Pollen

Chapter 1

MY EYES NARROW and my senses open up to the pulse of energy ahead of me. I can't see him, but I can feel his presence. I can almost hear his heartbeat and the quiet inhale of his raspy breath. My finger tightens around the trigger of the pistol in my hands, even though the handle is slippery from the sweat glazing my palms.

The tree that guards me is narrow, barely wide enough to hide my body, but that doesn't matter. It's *my* turn to pursue. It is Yoric who must run and keep hidden.

A stirring in the trees above me tears my attention away from my prey. It is Timber, a fitting name for a girl who loves to climb trees. Her short, ashen hair and muted gray clothing blend in so well with the tree bark it's nearly impossible for anyone to see her. She nods her head and signals me to move forward. I move ahead and stiffen at a cracking noise as I step on a twig. I remind myself to be lighter on my feet. There's a rustling about ten feet ahead of me, too unnatural to be the warm gusty breeze on this mildly blustery day.

The overcast sky kills any chances of seeing shadows among the trees. I haven't seen the actual sun since we've been here. In fact, I can't remember the last time the sky was cloudless. Even sunny days carry a thick reddish haze in the sky. Seems like air pollution has gotten worse since the virus, which is strange considering there aren't as many people around to cause it.

I inch closer and closer, gingerly placing my toes to make as little noise as possible. My own thumping heart bursts up into my throat at the sound of an explosive *POW* from behind me. The shot just barely grazes my right cheek, leaving a thin streak of cobalt blue upon my skin. I turn back and fire two rounds, which miss their target, but Timber is already firing at Jansen, who is now on the retreat. A splatter of red coats his back and he lies face down on the ground.

My attention turns back toward Yoric, who is now fleeing and within sight. I shoot at him and miss. Two more shots manage to hit a tree and a thorn bush. I curse at myself silently. I have one round left. I've got to make this count. I've found in my training that I'm a great shot when standing still. But on the move I can't hit a target if it was standing three feet in front of me doing a happy dance.

Unfortunately for me, Yoric is running and I have no time to stop and aim. He enters a small clearing and I know this is my only chance. I raise my pistol and charge forward, pulling the trigger just as my toe catches a protruding tree root and I land on my chest with my arms extended forward.

I raise my head in defeat. Yoric stands above me like a grisly giant, carrying an impish grin on his face. A splash of red drips down the sleeve of his army green shirt and onto his bulging bicep. Some clumps of long flaxen hair have come loose from his ponytail and hang clumsily over his baby blue eyes. He squats down and snatches my gun, which I dropped during my fall. After checking the magazine briefly, he stands up and shoves the gun down the back of his pants.

"Looks like you're unarmed, sweetie. Better luck next time," he says as he pulls a gun from his thigh holster. I thought he was out of rounds, but I was wrong. He pulls out some blue bullets from his pocket and begins loading his magazine.

Without giving it a second thought, I roll over and leap to my feet. My speed and experience being chased are now working to my advantage. I look back and see him chasing me, but I dodge left and right, evading the two bullets he shoots my way. Yoric is an excellent shot, but not a very fast runner, and I am able to put a good distance between us.

I find a large oak to hide behind while I catch my breath and compose myself. Sitting with my back against the trunk I unstrap my holster from my leg and unwind the rubber band from around my ponytail. I made my own holster shortly after I began training here at Celadon Botanical Research Center, CBRC or

Ceborec for short, headquarters of the Committee for the Oversight of Planetary Salvation, or COPS.

Residents are required to train in weapons combat and self-defense in case of an incursion by Crimson Enforcers. We were introduced to several different types of weapons; everything from a wide range of firearms to simple daggers for hand combat. I found that I had a knack for using a slingshot. But since slingshots won't do much damage, I was encouraged to take up firearm training primarily and use a slingshot as a back up. So, with Marcus's help, I built my own holster from molded leather and acrylic to act as a slingshot frame, complete with a foldout wrist brace. I use the elastic from the slingshot as a hair band so that if I am ever captured and my gun confiscated, I will still be armed. And since it is a primitive weapon, I can use just about anything I can hold as a projectile.

I quickly slide out the recessed forks until I hear them click into place and attach the elastic sling to the holster with snap-in rivets. I have a few extra bullets in my pocket so I load one of them into the sling and turn to face my pursuer. But he is not there.

My eyes shut instinctively so I can refocus my senses and listen. The faint sound of rustling leaves can be heard, but not near me. He must have doubled back to where Timber was in the tree.

Although I'm sure I'm in the clear, I peer around the tree to ensure nobody is around before running tree to tree to make my way back to Timber.

In the distance Timber is gracefully climbing down the maple. She makes tree-climbing look so natural. But beyond the tree I spot that familiar scruffy blond hair peeking up over a bush. Timber is facing my direction but before I can get her attention, a shot rings out and she is down. Yoric approaches her and bends over to whisper something in her ear. She swats an arm at him and misses. He stands back up, proudly grinning, and places one boot upon her back to hold her down.

As he stands there, reveling in his victory, I take aim. Squinting my eyes to narrow my focus, I pull back the pouch of the slingshot, holding the red pellet in place. The gust of wind blows from the west, adding an air of suspense to the moment. I release the sling and within a second, Yoric is on his back, red paint splattered across his chest.

"Damn!" he shouts, kicking his feet on the ground.

Timber climbs to her feet and brushes the leaves off her clothes as I approach them.

"Nice shot, Pollen," she gloats cheerfully.

"Thanks," I say. "And thanks for covering me. I didn't even hear Jansen behind me."

"Yeah," says Jansen stepping out from behind a tree. "I have twinkle toes. Ballet may not be manly, but it's definitely got its advantages." Jansen used to be a ballet dancer before the planet went to hell. He danced for a big company in Tarnov, one of the major cities in North Cythera known for its support of the arts. And by the look of him ballet definitely has its advantages. He is not much taller than me, but his small frame is extremely muscular. I swear he hasn't got an inch of fat on his whole body. If I were fighting hand-to-hand combat, I would definitely want Jansen on my team. I just hope he never gets hit in the face—his features are just too pretty to mutilate.

"Perhaps, but I had the advantage over you this time," laughed Timber.

Yoric gets up to his feet and studies the red splotch on his shirt. "Man, I would have won if you hadn't cheated!" He glares at me.

"Cheated? How do you mean?" I ask lowering my eyebrows inquisitively.

"Only one weapon allowed, remember? That's the rule. And since I took your weapon," Yoric says as he pulls my pistol from his pants and drops it on the ground, "you had to have brought another one. Therefore you cheated."

I pick up my pistol and dust it off, while Timber picks crinkled leaves out of Yoric's disheveled ponytail. "I didn't cheat. There are no rules against fashioning your own weapon upon disarmament. In fact that's what any skilled soldier would do. I simply crafted a slingshot out of my holster and hairband. You could have done the same."

"I'd have to agree with Pollen this time Yoric," says Jansen.

"Dude, you're on my team," shouts Yoric.

"Sorry, man. She's right," Jansen responds.

Yoric presses his lips together in frustration. He really wants to say something but can't seem to find the words. His agitation eats at him and he waves his arms around, pushing Timber's hands away from his hair.

"Don't worry, we'll get them next time," Jansen reassures.

"Damn right we will!" Yoric declares as he storms away.

"He'll be okay," Jansen says. "Good game today." He holds out his right hand in a friendly gesture. Timber takes it first and then I follow.

"Do you guys want to meet up again the day after tomorrow?" asks Timber.

"Sure," replies Jansen, "we'll meet you at the armory at two."

Jansen runs ahead to catch up with Yoric. I fasten my holster back on my thigh and nestle my empty pistol in it. As Timber and I walk back to the facility, I wrap the hair band back around my ponytail.

Timber is my best girlfriend here at Ceborec. I sometimes see Lynx, my old roommate from Crimson, here every now and then, but she was hired on in the aerospace engineering department, helping to design the Earth shuttle, and it seems like she's always working, so I don't get to spend much time with her. I met Timber on my second day here. She was working in the clinic when Evie, Marcus, and I went to get our medical evaluations. She has a nurturing quality about her and she made me feel human again after the ordeal at Crimson. We've pretty much been best friends ever since. Whenever I am not with Marcus or Evie, I usually spend my time with Timber, who has turned out to be a great training partner.

"That was awesome," says Timber. "Did you get any shots with the gun?"

"Just Yoric's arm. I really need to get in some more kinetics practice at the range. My coordination sucks."

"You'll get better. Maybe you can practice that with Marcus tomorrow. I'm sure he won't mind being pummeled with paint pellets. Hell, the way he feels about you I'm sure he'd take a few real bullets."

I laugh nervously, "Well, I won't let that happen. What are you doing this afternoon?" I ask.

"Well, I was going to help out at the clinic, but I called in this morning and they said it's really slow. I may just catch a movie or something. You got any plans?"

"Not really. Just hanging out with Evie while Marcus trains with Nicron."

"Why don't you two join me?" Timber asks. "Maybe we can go bowling or something."

"Sure, I'd—" I begin, but I am interrupted when Evie comes barreling down the hill and squeezes my legs in a hug. Evie just celebrated her fourth birthday. I can't believe how much she's grown just in the past few months. She looks so pretty wearing a frilly yellow dress and her hair neatly brushed. On her left temple she still bears the tattoo of the infinity fly as a reminder of our imprisonment at the Crimson Survivor Refuge, but her light brown locks frame her face and cover it up nicely. Sometimes she asks me about the tattoo. I tell her it's a stamp to make her look pretty, like makeup, and that she never has to wash it off because it's there forever. She seems to accept that cheerfully.

"Pollen!" My eyes draw up the hill to see Marcus, the love of my life. His shoulder-length auburn hair flows gently with the breeze, reminding me of the men on those silly romance book covers. He carries a large blue cooler, with a red and white checked blanket draped over his shoulder. Moments like this were once rare and hard to come by. But now they are more frequent. My life feels perfect and complete.

Chapter 2

Evie's arms stick to my legs like tar to a roof shingle. I gently peel them off and jog toward Marcus, swinging my arms around his neck and greeting him with a quick kiss.

"What's this?" I ask. "I thought you were training tonight."

"Nicron bailed on me. Sounded like he was hung over. Anyway, Evie wanted to have a picnic and I thought it would be nice to enjoy the outdoors while we can. We'll be underground in a few weeks, you know." I'd almost forgotten about that. The temperatures have been on the rise in the past month, but I've been so focused on my new life here that I barely even noticed. Summer begins in about six weeks and we'll be moving into the bunkers to keep from roasting in the unbearable heat. Last year, the highest recorded temperature almost reached two hundred degrees. I'm sure it will be worse this year with this cloud cover to trap the heat in.

"That sounds good," I say. "But only if Timber can join us."

"Of course," Marcus smiles. "I only brought three meals, but we have plenty to share."

I pull the red and white checked blanket off of Marcus's shoulder and hold it out, allowing the breeze to lift it into the air like a waving flag. Timber takes the opposite side in her hands and together we lower it to the ground, pulling out the corners to flatten out the wrinkles. Evie is the first to jump on and find a spot for her to sit.

"Can Timber sit next to me?" asks Evie.

"I'd love to," replies Timber in a child-like squeal. Marcus sets down the cooler and begins handing out sandwiches wrapped in brown paper and apples. Evie splits her sandwich in half and gives the other half to Timber.

"I love PBJs!" says Timber toward Evie. "I remember my mother used to make peanut butter and jam sandwiches. She used to make her own byrchberry jam from the bushes in our yard."

Unfortunately, the deep purple byrchberries are in short supply these days due to the infestation of infinity flies. There are two byrchberries in the greenhouse below, but I've heard that the scientists are struggling to keep them alive. The plant could possibly go extinct very soon. The infinity flies lay their eggs under the leaves of byrchberry bushes and when the larvae hatch, they burrow into the shaft of the plant, eating their way down to the root and the plant dies. The infinity fly is a bane to most farmers since they are nearly impossible to eradicate, and they are symbol of death to most plants, although byrchberries are among their favorites.

Now, however, it has become a symbol for life, for survivors of the virus. All the survivors, i.e. prisoners, at Crimson had the infinity fly tattooed on their temples to identify them. The ink contains a chemical that activates when exposed to high levels of electromagnetic radiation, causing short-term memory loss. Marcus and I lost our memories after we escaped Crimson the first time, but we were captured and taken back, before we escaped again. Here, at Ceborec, only four of us bear the tattoo: Marcus, Evie, Lynx, and myself.

Marcus digs out a bottle of dry white wine from the cooler and pours me a glass. Lucky for us Ceborec has a huge stash of wine and they even grow a vineyard in one of the underground greenhouses.

"Can I have some?" Evie asks. Marcus and I give each other a questioning look. We both know children shouldn't drink alcohol, but I remember my dad giving me sips of beer as a child, so I figure it can't hurt.

"Sure, why not?" I say handing her my glass.

Evie takes in a big mouthful, scrunches her face in disgust and spits it out all over the blanket, spraying some on my gray cargo pants.

"Evie!" I laugh. "Oh well, I need to take a shower anyway."

Marcus wraps his arm around me, squeezes my shoulder, and leans in to sniff my neck. "You smell fine to me," he says before delicately kissing my neck. I wince at the tickle of his plush lips and push him away playfully.

"Not with an audience, babe. How was work this morning?" I ask, abruptly changing the subject.

"Good," he replies. "We finished framing yet another level today."

Shortly after we arrived, Marcus was hired as a construction worker in one of the new bunkers they are building a few miles away. It's supposedly a "top secret" project, so he doesn't even know for sure what he is building. We've discussed some ideas, like a military complex or a secret bunker for the leaders of COPS in case we are ever attacked. Or possibly another launch pad for a spacecraft. Either way, despite the secrecy, he's happy to be back at work and people here are good to us.

My mind wanders and I find myself staring at his lush lips as Marcus speaks eagerly about his work. My memory drifts back to our early days here at Ceborec. After we escaped Crimson, we were found wandering the Web and brought here to live. They already had a furnished apartment ready for Marcus, Evie and me to move into. I was so nervous, that first night with Marcus. I wanted him so badly, and he wanted me. But it was awkward, since we still didn't really know each other that well and we had only recently regained the memories we had lost after our first escape attempt. Luckily, my broken ankle gave us an excuse to hold off physically. By the time it had completely healed, Marcus and I couldn't have grown any closer. We were like two puzzle pieces that fit perfectly together. The first night we made love was paradise.

I nod my head unconsciously while Marcus speaks, unaware of my conspicuous blank stare.

"I might as well be speaking another language," he laughs. "You don't understand a word I'm saying do you?" I grin, acknowledging his comment. Most of what he says about his work goes straight over my head. But I know he likes to talk about it so I always ask.

"I'm sorry," I say. "You know I don't understand that stuff."

"I know. Sorry to bore you with that. What about you? What did you and Evie do this morning?" Marcus asks.

I take Evie to preschool every morning. When we arrived at Ceborec I didn't want to leave her with anybody but Marcus. But as a resident everybody is required to contribute in some way. I told Myra about my desire to teach and she placed me as an apprentice in the preschool where I can always be with Evie in the mornings. There are only six kids there, so it's pretty quiet, and the head teacher, Lana, seems to view me more as a nuisance than an aid. But at least I get to spend more time with Evie. And I was given some textbooks to study in the evenings, although those focus more on how to discipline unruly kids rather than actual teaching methods.

"The usual. Lana is teaching them about shapes and colors. Then she berated me for paying too much attention to Evie and not the other kids. I didn't think I was."

"Lana's just pissed that she's got some competition now. Don't let her get to you," says Timber, reassuringly.

"Oh, I don't. I just wish she'd pull that stick out of her ass," I say. Turning to Evie I ask, "What did you two do this afternoon?"

"We saw snakes!" Evie said enthusiastically.

"We went to the library," Marcus corrected. "Evie found a book about snakes that she couldn't put down."

Evie loves animals of all kinds, but she seems to be going through a reptile phase now. It must have started when Lana read a book called *The Lizard of Bagizzard* at preschool. She was obsessed with lizards for about a week. When she learned that snakes don't have legs and must slither to get around, she became fascinated with them.

We all finish eating and as we are folding up the blanket, a female voice crackles over the intercom's outdoor speaker, "Marcus Stygma, please report to checkpoint three immediately."

"Damn. I must've left my pager in the room," Marcus scowls, as he pats the waist and empty pockets of his jeans.

Because the facility is so enormous, they created the checkpoints in order for people to meet at a particular spot quickly. There are thirty checkpoints and we had to memorize all of them. I still haven't gotten them all down yet, but the first ten are easy because they are in the more common areas. Checkpoint three is in the atrium, where the administrative offices are located along with the aerospace engineering department. In the center of the atrium is a huge holographic model of the Earth shuttle. Checkpoint three is a fairly common meeting area, so I don't think Marcus has anything to be concerned about.

"Go ahead, we'll meet you inside," I say to Marcus. Timber, Evie and I finish cleaning up our mess while Marcus runs up the hill to the building. I roll up the blanket and toss it in the cooler along with the garbage.

"I think I'll go see how Yoric is doing," says Timber. "I'll take your gun back to the armory if you'd like."

"Thanks," I smile, handing her the pistol. I know Timber has a thing for Yoric, but she won't admit it. To be honest I think she'd be good for him. Even though he's twenty-five years old, he acts like he's twelve. He could use some of Timber's maturity. I smile at the idea of hooking them up. I've never played matchmaker before, but I'd be willing to give it a shot for those two.

<hr>

At the entrance of the building is a handprint-scanning system for security. All adults must scan their hands to gain entrance to the building. Evie is exempt, of course, so she crawls under the gate and waits patiently by the door for me to enter. Security hasn't really been an issue here yet, but they're not willing to take any chances on stragglers who wander past the perimeter.

I take Evie's hand and we walk into the enormous glass domed atrium. In the center of the room, on the lower level, a crew of engineers are working on the spacecraft plans and fiddling with the computer systems surrounding the holographic model of the Earth shuttle. Encircling the central area of the atrium are railed walkways against the walls with stairways ascending the three upper levels.

Marcus is in the COPS central offices, deeply ingrained in a serious conversation with Chlamyra Rowan and General Granby, head of security here at Ceborec. Granby is a tall, lean and muscular man, a little younger than my father was judging by the sporadic grey strands highlighting his russet hair. His square jaw and heavy brow pose a sharp contrast to his gentle nature. I've met him a few times since I've been here, mostly in the armory. He is a very kind, temperate man, but hard and tough when he's with his soldiers. He reminds me of my father, who I've grown to miss dearly.

Marcus nods and shakes Granby's hand before leaving the offices and walking back toward us.

"What was that all about?" I ask, setting down the cooler next to me. Evie plops down on it, kicking her feet against the plastic surface.

Marcus's forehead wrinkles with concern. "Granby's organizing a formal militia. They're worried about security now that the shuttle is nearing completion. He wants to recruit me."

I drop my head and bite my lower lip. It's too difficult for me to look him in the eyes. I don't want him to see the pain in mine. Militia means he'll put his life at risk for the safety of everyone here. I can't bear the thought of losing Marcus after everything we've been through. I bite my lip harder when I feel the pressure build up behind my eyes.

"What did you say?" I ask, looking down at the floor. My voice is barely audible.

Marcus places his hands on my shoulders and rubs them, sensing my discomfort. "I said I would consider it. I told him I have a family now and I can't jump to a decision without consulting you first."

The tension building up within me diminishes and my muscles relax. I lean in to his shoulder, burying my face in his neck and fold my arms around him.

"Thank you," I whisper in his ear.

"We'll talk about it later," Marcus says.

As I nod, a ruckus at the entrance of the building behind me tears Marcus and me apart. We both turn curiously toward the commotion as other onlookers gather around.

Two men dressed in light brown uniforms wearing helmets and visors—the Watchers—barrel through the front doors, dragging a one-eyed man who is writhing against their restraint. Watchers are what we call the men who stand guard at the entrances and the vast perimeter surrounding Ceborec. They are kind of like the Crimson Enforcers, except they are volunteers; not bribed or threatened like the Enforcers are. They guard the facility because they want to.

Granby, Sage—his second in command, and two other soldiers who often accompany him, march to the entrance to take charge of the situation. The struggling man wildly thrashes about and the Watchers are quickly losing control of him.

"Let go of me!" he shouts. My heart feels as though it has leaped out of my chest, stretching against the tendons holding it in place, and I instantly feel like I am going to lose my lunch. I know that voice.

One of the soldiers that followed Granby raises a baton and thumps the flailing man on the back of the head and he falls to the floor, rolling over face up. I can't resist moving forward to get a better look. Dread tugs at my heart when my eyes rest upon the man bearing an eye patch over his right eye. He's still wearing the creepy indigo uniform of the Crimson Enforcers, though torn and grungy.

It's my ex-fiancé, Glenn.

Chapter 3

"What do you think they'll do to him?" I lie on the bed staring straight up at the blur of the rotating ceiling fan blades. I try to keep my eyes focused on one blade as it spins around but the rotation is too fast and after one orbit the blade dissolves into the spinning gray circle. Marcus restlessly paces the floor of our quaint closet-sized bedroom. The room is fairly empty except for the double bed, nightstand and chest of drawers, but it's all we really need since we don't have a lot of things to take up space. Hanging on the pale blue wall is a single unframed abstract painting on canvas Marcus painted about a month ago. Empty cardboard boxes, which at one point in time stored lab equipment, are stacked in the corner in front of the narrow closet, waiting to be filled with our sparse belongings when we move down into the bunker in a few weeks.

We should be discussing Marcus's offer from General Granby to join the militia, but I can't get that image out of my mind. Glenn's tattered body lying on the floor. *And that creepy eye patch, what was that about?* Was he trying to cover his eye as a disguise? What if he were sent here as a spy, to infiltrate the COPS headquarters? My happy, almost perfect existence is beginning to crumble around me like ancient ruins turning to ash and I'm helpless to stop it.

"They'll take him to the clinic until he comes to," Marcus says. "Then they'll take him somewhere for questioning. Other than that," he shakes his head, "I don't know."

"Do you think they'll torture him?" I ask, envisioning the scars on Marcus's back from his interrogation at Crimson, where Glenn took out his anger and jealousy toward Marcus through a brutal and savage whipping.

Marcus turns from me, obviously agitated by my concern for Glenn. "I couldn't say," he retorts, opening the top drawer of the bureau and peering in.

"Why do you think he's here?" I continue, ignoring his rising vexation.

Marcus slams the drawer shut, snapping me out of my trance. I sit up instantly in alarm.

"I don't know, Pollen. Look, I don't want to talk about Glenn okay?" Marcus barks at me. I coil back on the bed wrapping my arms around my knees and hugging them close to my body. Marcus isn't usually so snippy. In fact, I haven't seen him like this since we were at Crimson and he thought I had joined the Enforcers. And I'm usually not so sensitive around Marcus, but my heart sinks a little, given the tone of his voice. He paces over to the bed and sits down next to my feet.

"I'm sorry, Pollen. I didn't mean to snap at you like that. I just . . . I feel uncomfortable with him here. Knowing you two have a history. And what he did to us."

"Marcus, you have nothing to worry about. History is exactly what Glenn and I are. I could never love him again, not the way I love you." I take Marcus's hand and sandwich it between my own.

"I can't help feeling jealous," Marcus says. "I don't want to lose you."

"You won't," I assure him. Although Marcus lets the topic go, the tension on his face remains. We sit silently in a moment that echoes those days we spent in the woods after our first escape from Crimson, when we woke up with no memories of the virus that destroyed the entire animal kingdom. There was that eerie silence as we wandered the woods together, not only from the lack of animals, but that 'I just met you and I don't know what to say' feeling.

"What do you think I should do about Granby's request?" Marcus asks, breaking the silence, but building upon the tension in the room.

I inhale deeply, blowing out the air in one quick gust. "I don't want you to do it," I say bluntly. "I can't lose you Marcus. You and Evie are all I have."

"You won't lose me," Marcus says. "There's rigorous training and there's no guarantee I'll ever have to fight anyway."

"But you might," I mutter.

"Don't you want to hear about the benefits?" Marcus asks.

"No," I state impetuously. I don't care about benefits. We have all we need right here. Steady jobs, healthcare, community. This place is a virtual utopia. There's nothing we need that the COPS haven't already provided us with. But Marcus will tell me anyway.

"We'll be eligible for the first flight to A1D3."

That hooks my attention and pulls me back. Ever since I found out about the Earthcraft, as I like to call it, and the state of our own dying planet, I've been dreaming about a new start on A1D3. I'd get to experience life on a planet untainted by human destruction. A place where the air is fresh, the water is clean, and there's no need to spend half the year underground, although I'm not sure what to expect of the freezing temperatures. It's the kind of thing I fantasized about since childhood, but never really thought it could be reality. This definitely throws a millstone in my argument.

"Eligible. Does that mean we're *guaranteed* a spot?" I ask, hopeful that we may have a blissful future ahead of us.

"Not exactly," Marcus says, crushing my hopes to bits of confetti. "There's going to be a lottery. Only the names of eligible candidates will be included. If chosen, each will be able to bring up to three family members." Interesting. Most people here don't actually *have* any family members. There are only a few who have one surviving child. Or the occasional sibling. I think our family is actually the largest here with Marcus, Evie, and myself. The COPS don't actually bother with technicalities such as nuptials. It's assumed that if a man and woman are living together, they are a family. Which is fine with me. Sure I'd love to marry Marcus. But what is marriage really, other than two people living together? Just an overly stressful, money-wasting ceremony where two people flaunt their pretentious and exaggerated love for one another in front of a crowd of envious onlookers pretending to weep tears of joy for them. I could do without that.

"How many will be chosen?" I ask.

"I don't know yet," Marcus answers. "Look, if you don't want me to join, I won't. I won't do anything you're uncomfortable with." I really want to be on that first flight to A1D3. But I don't want to go without him. And I'm not willing to risk his life for that opportunity.

"I don't want you to join," I say flatly.

Marcus opens his mouth to speak when the squeak of the doorknob turning interrupts him and Evie shuffles in from the darkness.

"I had a bad dream," she whimpers.

"Come here, sweetie," Marcus opens his arms out to her and she fills them happily. Marcus has become such a wonderful, loving father to her, I sometimes worry that she's forgotten who her real father was, my brother Drake. He was killed by a landmine in the Deimosian War, before the virus was released. I know he'd be happy with Marcus raising Evie. I wish he could have had the opportunity to meet him.

"What did you dream about?" Marcus asks, holding her close and rocking her against his chest.

"Uncle Glenn," she says, and Marcus looks at me painfully. "And there was a fire. He looked mad. Is he dead?" Even though Evie was there when he was brought in, thrashing about, she made no mention of him earlier. She's always so quiet I don't really know how much she takes in. I didn't realize that she had recognized him.

"No, Evie, he's not dead," I say. Her shoulders droop slightly and she looks a little relieved. Despite the problems I've had with Glenn, he's always been good to Evie and she's always liked him.

"Can I sleep with you tonight?" From the way Marcus leers at me I can tell he had other, naughtier, intentions for us tonight. Tempting as it is to give in to his wanton desires, I'm too concerned about Glenn to be intimate with Marcus right now.

"Yes, but just for tonight," I say. Marcus silently accepts defeat and helps to tuck Evie into the center of the bed. He crawls in and snuggles next to her, while I get up to go to the bathroom.

"Where are you going?" Marcus asks.

"I forgot to brush my teeth. I'll be back in a few minutes," I say. But that's not fully my intention.

I just need a few minutes on my own to gather my thoughts and compose myself.

The door clicks shut behind me and I lean over the sink, staring at my image in the mirror. My long chestnut hair, still damp from the shower I took an hour ago, is pulled back in a loose bun, revealing the infinity fly tattoo on my left temple. A faint pink line of taut skin across my face is all that remains of the scar I inherited when I crashed the van during my first escape attempt from Crimson and the shattered glass sliced my face open. Like the tattoo, it will always be a constant reminder of what happened and what I had to go through to safeguard Evie's future. It also reminds me of what Glenn did to us. And *for* us.

I'm so torn over Glenn. I want to be angry with him and hate him. But he is also the reason we ultimately escaped and came to be here, living this perfect life. And as much as I hate to admit it, deep down there will always be a part of me that loves him. We were together for five years, had a child together, planned to spend the rest of our lives together. That's a connection I can't sever no matter what awful things he did to Marcus and me. But I'll never be in love with him again the way I am with Marcus. That love died when he betrayed me to become a Crimson Enforcer.

For the most part, I've overcome my instinctual urge to cry every time I get emotional. But I feel my eyes welling up out of the frustration of my chaotic thoughts. As tears begin to escape down my cheeks, I splash water on my face to wash them away. I can't cry about Glenn. He's not worth it, I tell myself.

I've got to organize my thoughts. *Focus, Pollen.* There's an inescapable chance I will run into Glenn sometime in the near future and I need to be prepared, emotionally and mentally. I cannot allow him to peel through my shell and into my heart. I need to remain calm, collected, and tenacious. He will not break me.

I just hope I don't shatter under the turmoil thundering inside my head.

Evie's delicate hand strives to hang on to mine as she excitedly pushes into the sticky, warm aisle lined with tangled vines of watermelon and honeydew. Evie's class is taking a field trip to the warm-zone underground greenhouse in the lower levels of Ceborec to learn about how plants grow. I suggested to Lana that we divide the children into two groups of three and split up so the kids can see and do more, but she opposed the idea, most likely because it was *my* suggestion.

The warm-zone greenhouse is where the botanists at Ceborec grow warm weather crops. They have another greenhouse for cool weather crops, but it is much smaller, since the planet hasn't really experienced cool weather for the past thirty years. Most cool weather crops went extinct with the harsh winters, with the exception of a few hardy varieties. There is also a tropical greenhouse, orchard, and vineyard down here, as well as an aquarium and pastures for raising animals for meat.

As we walk through rows of beans, tomatoes, squash and cucumbers, one of the scientists, a petite and very stoic man, acts as our guide and lectures about how they grow the plants down here. The kids are so young; they couldn't be less interested in the plants. The scientist's lecture is even putting me to sleep. But the boys and girls perk up when we are shown the worms that were used for composting. Ceborec already had an outstanding composting facility before the virus struck. Shortly after, researchers dug into the soil to determine how far the virus reached and how many life forms were affected. They found a few worms, beetles, and other subterranean insects well below the surface, but they let them be for fear they might contaminate the established colony. The children each held out their hands to hold the wriggly creatures.

Toward the end of the tour we are given the chance to sample the delicious fruits grown here. Of course the kids come alive when they are offered paper cups filled with berries and wedges of watermelon to eat.

On the way out, a little boy named Garner runs back and forth with his friend Cameron playing a little too rough. Lana reprimands them both harshly, but he might as well be wearing earplugs. Garner continues to romp around and falls over into the cucumber patch. His cries interrupt the researchers as they stop to look over at our group. Lana lifts him from the patch, revealing a nasty gash on his knee from scraping one of the trellises.

"Pollen, I need you to take him up to the clinic, while I get the kids back to the classroom," Lana commands, as we are boarding the glass elevator.

"Okay, but I'm taking Evie with me," I say.

"Our school day is not finished, Pollen," she challenges. But I remain adamant.

"Evie does not leave my sight," I glare at Lana, unyielding.

She flips her chin-length raven hair and rolls her eyes. "Fine. Bring them both back to the classroom when Garner is attended to." I nod and the elevator stops at the medical floor.

Timber is in the lobby and greets us with a smile as usual. She's dressed in a cute set of light blue scrubs splotched with red apples all over.

"And what brings you here this morning?" she smiles at Evie.

"Garner has a boo-boo," Evie replies.

Timber squats down to Garner's eye level. Her forehead wrinkles with exaggerated concern as she asks, "Where's your boo-boo?"

While he points to the bleeding gash on his leg, a nurse walks through an open set of double doors on the right and something draws my attention down the hallway. A tall, dark-haired figure stands motionless, flanked by two Watchers, who appear to be restraining his arms. My throat swells up and I find myself unable to breathe, choking on my own flesh. Glenn's lonely eye is staring directly at me.

Chapter 4

I HUDDLE IN THE CORNER of the examination room where Timber took us to dress Garner's wound, breathing deeply into my fist. Despite my relief that I don't have to face Glenn yet, reality is setting in. He has regained consciousness now and I know it's only a matter of time. My heart hammers into my sternum as I imagine the confrontation. *How do I prepare for this?*

Timber lifts Garner onto the paper-lined, cushioned table while I stare blankly at the wall beyond them. There is a mural of cartoon fish in the ocean painted on the wall. My eyes seem drawn to one orange and blue striped fish in particular, even though my mind is so buried in anguish that I'm not really looking at it.

While Timber attends to Garner's leg, she speaks to me. "You look as though you've seen a ghost."

"Not a ghost," I say. "Possibly a demon. Or an angel. I'm not quite sure yet."

"You want to talk about it?" she asks. That's one thing I like about Timber. She's concerned enough to ask me if I want to talk about what's on my mind, but doesn't force the issue if I don't. Most people seem to get this offensive look on their faces if I don't say exactly what I'm thinking. Timber gets me. I've grown to trust her sincerely.

"I do," I say, "but I need to get these two back to class or Lana will have my head on a stake."

As we leave the exam room and enter the lobby, I glance up to see Glenn once again, this time in the elevator. My heart jumps so suddenly a pain shoots through my chest, stopping me in my tracks. The doors have already closed, but through the glass he sees me. I could swear he mouths something to me, but I just can't make it out before the elevator begins to descend.

Timber leans against the wall just outside the glass door of the elevator, combing her snakelike fingers through clumps of her spunky blond hair. I smile and wave at her as I wait for the door to slide open.

Timber and I always meet for lunch every other day while I wait for Marcus to get off work so we can train together. I usually alternate my training days with Marcus and Timber so that I can spend time with both of them, and benefit from their different strengths and weaknesses. On the days I train with Marcus, I have lunch with Timber in the food court, then she babysits Evie for us.

The food court is laid out like the ones I used to see at typical overcrowded shopping malls. There are a variety of 'restaurants' where they prepare different cuisines. The only difference is that there is no exchange of money here at Ceborec. Everybody who lives here is assigned a job based on their skills and desires, whether it's treating patients in the medical clinic, or flipping burgers at the grill. And no money is required for any of the services here. In a way, everybody is equal. It's about as utopian as can be in the current state of the world, I suppose.

Timber and I find a small round table in a quiet corner of the cafeteria where we can talk without any prying ears.

"So what's going on?" Timber asks, taking a bite of her BLT sandwich on rye bread.

"That guy they brought in yesterday," I start, skewering lettuce leaves with my fork in the plastic salad bowl in front of me.

"The one with the eye patch?" she interrupts.

"Yes," I say. "Did you attend to him?"

"No. They called me in last night, but only to cover scheduled patients. I just heard Orla talking about him. Do you know him?"

I push the lettuce leaves around in my salad bowl with the fork, taking tiny nibbles but not really eating. My appetite is virtually nonexistent today.

"He was my fiancé."

Timber drops her sandwich, scattering the pieces of bread and lettuce all over her plate. Her eyes bulge and her bottom jaw falls open. I explain what happened when the virus hit and we were taken to Crimson. She knows most of the story already, but when I told her before I intentionally omitted the role Glenn played. As she leans in, I tell her about Glenn's involvement with the Enforcers and how he helped us escape by opening the Web for us.

"I can see now, the angel or demon thing," says Timber. "What are you going to do?"

"I don't know," I utter.

"What about Marcus? How does he feel about all this?" Timber asks.

"He's angry. And jealous, of course. He thinks that we'll somehow rekindle our old relationship."

"Is that possible? I mean, you *were* engaged."

"Of course not!" I assert. "After everything he did to us? Helping us escape does not erase the scars off Marcus's back. Or those in my heart," I say. I fight the swelling under my eyelids, but I can feel the blood vessels thickening.

Timber takes my hand and gently squeezes. "I'm sorry, Pollen. I didn't mean to bring up old emotions."

"There are no emotions," I lie. "There will never be anything between me and Glenn. It was over a long time ago. I just don't know what to say to him. You know, if they let him stay. I know I'll have to confront him at some point."

"This must be tearing you apart," says Timber, kneading the skin on the back of my hand.

"It's just that, I'm angry with him . . . but I don't want him to get hurt. Tortured, I mean. Yes, he tortured Marcus and part of me wants him to know that pain. To feel the same agony he inflicted on Marcus. I hate him and love him at the same time. I don't know. I don't even sound coherent, do I? This is why I can't face him yet."

"Don't worry," says Timber. "We don't even know if he'll be staying here."

"Let's hope not."

A few days pass before I see Glenn again. Marcus and I are hopeful that Granby got rid of him. That would make life so much easier on me, not having to face him. In a way, life goes back to normal and I almost forget that he's here.

After school, I take Evie down to the shopping area, just behind the food court on the commerce level, to trade in her old clothes for new ones. Kids her age tend to outgrow their clothes every couple of months.

The shops are categorized by the type of merchandise they carry, followed by age and gender, just like they would be at a typical shopping mall. The children's store, called KidsWear (not the most clever name for a store, but what can you expect from a community of scientists?), is by far the largest of the clothing stores, followed by women's, then men's.

Evie loves going shopping with me. She grabs armfuls of frilly dresses, floral skirts, and dainty blouses to try on in their pint-sized dressing rooms. It reminds me of old times back at home when I used to make her up like a runway model. I used to have to help her get dressed, but nowadays she likes to do it independently. I don't mind because it gives me time to study my textbooks.

It takes Evie almost an hour to decide what clothes she wants to keep. And an extra ten minutes of me explaining to her that she can't take everything.

"Only what you need, Evie. You don't need this many clothes. You can get three outfits. That's it."

As we are walking out of KidsWear my arms lose all feeling and my textbooks drop to the floor with an echoing thud. Glenn is in the menswear store across the corridor, unattended. No Watchers, no escorts. He is all alone. I can't believe they trust him well enough to set him free in the facility. I shudder when I think of all the times he'd betrayed me.

Glenn holds up an olive green button down shirt and examines it when the loud thud diverts his attention. He looks up for a brief moment and we make eye contact. He is still wearing that bizarre eye patch. I feel a flutter in my stomach and my knees begin to go numb. I silently swear at myself for being so clumsy. I could have easily gotten away from here without him seeing me, but now that is impossible.

Grabbing Evie's hand, I speed walk down the corridor toward the elevator, dragging her shuffling feet as we go.

"Pollen!" I hear Glenn call out behind us. But instead of turning around, I move faster.

"Hi Uncle Glenn," Evie calls out. I flinch at the words.

At the edge of the food court I can see two men and a woman boarding the elevator. I make a dash for it, ignoring Evie's protests. I curse at the tables and chairs I have to dodge and push aside in order to cross the huge cafeteria. But my nightmarish prediction has come true. We're too late. The glass doors slide shut as we approach and we are left to wait for the next one.

I turn back, hoping sincerely that Glenn chose not to follow. Much to my dismay, he is walking towards us. I try to swallow the lump in my throat, but it persists, threatening to choke me.

As he pushes through the last set of tables and chairs my eyes drift down to something he is holding. My textbooks. Damn, I forgot to pick them up.

"I think you dropped something back there," he says, looking boldly into my eyes. His voice, which used to set my heart fluttering, now sends icy chills down my spine. I find it difficult to make eye contact with him so I just glance at him quickly then look down at the floor.

"Thanks," I say quietly. He passes the books to me and I hug them against my chest. Evie stands by, swinging her bag full of clothes around in a circle like a lasso.

"Pollen, can we talk?" he asks. It's the question I've been dreading since he arrived. Talking to Glenn the last thing I want to do. I just want to get away from here. I struggle to come up with an excuse to avoid it.

"I can't right now, Glenn. I've got to get Evie in bed for her nap and then I need to study."

Glenn eyes my textbook. "So you're actually going to be a teacher, huh? That's great." His encouraging words soften me a bit, but I don't respond. I just don't know how to react to him.

"Look, Pollen, I have some things I really need to talk to you about. If now's a bad time, I understand. Just please find some time to come see me. Okay?"

I glance up at him one last time and nod. "Okay," I mutter. I'm sure he can see the flashing neon signs in my eyes that scream 'Liar!' Of course I have no intention of seeing him.

"I'm on the third residential floor. Room 824." I nod once.

The glass doors of the elevator open and I barge my way in dragging Evie behind me before the passengers have a chance to exit. Glenn stands in front of the elevator and watches thoughtfully as we ascend the glass tube.

After my meeting with Glenn earlier today, I'm feeling quite jittery, so I convince Marcus to take me out on a date for a much-needed respite. Timber volunteers to stay with Evie while we go out. She is the only person here beside Marcus who I trust to care for Evie and I know she won't mind if we stay out late.

Marcus takes me to the bowling alley on one of the lower levels. Despite the noise, it actually has a calming effect on me. The dim lights. The low rumble of the balls rolling down the lustrous wooden lanes. The frothy mugs of McMullin's Pride beer, to commemorate the first drink Marcus and I shared together. This is exactly what I need to relax.

Marcus and I had intended to take a lane for ourselves, but apparently everyone in the facility decided it was a good night for bowling and the eight lanes are packed tighter than a cow in a corset. We end up sharing a lane with Jansen and Yoric, of all people. I already know how this night will end. Yoric will storm off like a ranting lunatic when he doesn't win. Perhaps Marcus should have taken me to a movie instead.

Since I'm the only female playing on our lane tonight, I get to bowl first. I find an eight pound blue ball marbled with specks of silver that attracts me and lift it up on my fingers, resting its weight on my palm. I eye the pins and do my best to aim for the center pin.

Bringing the ball back, I take a few steps then swing my arm forward, releasing the weight of the ball onto the lane. As it glides down the glossy surface, I stare at it with narrowed eyes, willing it to stay in the center. But just at the last moment it the ball veers to the left, taking down only two pins.

"Better luck next time," Yoric heckles. I flash him a dirty look before retrieving my ball. This time, I drop my focus and let my emotions run wild. The anger, the sadness, the frustration. I release all that energy into the ball and I let it fly down the aisle. We all watch intensely as it knocks down all eight of the remaining pins.

"Spare!" Marcus cries out and marks the scoreboard. I glance over and smirk at Yoric, who is forcing a painfully fake smile. Throughout the game, he does a remarkable job of controlling his reactions, both the facetious sarcasm and the animosity. I wonder if it's something that Timber said to him the other day. Perhaps she bribed him. Or threatened him.

"Got room for another player?" a deep, husky voice calls out behind us.

"Hey, Nicron," Marcus calls out.

Nicron works with Marcus on the construction team building the bunker. His dark chocolate skin and ebony dreadlocks blend in to the darkness of the bowling alley, giving him a shadowy appearance. I used to be intimidated by Nicron when we first moved here. He's got this tough as nails, inner-city appearance, but as I soon learned, he's very even-tempered and friendly.

"We're already two on two," says Jansen, "but you can keep score until the next round."

"Sure," he smiles.

For the first time in almost a week, I feel really good. Marcus and I are losing the game to Jansen and Yoric, but that doesn't matter to me. We're all having a great time sipping on icy cold beer, telling jokes, and just being goofy. I haven't laughed or had this much fun since before Glenn arrived.

Much to my surprise, Yoric cuts out on us early.

"Why are you leaving?" I ask. "We haven't even finished the game yet."

Yoric averts his eyes and picks up his empty beer mug. "I'm tired. Plus I've got the early shift tomorrow." Yoric is a barista in the coffee shop at the food court. It's not a very notable position, but it suits him.

"Have a good night," says Marcus. "I'll probably see you in the morning."

Yoric nods and smiles as he rambles off into the crowd.

Nicron shakes his head, smiling. "You guys don't really buy that, do you?"

Marcus and I quickly glance at each other with creased brows and back at Nicron. "Why, what do you think is going on?" I ask curiously.

Jansen cuts in, smiling, "Yoric couldn't care less about work. Never has before. And you saw how he was tonight. No crazy remarks. No outbursts. He didn't even stay to finish the game and we were winning! There's a special lady on his mind."

"Who?" I ask.

"I don't know, but whoever it is, she's definitely got a hold on his heart, or his handle," Jansen says smugly and glances over at Nicron. I blush as laughter pours out of me. My grin instantly disappears when I discover the dark figure approaching us.

"I see you're out a player," he says. "Mind if I join you guys?" Has he been watching us this entire time, waiting for an opportunity? It's kind of weird seeing Glenn wearing normal clothes: a pair of jeans and a grey tee shirt. He's been forever etched in my memory wearing that hideous blue jumpsuit of the Enforcers.

Jansen jumps up and holds his hand out to Glenn in a polite gesture. "Sure, man. I'm Jansen. We'll start a new round. Why don't you double up with Nicron and I'll take score." Obviously Jansen is totally oblivious to the animosity between Marcus and Glenn. But Nicron is not. His eyes narrow and he shakes his head at Jansen.

As Glenn shakes Jansen's hand, I turn to Marcus, who is clenching his jaw with such force I swear I could hear his teeth grinding. I place my hand on his and whisper, "Let's go." He nods and we both get up to leave.

"We're gonna get out of here," I say to Jansen and Nicron, trying to ignore Glenn. Marcus storms past Glenn, not even acknowledging his presence. I have to admit I'm impressed. After what Glenn did to him in that torture chamber at Crimson, I almost expected him to attack Glenn with the magnitude of a nuclear missile. And I can't believe Glenn actually had the nerve to approach us while we're together.

"You too?" Jansen asks, confounded.

"Yeah, we don't want to keep Timber too late. I'll see you later, Jansen." He frowns.

As I try to pass Glenn, ignoring him, he reaches out and grasps my wrist, stopping me from proceeding. I look up and his single eye gazes deeply into my eyes, but he does not say a word. I can feel my pulse throbbing against the warmth of his hand. I wish I had moved faster so he wouldn't have had a chance to stop me. My heart trembles momentarily. The look in his eye is different. It reminds me of the way he used to look at me in the beginning of our relationship. When I try to swallow I can't; my throat is paralyzed. I can't deny the connection that still exists between us, but I can't allow myself to acknowledge it either.

I thrust my arm away and maneuver my way through the crowd to join Marcus. He is already waiting by the elevator.

"What took you so long?" he asks, flatly.

"Well, I couldn't just leave Jansen and Nicron there without an explanation," I say.

"Nicron doesn't need an explanation." Marcus presses the button for the elevator repeatedly and stares up into the glass.

"Well, it looked to me like Jansen did. And I'm not going to be rude and just take off."

Marcus takes a deep breath and flexes his fists. He's really struggling to hold it together. Had I not been there tonight, I'm sure Marcus would have attacked Glenn without hesitation.

We travel back to our apartment in silence. Walking down the corridor to our room, I take his hand in mine. It must strike a chord in him because he stops just outside our door and turns to me.

"I'm sorry for the way I acted," he says. His hardened face has softened significantly.

"It's okay, Marcus. I know the way you feel about Glenn. I don't blame you. In fact I'm proud of you for holding yourself together. I know that couldn't have been easy."

"I trust you, Pollen. I know I don't act like it sometimes. I can't help but be jealous after what Siera did to me." Siera was Marcus's ex-wife who left him when they discovered he couldn't have children. After she broke his heart, he had a difficult time trusting any woman in a relationship. Until I came along, that is.

"I'll never do that to you, Marcus," I say. "I'll never leave you." The tension behind his eyes fades. I only wish I could convince myself of my own words the way I've convinced him. The feelings that came back to me tonight when Glenn touched me frighten me. Glenn is my past. My history. I shouldn't feel *anything* for him.

Our embrace is interrupted when we hear cries echoing from our apartment. Marcus storms in to see what is going on. There on the grey couch are Timber and Yoric, half-naked and tangled in each other's limbs. I have to stifle a laugh at the unexpected discovery. I knew Timber liked Yoric, but I had no idea anything was actually going on. Huh. Jansen was right about him all along. I just hadn't expected the woman on his mind to be Timber.

"What the hell?" Yoric cries out. "I thought you were still playing." Timber blushes as she reaches for her white peasant blouse, which is draped over a plant on the other side of the couch, and holds it over her chest in a feeble attempt to cover up.

"I got a, uh, cramp in my wrist," I say, caressing the spot where Glenn grabbed me, "so we decided we'd had enough."

After the serious nature of the last twenty minutes, I'm surprised to see Marcus uplifted. He snickers and teases Yoric, who is looking around the room for his own shirt.

"We're going to bed," Marcus says. "You two get dressed and find your way to your own beds."

⸘

I wake up to find empty sheets next to me. Marcus must have left early for work today. Evie and I don't need to be at class for another hour, so I lie in bed staring up at the revolving ceiling fan and try to figure out what I'm going to say to Glenn, since it's inevitable that I will see him again.

A rapping at the door startles me. Who could be here now? Probably Timber coming by to apologize for last night. She's the type who would do that. I really don't feel like getting up now. Perhaps if I ignore it she'll go away. She doesn't really need to apologize anyway. I probably would have done the same had it been Marcus and me.

The knocking continues, so I get up and approach the door. When I reach my hand to the doorknob, I realize that I'm way underdressed for answering the door. But if it's only Timber it's no big deal. And really, who else could it be this early?

Just my crummy luck. *How did I not see this coming?*

Chapter 5

I SLIDE MY SCANTILY clothed body behind the door to hide from Glenn's wandering eyes. Or eye.

It's really weird and disconcerting, seeing only one eye when I'm used to seeing two.

Awareness that I am still wearing my dainty rose nightgown trimmed with lace causes goosebumps to form on my flesh. I never used to wear these kinds of things before—I'm a tee shirt and sweats kind of gal—but Marcus likes feminine lingerie so I wear them for him. They are so skimpy, sometimes I let Evie wear them as dresses when she plays dress up.

"What are you doing here, Glenn?" I whisper, hoping that the knocking did not awaken Evie.

"Pollen, I really need to speak with you. I can't wait any longer," he says as he starts to walk forward. I stretch my arm out to stop him.

"How did you know where I live?"

"I followed you guys home last night. I'm sorry, I just didn't want you to keep evading me every time you see me," he says.

I try to shut the door before he gets any further, but he raises his arm to hold it steady and wedges his shoulder in the opening.

"Marcus isn't here," I whisper. "What if someone sees you?" My mind drifts back to the old days, when it was Glenn's jealousy I worried about. He of all people should understand the implications of the situation.

He ignores my question and says, "If Marcus isn't here, that's probably best. It's you I want to talk to, not him." Despite the firm obstruction his body poses, I continue to push the door against him, but without much avail.

"Pollen, this isn't about us," he assures. I study his face but Glenn is hard to read, especially with that patch masking his expression. I don't know if I can trust him yet, but I find my determination to stay away from him faltering. He won't give up until we get this over with.

I loosen my grip on the door and allow him to come in. The living room is brimming with darkness in the early hours of dawn since the sun hasn't fully risen yet. I grope the wall, searching for the light switch and flip it on.

"You look good," Glenn says, eying my nightgown. My arms fumble clumsily over my gown as I feebly attempt to cover myself. I recall leaving my robe hanging in the bathroom so I retrieve it and hastily wrap it around myself. I could think of nothing worse than Marcus walking in and seeing Glenn here with me in my lingerie.

"What do you want, Glenn?" I ask tersely. He peers around the room taking in his surroundings and helps himself to a seat on my couch. My feet remain planted on the floor where I stand and I cross my arms shrewdly.

"I came to apologize," he says. I grunt dubiously. This surprises me, considering Glenn has never apologized for a thing in his life. "No, really.

What I did to you and Evie . . . and Marcus; it's unforgivable. I want you to know I've changed. I really have. Okay, I understand you may not trust me now. But I'll prove it to you. I'm not here to hurt you, Polly."

"You expect me to believe that? After what you did to Marcus? I've seen the scars, Glenn." I shake my head.

"I'm sorry you had to see that. Even more, I'm sorry for what I did. He wasn't the only innocent I tortured," his eye gazes away in a blank stare, like he's recalling some horrifying memory. "But I admit, I was much harsher on him than the others because ... he took you away from me."

"He didn't take anything from you. You left *me*. You pushed me out the door and turned your back on me."

"You're right, Polly. I was callow and stupid."

Well, at least he admits *that*.

"You say you're sorry. And I want to believe you. But how can you expect me to after everything you've done?" I squint at Glenn.

"It'll take time, I guess. I did open that door for you. Doesn't that count for something?" I should have known he'd bring that up. He's right, though. He *did* put himself at risk to help us. But is that enough to negate everything else he did?

My eyes keep drawing to his eye patch as if it were magnetized. "What's up with the patch?" I ask.

"You want to see?" he asks. I hesitate. Do I really want to see what's behind there? I'd managed to convince myself that he's simply covering up the mark of the Trinity—the eye tattoo shaped like a triangle with a dot in the center. I'd never really considered the alternative.

Glenn removes the patch to reveal an empty eye socket. I gasp at the void but sit down next to him to get a better look. This skin of his eyelid droops into an empty pink cavity where his eyeball used to be—the eye that once bore the mark of the Trinity that all Enforcers are branded with.

"They did this to you," I start, but my voice fades as I'm at a loss for words.

"Because I helped you escape," he finishes. My heart sags in sorrow. I admit I wanted Glenn to be punished for the pain he inflicted on Marcus. But I hoped he would get a lashing or beating, or something else. I didn't expect him to lose his eye. But I guess that makes sense. If he is no longer an Enforcer he can no longer bear the mark. And how else would they remove it?

"And also because I shot three of our own," Glenn continues. He replaces the patch. "Now do you see that I am on your side?"

"Yes," I utter, lowering my head in shame. Guilt washes over me as I remember the good times Glenn and I shared, before Crimson or the Trinity came into our lives. The late night movies, the camping trips, sleeping together under the stars. Glenn lifts my chin up with his fingertips. "Don't blame yourself, Polly. I know that's what you do. It's not your fault. And trust me; it could have been much worse."

My eyes widen, "What do you mean?"

"They intended to do much more. They were going to cut off a finger for each of the Enforcers I shot. And I was scheduled to be tagged and put in the hole for a few months. After they gouged my eye out, I had a rare opportunity to escape, so I took it."

"And you came here," I finish. "What happened, after you were released from the clinic? Did they interrogate you?"

"They took me to a room and questioned me, yes. I was there for hours while they drilled me, probably waiting for me to screw up. They only let me out after I gave them some valuable intel."

"Like what?" I asked, leaning forward, my eyes imploring him. Glenn looks away, as if he's searching his mind. I know that look. He's trying to decide whether or not to tell me. He always used to do that before, when he thought I was too young or naïve to understand something.

His lips press into a hard line. "I'm really not supposed to say," Glenn says.

"Right," I mutter, disappointed. I should have known he wouldn't be forthright with me. He has always carried the notion that I can't handle anything serious.

"No, really, Pollen. They don't want any of this getting around the complex right now. Look, I know you're not a gossip, but I'm really trying to do the right thing here, okay?" It makes sense, I guess, even if I am a little offended that he won't tell me. I nod, accepting his explanation and glance over at the clock.

"Oh my god!" I exclaim. It's seven forty-two. I've got to get dressed and wake Evie for school. Lana would murder me for being late if she could get away with it. But since she can't, she'll probably have me scrubbing toilets, which is only one notch above murder in my book.

"Is everything okay?" Glenn genuinely looks concerned.

"We're going to be late for school. Could you go wake Evie for me?" I ask, pointing to her closed door. "No problem," he says, approaching the door.

I rush into my bedroom and close the door behind me. I quickly brush my teeth and splash some icy cold water over my face. I can't believe I lost track of time. Lana is going to enjoy chiding me for my tardiness.

As I slide into my clothes, I hear some shouting coming from the living room. I button my pants hurriedly and grab my shoes when I hear a crash. My primary concern is Evie. Oh god, I hope I'm not wrong about Glenn.

I dart through the door. There, in the living room, is Marcus, standing over a shattered lamp, his hand clasped firmly around Glenn's throat.

Chapter 6

"STOP IT!" I shriek as I scramble toward Marcus. His enraged eyes rise up to meet mine, but he keeps his fingers clamped around Glenn's neck. Evie stands in the doorway, cradling her baby doll. She looks like a frightened mouse that has backed itself into a corner with no way out.

Marcus draws back his left arm, which only means one thing. I can't let him hit Glenn. Especially not his right eye—or empty socket. I feel bad enough that he's lost his eye, even if it is his own fault. I charge forward, straining to pull Marcus's arm down.

"Please, Marcus! Don't!" I plead. At first Marcus struggles against me, his intent to make Glenn pay stronger than his own self-control. "He's not one of them anymore."

Finally, with conflicting emotion, Marcus loosens his grip and Glenn drops to his knees with a thump. He rubs his neck but that does little to remove the inflamed hand imprints Marcus left there.

Marcus turns and glares at me, "What the hell is he doing here?" His piercing sapphire eyes are usually a source of comfort for me, but not now. Now the color has drained from them, leaving them icy, and they seem to carve into my heart, leaving an empty hole where that sense of security used to be.

"He came to the door this morning. He just wanted to apologize. Then I realized I was running late, so I asked him to wake Evie. That's all," I explain.

"And you let him in?" he asks incredulously.

Glenn rises to his feet, still massaging his neck. "Don't be angry with Pollen," he says.

"Don't talk!" Marcus snaps, never taking his eyes off me.

"Marcus." I take his hands in mine. "I wasn't exactly thrilled when he came here. I can only imagine how you must feel. Please, just let him explain."

Marcus grits his teeth and lowers his eyebrows, sending a shiver down my spine. But he turns and looks at Glenn in silence, giving him an opportunity to talk.

"Look, I'm sorry this happened this way," says Glenn. "I'm not here to come between you two. I know that what happened between Pollen and me is over. I accept that. I just needed to apologize. And I wanted to do it with each of you separately, because I wronged you both in different ways. Marcus, I know nothing I can say that will take back the pain I inflicted on you, but I really am sorry. I hope that one day you could forgive me, and we could be friends."

Glenn really sounds sincere—to me anyway. I'm not sure Marcus is buying it though. We stand in silence with only the hushed murmurs of our breathing adding to the tension.

"If you're done, get out," Marcus declares in such a low tone I'd almost think he was possessed by a demon. Glenn nods and leaves, closing the door behind him. I'm so glad I got dressed when I did—if

Marcus had come in about five minutes earlier, this would not have ended so conciliatingly.

Evie is still standing in the doorway, rubbing her eyes. "I've got to get Evie to school. She hasn't even had breakfast yet."

Marcus aims his dagger eyes at me once more, and I can sense his bruised emotions. "We'll talk about this later," he says. "I have to get back to work." He picks up a clipboard from the side table next to the couch before he leaves, slamming the door behind him.

I know Marcus feels hurt, but I wish he'd let it go. It's not worth carrying around that baggage, always worried if I'm going to leave him. I understand his anger and resentment towards Glenn for the physical torment he was put through. But my past relationship with Glenn is none of his business. It's my burden to carry, not his.

Now that Glenn finally got his chance to speak with me, he keeps his distance for several days, giving Marcus and me a chance to talk things out and reconnect. Marcus is still embittered about Glenn living here at Ceborec, but each day his hostility seems to lighten. He can pass by Glenn in the same room without the insatiable urge to beat him, though he still won't acknowledge him.

I run into Glenn again on my way to meet Timber for training. He seems to be in higher spirits now; maybe it's the relief of releasing the burden of his past crimes. Or the freedom that Ceborec offers in stark contrast to the repression of Crimson. His smile seems to glow brighter and he walks with a slight skip in his step. This is the Glenn I remember from years ago.

"On your way to training, too?" I ask, as we walk side by side down the hill toward the armory.

"Nah, they don't trust me with any weapons yet," he says. Glenn's been given a trial period, to make sure he's not a spy, planted here to gather valuable information and plan an attack. I could see a real possibility in that theory, but I hope I'm right to trust him. It's nice to have him back in my life as a friend. "I volunteered for a grounds keeping position. I'm so sick of being inside all the time."

I burst into laughter, "What are you going to do when we go underground next month?"

Glenn smiles, sensing the irony. "We'll be doing general maintenance around the bunkers." That suits him well, actually. He's always had that handyman knack. Fixing mechanical stuff and working on cars. He always wanted to help my dad out in the garage, but after we got pregnant with Lex, my dad let him know under no vague circumstances that he was no longer welcome at our house.

"Plus we'll be able to come up for short periods of time to clear the vents and stuff." Glenn pauses and there is an awkward moment of silence. I sense he wants to say something, but he's hesitating.

"How are things with Marcus? After the other day, I mean. I hope I didn't mess things up for you," he asks. No wonder he hesitated. I'm sure he didn't want to imply any selfish intentions by asking that question, but given our history it's plausible to think he may be looking for an excuse to get back with me.

"We're fine. He just needs some time. I think he's angrier about the prospect of losing me than he is about the scars. He's been burned in the past and hasn't really gotten over it," I explain.

"What happened? If you don't mind asking."

"Marcus married his high school sweetheart. She wanted children and they tried for a year without success. Then he found out he's infertile. Apparently that was a gamechanger for her and she divorced him."

"I'm sorry to hear that," says Glenn. "So, why don't you want any kids?"

I'm taken aback by the intrusiveness of the question. *What business is it of his if I want kids or not?* I've never known Glenn to speak so bluntly. He's always had a way with words—this keen ability to make some awful comment sound sweet, or an intrusive question sound innocently curious. Maybe this is some part of his atonement—to stop being so conniving and manipulative. I hesitate, but decide to answer anyway.

"I didn't say that I don't want kids. It's just . . . after Lex, I don't think I could handle losing any more children. Glenn, you know how that tore me apart when he died. Plus, I've got Evie to take care of. That's all I need." I do want kids, but my life won't be over if I don't have them. And Marcus and I have a bond that could never be broken because of his condition. I love him too much to abandon him for my own selfish motives.

"Evie's really special to you, isn't she?" Glenn observes.

"She's the only blood relative I've got left," I remark, "the only link to Drake." The memory of my late brother saddens me. He was a captain in the National Army of North Cythera and died in the Deimosian War a few months before the virus was unleashed.

"She misses him. But Marcus is a perfect substitute. He treats her like she's his own daughter and she loves him dearly." I glance up at Glenn, who has that conflicted look on his face again. I can't help feeling there's something he's holding back.

I stop and turn to him, vexed by his disconcerting silence. "Glenn, I know that look. Is there something you want to tell me?" I boldly ask.

He shakes his head, turning his head away to ensure his gaze doesn't become ensnared in mine. "It was good seeing you again, Pollen. I've got to get to work. I'll see you later." Before I can protest, he trudges off to the maintenance shed, where they keep the mowers and other grounds keeping equipment.

I continue on to the armory by myself, a few hundred yards from the maintenance shed. Upon entering the building I have to scan my hand, both for security and to check in for my daily training. The armory is divided into five sections: firearms, ammunition, alternative weapons, sparring arena, and shooting range. There is an additional outdoor shooting range in the valley behind the armory, as well as the full-scale training arenas throughout the acreage, where we do tactical group training.

I report to the firearms checkout counter where Timber is adjusting a holster around her hips.

"Hey Pol, what's up?" Her bright green eyes greet me with a concerned look. I'm still thinking about Glenn and that feeling that he's hiding something. I'm doing a horrible job of masking my emotions.

"Nothing. Just thinking, that's all," I reply. The attendant at the counter returns with Timber's handgun and places it on the counter.

"Must be some deep thoughts, by the look on your face," says Timber, placing her gun in the holster at her hip.

The attendant stares me down for a few seconds as if I'm wasting his time. I place my left hand on the countertop scanner and tap the fingers of my right as I wait for the green laser to sail back into the darkness.

"DS-42," I say to the attendant, who disappears into the storage room behind a high security steel door.

"It's Glenn," I say. If there's anyone here I can talk to about him, it's Timber. Maybe she can give me some helpful advice. "We're getting along better now. Becoming friends again. But I can't help feeling he's keeping something from me."

"Like what?" asks Timber.

I pause when the attendant returns with my pistol, pressing my lips together. Nestling it in the holster on my thigh, I grab Timber's arm and amble toward the ammunitions counter slowly, speaking in a hushed tone.

"I don't know. That's what bothers me."

"Do you think he's still one of them?" Timber asks, wide-eyed. The thought had occurred to me. He's got a trademark for deception. But that's not really the gut feeling I'm getting from him. And my gut feelings are usually pretty dead-on.

"I don't think so. It feels . . . more personal. Like something specific to me."

"Do you think he still has feelings for you?"

"Oh, I *know* he still has feelings for me," I remark. "But I don't think that's it either. And when I asked him about it, he just made an excuse to cut the convo short."

"Interesting," she says, gazing upward.

We approach the ammunitions counter where Harrison, the attendant, casually leans over on his tattooed forearms. One of his tattoos looks like his skin has been ripped away and reveals a gorgeous representation of a double helix. He told me he got that done after his son was born six years ago. Harrison didn't see him that often because he lived with his mother, Harrison's ex-girlfriend. But he meant the world to him. His little boy did not survive the virus.

"Hello lovely ladies," he says with a smirk. Harrison is in his late twenties and he is an incurable flirt. It's annoying sometimes, but it's also kind of cute. I'd feel sorry for the poor girl that falls for that contagious smile and long black hair streaked with gold. He's not the type to commit to anyone for very long. A love 'em and leave 'em type. He's been trying to get into my and Timber's pants since we got here. Normally I'd be put off by it, but somehow I find it flattering coming from him. At least he's good-humored about my sanguine rejections.

"Hi, Harrison," I say. "I'll take red today."

"Yellow for me," Timber jumps in.

From under the counter, Harrison slides out two long, narrow wooden boxes and places them on the counter. Inside the boxes are rows of training bullets filled with paint. The coating that shapes the bullet is a substance that dissolves upon firing so that target is hit with only a splash of paint. It's a little painful at first, like being slapped with a rubber band, but you get used to it after a while. The purpose for using paint bullets at the shooting range is not only for safety, but also for conserving real bullets for when they are needed.

Harrison pulls out some empty magazines from below the counter and begins to load them up with paint bullets. He hands me, and then Timber, five magazines, each containing eight training bullets for a total of forty, the maximum we are permitted for each training day.

"So when are you going to dump that boyfriend of yours for me, Pollen?" Harrison asks jocosely.

"When the compound gets snowed in," I answer, smiling back.

"Maybe we'll get lucky and have a blizzard next winter," he quips. Snow hasn't fallen on the planet since before I was born because of the rising temperatures and greenhouse gases. He won't be getting lucky any time soon.

Harrison takes my hand in his, and with an impish smirk on his face he raises it up to his lips. As he gently kisses my fingers, I can feel him curl them around something. He winks at me as Timber drags me away. I open my hand to find three extra bullets, which I slide into my pocket. Harrison often slides me a few extra bullets. So, yeah, I guess I do cheat sometimes. I just hope Timber doesn't tell Yoric—he'd either go ballistic or gloat that I have to cheat to win anything.

Timber and I stroll out to the outdoor shooting range. I prefer the indoor range, because the distance is shorter and, therefore, easier to hit the targets. But Timber wants to get some fresh air, and I could use some as well. Plus it will give me an opportunity to challenge myself beyond my comfort zone.

The outdoor range resembles a football field. Shooters line up at points along the short end, thirty in all, and shoot at targets at the other end of the field. The targets are a strong, bubble-like substance, which pop upon impact with the paint. They are blown up from an automated machine, so as soon as one target pops, another one appears in its place.

There are ten other residents out here shooting, so it's pretty quiet for a training session. General Granby paces leisurely behind the shooters, observing and giving pointers when he can.

My first round of shots fails miserably. Out of eight bullets, only one made contact with a target. My disturbed thoughts are affecting my skills. I shake the thoughts of Glenn from my head and try again. My second round improves and I manage to hit the target four times. I strike luck on my third magazine, popping seven out of eight targets.

"Very nice," says General Granby, startling me. I holster my gun and turn to address him, "Thank you, sir."

"Could I have a word, Miss McRae," he asks in a gentle, paternal tone.

"Yes, sir," I say. It's not really a requirement to address him as "sir" all the time since I am not a member of the militia, but I find it hard not to when he looks so dignified in his dark green military uniform, donned with medals and decorations. Before the virus, he was a well-respected general of the eastern division of the National Army of North

Cythera and served four tours of duty in the Deimosian War in the south, which has been going on for years. His wife and two little girls perished from the illness. He came to serve COPS after learning about the Trinity and their betrayal to our country. He is now considered a traitor by the Trinity and there is a monstrous price on his head for potential bounty hunters.

Granby walks with me around the side of the armory building, away from the shooting, so we can talk.

"I've noticed you have improved greatly on your targets since . . . when did you arrive?"

"About three months ago, sir, but I've only really been training for two," I reply.

"Two months. That's quite impressive," says Granby.

"Thank you," I say. When I first arrived I barely knew how to hold a gun, much less shoot it and hit a target. In fact, I've always been scared of guns. My first training session here was a nightmare. All I can say is thank goodness we only use paint bullets or the medical clinic would have been very busy that day.

"What I really want to talk about is Glenn Malek. How well do you know him?" Granby asks. He must have seen us talking earlier, or maybe Glenn told him that he knew me.

"We were engaged. Before all of this happened, anyway," I say.

"So you have a personal relationship with him?"

"Used to. We were together for five years. When he became an Enforcer at Crimson I broke it off. We're still on speaking terms, but that's it."

Granby pulls out a small yellow notepad and pen from his back pocket. "I need you to tell me everything you know about him, beginning at the outset of the virus."

"The early memories are still a little fuzzy," I say, "but after my parents died, I didn't see him until I arrived at Crimson. I thought he had died already, because I read his name in the newspaper—the list of the deceased."

As I speak, Granby jots down some notes. I feel like a witness at Glenn's trial. I know I must be honest in my recount, but I hope what I say doesn't have a negative impact on Glenn. I can tell he's trying to be a productive part of our society.

"When I discovered him at Crimson," I continued, "he blew me off. Made it seem like he wanted nothing to do with me. Then he got insanely jealous when he saw me with Marcus. That's when I officially ended our relationship. When we escaped the first time, he grabbed my niece, Evie, just as the van we stowed away on was leaving. He knew I would be forced to come back to get her."

Granby stops writing and I take notice, expecting him to dismiss me. "Please continue," he says. I tell him all about how Glenn caught up with us at my house, after my memory loss, and deceived me in order to take Marcus and me back to Crimson, and about how Glenn encouraged me to join the Enforcers to save myself. Granby seems more than attentive when I explain Glenn's role in our second escape attempt.

"If you don't mind my asking, sir, what is this all about?" I ask.

"I need to know if Glenn is going to be a threat to our people. He gave us his story of what happened at Crimson. I wanted to hear it from you to see if the stories corroborate," says Granby.

"And?" I ask with anticipation bubbling up inside me.

"Your stories match precisely. Unless you have good reason why we shouldn't trust him, we will probably grant him limited unrestricted access to the facility and armory." Granby looks at me, as if expecting an answer.

"I think he's okay," I say. "I trust him."

"Very good," says General Granby. "Proceed with your training, Miss McRae."

Glenn will have access to weapons now. I hope I didn't just make a horrible mistake in judgment.

Chapter 7

I'VE MANAGED TO FIND the tiny minnow in a sea of fish: a small round table in the boisterous food court, which is bustling with activity at this hour. I already have my dinner of black beans and quinoa with red peppers, so I just sit here alone, pushing the beans around my plate letting them get cold, and scan the room for a familiar face. Lynx and I have a dinner date tonight. We try to meet up once a week to catch up since we hardly see each other any more. Tonight she's running late.

Yoric approaches the table and startles me out of my intense focus. His golden hair is loose and frames his square face nicely.

"Hey, Pollen. Mind if I sit down?" he asks politely as he pulls out the chair across from me and plops down, not bothering to wait for a response.

"Actually, I'm expecting somebody, Yoric," I say, scanning the crowd behind him.

"Which one of your boyfriends?" he asks facetiously, with a grin the size of the moon stretching across his cheeks.

"Neither," I glare at him. Apparently, word has gotten around about my past relationship with Glenn, and as with any large enclosed facility, people *will* talk. I'm not worried about what they think, though. My only concern is the people closest to me: Evie, Marcus, and Timber. "Actually, I'm waiting for Lynx. She was my old roomie at Crimson."

"Oh," says Yoric. "Well, I'll get out of your way when she gets here. I wanted to ask you something." Yoric averts his eyes and fidgets with his hands like a nervous twelve-year-old. "I want to do something for Timber and I need your advice. Can you keep a secret?"

"Sure," I said. "Especially if you're planning something nice for Timber. She deserves it."

"I think I'm going to propose to her," Yoric says.

My jaw drops. After a few seconds I giggle uncontrollably. "Stop it, Yoric. You're killing me!"

He looks dead in my eyes. He isn't kidding. "I mean it, Pollen. I love her and I want to marry her." He can't be serious. It's way too soon for them to marry. They've barely just started dating. Then again, I've only just found out about their relationship a few days ago. Maybe they've been keeping this secret for a long time now.

"Yoric, how long have you two been—"

"Three months," he interrupts me. "But I'm really into her. And it's not like I have a ton of options anymore. None of the other women here do it for me."

"Yes, but marriage? Do you really want to take it that far? Maybe you two could just live together for a while and see what happens."

He didn't seem to hear me. "I want to do something really crazy for the proposal, but something she'll like. That's why I need your help."

"Yoric, I'd love to help you, I'm just not so sure this is a good idea," I say. "Timber's got a good head on her shoulders. I don't think she'd say yes, no matter how much she loves you. You should give it a little more time."

Yoric slumps his shoulders, defeated. "Really?" I feel kind of bad now. He truly does love her. I try to think of something to lift his spirits.

"Yes, but that just gives us more time to plan something really spectacular," I reassure. Yoric looks up with a glint of hope in his eyes. Just behind him I spot Lynx approaching.

"Hey, Pollen. Sorry I'm late. I just spent the last hour arguing with Curtis about the placement of the auxiliary coolant system," she says. Lynx looks like she just came straight from work: shoulder-length blond hair pulled back carelessly into a ponytail, creases etched into her forehead, and a wrinkled lab coat hanging over her forearm.

"Thanks, Pollen," says Yoric as he stands, nods to Lynx, and disappears into the cloud of hungry Ceborec residents.

"Hey Lynx. Sounds like Curtis is—"

"A pompous nerd who thinks a couple of degrees earns him the privilege of being my superior,"

Lynx finishes. A brief pause and a questioning smile prompt her to elaborate. "Okay, yes, he's had a formal education in engineering, but I've had just as much education as he has. And just because my degree isn't in engineering doesn't mean I don't know as much as him. *I do read,* you know." She drops her plate of pasta marinara on the table and begins to slurp it up.

Lynx used to be a research librarian at a prestigious university before the virus struck. She truly is one of the most intelligent people I know. When she first arrived here, the only one of our escape party to successfully escape from Crimson during our first attempt, she took up a post as an inventory analyst for the aerospace engineering department. The library had no need for another librarian and she wanted to be involved in the development of the Earth shuttle. It was a stroke of luck, really, how she ended up where she is now. One of the lead engineers passed away and they needed an immediate replacement. Of course, since the virus depleted most of the population they had quite a small pool of candidates to choose from. Lynx somehow managed to convince the chief engineers that she was the most capable and competent for the job. Now she is a lead engineer and has unescorted clearance throughout the entire facility.

"Sorry you're having a bad day," I say.

"Yeah, enough about that. How are Evie and Marcus? It seems like ages since I've seen them." Lynx asks with her mouth half full.

We chat for a while, talking about things that have happened since we saw each other last week. Lynx updates me on plans for the Earth shuttle, most of which I don't understand, and I tell her about Marcus and Glenn.

"How's Marcus dealing with that?" she asks.

"He's suspicious, to say the least," I say.

"Well, who isn't?" Lynx laughs. "Just about everyone here has got their eyes on him. What do you think? Do you trust him?" That must be the question of the week for me.

"You know, I hate having the pressure of that question weighing down on me," I say. I push my plate away and wipe my hands on the napkin in my lap.

"I'm sorry, I didn't—" starts Lynx.

"Oh, I'm not directing that at you, Lynx. It's just that General Granby took me aside and asked me that earlier."

"Well, you are the only one here that really knows him," she says.

"Do I? I'm not sure I ever really knew him. I mean, since he's been here, it's like the last year never happened. Like he's the old Glenn I knew and fell in love with years ago."

"But, and correct me if I'm wrong, Glenn was quite the master of deception. It could just be a facade to gain your trust."

"Of course I've already considered that. Despite his past, I think I do trust him. And Granby trusts my judgment. The problem is; what if I'm wrong and something really bad happens? What if more people die as a result of my trusting him? I can't handle carrying that burden."

"I'm sure you are right about him, Pollen. You do have good judgment. Don't doubt that for a second." Lynx smiles.

The dinner crowd begins to thin out and as the noise in the food court dies down, Lynx takes notice of the late hour.

"I need to get going," she sighs. "I've got some CRTs to sign off on before it gets too late."

"Thanks for the talk. I feel much better about my decision. Same time next week?" I ask.

"Of course," says Lynx, standing up to push her chair in.

"Oh, and Lynx," I call out as she begins to walk away. She turns back. "Take a vacation. You can't work all the time." She smiles and nods before she walks away.

I've already finished eating my dinner, but I don't really want to go back to the apartment yet. My mind is whirling with thoughts of Glenn and Marcus. If Glenn is to remain here, I've got to figure out how to bridge the resentment between those two.

"Is this seat taken?" I look up to see Marcus smiling down at me.

"Lynx just left," I say. "I was just getting ready to go home. Where's Evie?"

Marcus relaxes into the chair and rests his arms on the table, fidgeting with a green piece of paper.

"Timber's with her. I think I might get promoted," he says.

"Really? That's great!" I say as my face lights up.

"I've been invited to go hang out with Hagar and the guys tomorrow afternoon." Hagar is Marcus's boss and the superintendent on the job site. He is often seen associating with lead engineers and scientists in his off time. But my smile fades when I realize I'll be on my own for training tomorrow.

"What about our training?" I ask.

"Why don't you see if Timber can train with you again?" he says.

"Then who's going to watch Evie?" I stare intently at him with a *'didn't you think this through first'* look.

"I don't know," he shrugs thoughtlessly. "Send her to the daycare."

"Daycare? You know I can't do that."

"Pollen," Marcus sighs restlessly, "they watch kids every day. You need to loosen the reins a little."

My blood begins to simmer and I can feel the veins on my face spill over with raging hot blood. My voice takes on a stiff, staccato tone. "I won't let her go with anyone I don't trust. You know that, Marcus. Why can't you just go another time?"

"This is important," his voice lowers, taking a more serious tone.

"And I'm not?"

His face reddens and his eyebrows descend, hedging over his eyes. The blue irises stand out in stark contrast to his magenta skin. "Pollen," he says in a deep low voice, "Ever since we've been here I'm either with you or Evie or at work. I need a life, too!"

"What's that supposed to mean?" I snap.

"It means, I need to hang out with some guys for a change."

"You hang out with them every day at work," I remark.

Marks shakes his head as he looks away, "Do whatever you have to do. I won't be training with you tomorrow."

Marcus nearly knocks over the chair as he stands and walks away, leaving me to brew in my own fury.

I can barely sleep when I return to the apartment. Marcus and I avoid each other as much as possible despite sleeping in the same bed. We don't talk. We don't touch. We don't even look at each other. This is our first real fight and, I don't know, maybe it's this tension with Glenn around, but although I should know better, I can't help but feel our relationship is beginning to break down.

Chapter 8

MARCUS WAS ALREADY GONE when I woke up this morning, presumably to avoid me and any argument I might start. Or continue rather. Maybe I was being a little selfish last night. I understand he needs his own friends. But surely he could find time outside our training schedule to socialize. And he didn't have to make those biting remarks about my handling of Evie's care. He knows the hell I went through, *we* went through, to get her out of Crimson and how difficult it is for me to let her out of my sight. I won't let that happen again.

I thought about staying home with Evie myself so that Timber could go train with Yoric, but I have so much pent up aggression I need to go shoot some stuff to allow myself to vent. I had to bribe Timber to stay with Evie and let me go alone. I now owe her a girls night out at the new nightclub that's about to open when we move underground.

It's a dark, overcast day, the kind of day people usually stick to the shooting ranges because the smoky clouds appear engorged with rain. I have no intention of using the range. I want to be out in the woods, away from everybody. Alone in my sanctuary—the way I used to escape into the woods when I was younger. I've just got to figure out how to convince the Watchers to let me out there without a training partner. Or maybe I don't.

As I wait for the attendant to return with my pistol, Glenn reluctantly approaches me.

"Hey Pollen," he says. "Shooting at the range today?" The attendant appears and places my gun on the counter while warily eying Glenn.

"Nope," I say, placing the pistol in my holster. "I'm going out to Arena Five." Arena Five is one of the wooded training arenas surrounding the complex. It's usually reserved only for group training.

Nobody's ever allowed to go to the outdoor arenas alone. The threat of bounty hunters makes it too dangerous—even with the barricade of Watchers on duty surrounding the perimeter.

"Where's your partner?" Glenn asks, looking around.

"He's got more important things to do today than train with me. I'm going alone." My tone is thick with resentment.

"No, you're not," he says, placing his hand on the scanner. The attendant looks up at Glenn nervously after reading the scanner, then disappears into the back room.

"Glenn," I start, but he puts his hand up to stop me.

"Pollen, it's not safe out there by yourself. Trust me. I could have easily gotten past the Watchers unseen if I'd wanted to. We'll train together today. I won't tell Marcus, I promise."

The attendant returns with a beginner's training rifle. Unlike the other firearms, these were designed *only* to use paint bullets, and not real ones. I'd expect Glenn to argue his way into getting a real gun, but he surprises me with his graceful acceptance of the rifle.

"Okay," I give in as we walk to the ammunitions counter. "But remember, we are training. Nothing more."

"Give me a full minute," I direct Glenn, and then dash off into the gloomy wooded abyss.

"One thousand one, one thousand two, one thousand three," I count silently to myself as I dodge the trees, looking back every now again to make sure he's not following yet. My speed has picked up in the past few months of training. I'm still not as fast as I used to be when I ran track in high school three years ago, but I'm getting there.

When I reach "one thousand fifty two," I duck behind a giant elm with a hollowed out trunk where some small woodland creatures probably used to take shelter before they were decimated by the virus. As I slow my breathing I hear the pit-a-pat of raindrops bouncing off of the leaves above me. A rumble of thunder hums in the distance, announcing an approaching storm.

It's so peaceful, being alone out here; I almost forget that I'm supposed to be on guard. I close my eyes and open my other senses to the world around me: tiny splashes of rain plopping on my exposed legs, the surging breeze winding its way around the tree trunks surrounding me, the creaking of the trees above as they sway with the turbulent wind. And the crunching of leaves under the heavy boots of a pursuer.

He's here already? How long have I been sitting here?

My eyes flash open and I pull my pistol from its holster around my thigh. I hold the gun softly against the slightly scarred skin of my cheek, preparing my tense body for action. Spinning around I point my gun in the direction of the footsteps, but no one is there. I rise to my feet and step forward, puzzled, looking behind the tree. *Where could he have gone?* Then I think of Timber and her expert tree climbing skills. *Can Glenn climb?*

I turn my attention upward, toward the fierce battle of blustering tree branches above, but there's no sign of him. Before I even have time to process this, I am grabbed from behind. I can't believe I was caught off-guard. It's one of the first things we learned here during training—to always be aware of our surroundings.

I feel the warm moisture of his breath behind my left ear. I writhe in his arms but his grip tightens, securing me in place. Fury rushes through my veins, but when his husky voice whispers into my ear, the terrifying awareness that it's not Glenn takes over and the gun slips from my trembling fingers as an icy chill jolts down my spine.

"Scream and I'll blow your head off, pretty girl."

I can feel the sharp edge of the barrel just behind my right ear. I don't know how I got myself into this situation or how I'm going to get out. I can only hope that Glenn finds me. But then what? What can he do with a simple training rifle? I never should have come out here. I should have stayed at the shooting range with everybody else. Now I've put myself and Glenn in danger.

My captor turns me around and leads me through the woods, never taking the gun away from my head. The rain is pouring buckets now and I can barely hear Glenn calling for me. But my captor won't let me stop; he continues to push me forward, silencing me with the cold metal shaft.

I know that once we are out of the perimeter there is no hope for me. I have to think of something quick. There's a tricky move I learned in the sparring arena where we do unarmed combat. It could work now, but only if I catch my captor off-guard. Otherwise I'll be on my way to joining my parents and Drake.

I continue to walk, trying to appear as submissive as possible. In one swift move I duck down and twist my legs around his, jabbing the back of his knee, causing him to fall backward. Now is my chance. I make a run for it.

In my mind, I'm back in the woods that fateful day, when I woke up with no memory and found myself being pursued by a band of redneck bounty hunters. Only this time, I've got the rain and wind to run against as well. I berate myself for not taking his gun when I had the chance. But it's too late now. All I can do is run. I glance back to see that he is right on my tail, only a few paces back. I charge forward, but I can't seem to lose him.

As I sprint, I tear my holster away from my thigh and yank the band from my hair. If I can't escape him, maybe I can stall him long enough to get away. I still have four full magazines and in my left pocket are three loose paint bullets I saved from my last training session.

Up ahead I spot the elm I was hiding in. I'm getting close to Glenn and the complex. If I can just make it out of the woods I'll be okay. He won't pursue me out in the open. But I won't make it that far.

Just as I am passing the tree, I feel a tug at my feet and I am on the ground, scraping my fingernails through the mud, trying to get away. The man is right on top of me. I reach into my pocket and load my slingshot. Turning to him I pull back the band and release the bullet straight into his right eye. It doesn't do any permanent damage, but does cause some extreme pain as the paint stings his eye. His agonizing wails echo through the woods over the booming thunder and pounding rainfall. But he doesn't release me as I had hoped. Instead he sits atop me and aims his gun at my left eye.

This is it. This is the end.

I clench my eyes shut, ready to make my peace, when the weight lifts off me. When I release my eyes I find Glenn gripping the man by his neck and striking his head against the tree repeatedly until he is unconscious. I stagger backward in the mud, trying to physically and psychologically distance myself from violence in front of me. Glenn takes the loaded gun from the ground and without hesitation, fires a bullet into my captor's left eye. An eye for an eye.

Chapter 9

THE ROTUNDA IS A HAILSTORM of utter chaos and pandemonium. The moment Glenn announced to General Granby that the perimeter had been breached, alarms blared, the militia were called in and everyone pretty much stopped what they were doing to follow emergency procedures. I just stand, hair and clothes dripping from the torrential downpour, shivering against the wall, blending in with the glossy white paint, and watch, still rattled by the attack and unsure of what to do. Glenn hovers by me, holding me close, comforting me. I search the men and women charging past, but Marcus is nowhere in sight.

"The Watchers are launching a full-scale run of the perimeter. Take the men to the armory," General Granby addresses Sage, who stands rigid and alert. Beyond him are neatly stacked lines of men and women, all in muted green uniforms, standing at attention. There must be about fifty of them. There's no way we could survive a full-scale attack with only fifty soldiers. There's hundreds of Enforcers at Crimson. No wonder Granby's been on the hunt for recruits. "Get them armed immediately. They are to fan out and scour every square inch of the property."

"Yes, sir," Sage salutes and the marches the men and women out the front entrance.

General Granby turns to Glenn and me, still standing against the wall, trying our best to stay out of the way.

"Come with me," he commands and leads us down a seemingly endless corridor and into a dimly lit office. A huge, mahogany desk in front of a bookcase backdrop takes up nearly half of the room. In the other half are two simple wooden chairs and a plush loveseat cushioned between two side tables with lamps built into them.

"Please, sit down," says General Granby. I sink into the loveseat, which swallows me into a soft cocoon. Glenn sits next to me, clearly unwilling to leave me alone for any period of time. Granby pulls one of the wooden chairs over to face me and sits with his elbows resting on his knees.

General Granby places one hand gently on my knee and asks, "Are you okay, Pollen? Are you hurt?"

"Just a little shaken," I say. "But I'm okay." Shaken is an appropriate word at this point. It's not cold at all in the building, but my entire body is shivering. I could lie to myself and assume that it's my wet hair and clothes causing the chills, but deep down I know the temperature has nothing to do with it.

"I'm sorry this happened to you," says Granby with a sincere look of concern in his eyes. My heart breaks, thinking about my father. As tough as he was on me, he had this same tenderness in his eyes whenever he could sense that I was hurting. Granby turns to look at Glenn, "I need you to tell me what happened."

"I'll tell you," I say, trying to straighten my body to sit up in the loveseat, but it just sinks back down. "We were in Arena Five. I went out ahead of Glenn. The guy caught me by surprise and took me from behind. I could feel the gun on the back of my head as he led me away from the complex. I was able to get away from him but he caught up with me and pinned me on the ground. By that time Glenn had found me and . . . took care of him."

The image of that man haunts my mind. One eye spattered with blue paint from my bullet. The other a black hole, framed with brilliant carmine blood. Try as I might, I can't release that vision from my head.

"His body's a little over a hundred yards in. Next to an elm with a hollowed trunk," Glenn adds.

"I know where that is. You're sure he's dead?" Granby asks.

"I shot him in the eye with his own gun. He's not going anywhere." Glenn confirms.

Static sounds from the walkie-talkie on Granby's hip. A voice comes over the radio, but I can't make out what is being said. Granby puts it to his mouth and says, "Ten-four. Be right there."

Granby stands and walks behind his desk, where he opens a drawer and pulls a handgun, checking that it is loaded. "Pollen, you stay here as long as you need to. Glenn, stay with her. I'll be back." Granby leaves and shuts the door behind him.

The room fills with a shroud of uneasy silence. Glenn is trying to maintain his distance emotionally and be respectful, while still remaining close enough to console me.

My emotions turn to anger—anger with Marcus for abandoning me today and allowing me to go out on my own. Today, he put himself first. He put his friends first. And look what happened. His friends were more important than my safety. I can't even bear to think of him right now, so I focus on Glenn. He's the one who was with me today. He's the one who saved my life. He really is a good friend. The doubt that clouded my vision begins to clear. I do trust Glenn.

"Thank you Glenn," I say, cutting the veil of tension that separates us.

"It's nothing," he says. "In fact, I think I enjoyed pulling the trigger. Payback, you know?"

"I'm not thanking you just for saving me, but for being there. If you hadn't shown up at the armory when you did, I would have found a way to go out on my own. I wouldn't be here if it weren't for you."

"Pollen, you know I would never let anything bad happen to you," Glenn says.

I flash him a look of discernment, reminding him of our past at Crimson. "Oh, really?"

He lowers his head shamefully, "You know I wasn't myself then, at Crimson. I was wrong and I admit that. When the virus hit, and everyone started dying I got scared. Everyone was dying and I didn't know what to do. I only cared about myself and my own survival. I was selfish. But I've grown up, Polly. When I saw you and Evie there on the floor in the solitary level, with Damon's gun pointed at your head, it just clicked. You ignited a spark in me that day and I realized that my life means nothing. It doesn't matter if I live or die anymore. What matters is that you and Evie are the only people I know that are still alive, and I intend to keep it that way."

"That day at Crimson," I say, "when you shoved me out the door—"

"I was following orders. They're extremely strict about who the Enforcers are allowed to associate with. Since I was a new recruit, I didn't want to get into trouble with them. I tried to find you later, to explain. But every time I saw you, you were with him."

"With Marcus," I state.

Glenn nods. "You know how I am. Dr. Nesbith says I have unresolved abandonment issues."

"You're seeing the shrink?" I stifle a laugh.

"Yeah," Glenn smiles. "Granby wanted me to be analyzed before allowing me to take up arms. Dr. Nesbith recommended that I continue seeing him for a while."

"You said abandonment issues," I remark.

"Remember what I told you about my mother?"

"She died when you were three." Glenn never spoke of his mother. He only gave up that information when I got upset with him for not introducing me to her. He was raised by his father alone, who was rarely around.

"She didn't die. She took off with some other guy. Abandoned us." My jaw drops suddenly.

"Glenn, we've known each other for five and a half years and you're just telling me this *now*?"

"I'm sorry, Pollen. It's always been hard for me to deal with. It's easier for me to cope if I just think she's dead."

"Wow," I whisper. "Now it's beginning to make sense—why you've always been irrationally jealous."

"Yeah. And it's done nothing but create a monster in me. I only hope that one day I can regain your trust again."

"You already have," I sigh, looking into his single eye. For a moment, I am back with Glenn on an autumn night, staring up at the stars, dreaming of our future together. This is the Glenn I remember.

What am I doing? I can't start having feelings for Glenn again. I'm with Marcus. Marcus is my future. We're meant for each other. Yes, I'm angry with him, but that will pass, as it always does. But the serenity in Glenn's single hazel eye is pulling me in. I need to get out of here before I say or do something stupid.

"I'm going to go back to the apartment and wait for Marcus," I say as I try unsuccessfully to stand from the loveseat. Glenn has to hoist me up since every attempt seems to suck me deeper into the cushion like quicksand.

Upon standing the power shuts off, blackening the room except for some yellow emergency lights in the corners of the ceiling. I freeze. A voice announces over the intercom, "Attention Ceborec residents. Due to a system power failure, facility lockdown has been initiated. Secure areas have been sealed for the protection of officers and classified materials. Please remain in your current location for the remainder of the lockdown. Thank you for your patience."

Glenn and I instinctively rush to the door and try to open it, to no avail. Long after I give up, Glenn continues to kick and barrel the door with his shoulder.

"Don't bother, Glenn," I say. "We're stuck here for now. It's okay."

"I know you're worried about Evie," Glenn says spinning toward me.

"I am. But she's with Timber. I know she's alright."

"And you trust her with Evie?" Glenn eyes me suspiciously.

"I do. She's great with Evie. In fact, I trust her with my own life," I assert. "Why, is there any reason I shouldn't?"

"No," says Glenn. "I just know how protective you are of your niece. If you trust Timber, she's in good hands. You always were a good judge of character. What about Marcus?" he asks with a slight air of jealousy.

I turn away from Glenn, trying to hide my frustration, even though the darkness disguises it well enough. "What *about* Marcus?" I ask tersely.

"I'm sure you're itching to get back to him. Especially after what you've been through."

"He's the last person I want to see after what I've been through. If it weren't for him, none of this would have happened. I only went to the outdoor arena because I was furious with him. I needed to be alone—to work out my aggression. You know how I am."

"Yes, I know," says Glenn. "What did he do?"

"He chose to cavort with his buddies from work over training with me. And he had the nerve to criticize the way I handle Evie's care." My voice begins to break as I try to stifle my emotions.

I flinch as Glenn places his hands on my shoulders and lightly kisses my forehead. "Sorry," he says. "That was probably inappropriate."

"It's okay," I say as I lean in to accept his arms around me. I close my eyes as I lean in to his body. He could be Marcus for all I know. The darkness masks his face and I picture Marcus and me standing together, embracing each other. The way things should be; without the distance that sprouted between us last night.

Glenn releases me and walks behind General Granby's desk, opening drawers and peering inside. My eyes have adjusted to the darkness, and under the golden emergency lights the room glows with mysterious intimacy.

"What are you doing?" I ask. "You can't go through Granby's things."

"Looking for something to calm our nerves," he says as he pulls out a handful of tiny bottles from one of the drawers. "These should do the job."

I glare at Glenn with disbelief. I can't believe he's just going to take those as if Granby wouldn't notice.

"What? Who knows how long we'll be in here," Glenn retorts. "Besides, he's the one who told us to stay, remember?"

That's a good point. Last time they had a lockdown here it was for no less than three hours. I'm sure Granby won't mind if we nab a few drinks. Besides, my nerves could use a little numbing right now.

"Okay, but just one," I clarify.

Glenn opens a bottle and hands it to me. It's too dark to read the label, so I'll just have to take a swig and hope it's palatable. As I draw the bottle to my lips I feel like a giant of my childhood fairy tales, living in the clouds and consuming the stolen goods of the tiny humans who live below.

I fight the innate urge to spit out the repulsive liquid fire in my mouth. I can't say for sure what it is, since I'm not well schooled in hard liquor, but it's definitely not a sweet, fruity, girlie drink. It continues to burn my insides, as it blazes a fiery trail down my throat. But the moment it hits my stomach, the warmth spreads and softens the tension throughout my whole body. I fight the gag reflex and take another swig. Each repulsive sip seems to build upon that serenity. Before I know it, the bottle is empty and I'm asking Glenn for another.

Glenn and I have submerged back into the depths of the cushy loveseat, with no hope of getting out on our own. As the liquor takes over our bodies, our inhibitions seamlessly slide away and we find ourselves reminiscing about the past and giggling over every word that exits our mouths. I even dare to lay my legs across his lap in an attempt to lie back on the loveseat and relax.

"Seriously, Glenn," I say, "thank you. I needed this. I feel so much better now."

Glenn massages his warm hand over my thigh, a sensation that sends tingles crawling up my skin higher and higher. "Good, I don't like to see you upset," he says, keeping his hand on my leg. My mind is screaming at me *"take his hand off your leg!"* but my body is resisting, as if his touch is a piece of sticky tape, keeping me from shattering into a million tiny pieces. I reach my hand out, but rather than push his hand away, I find myself holding it in place, not letting him go.

I finish the last swig of my bottle and toss the empty shell on the floor. "Any more?" I ask.

"Sorry, babe. This is the last one," says Glenn as he takes his final swig. Before my brain can even register what I'm about to do, I'm on top of Glenn, straddling him with my thighs, and placing my mouth over his to suck out the last sip of fiery madness from his mouth. But I don't let go after I swallow the last drops. My mouth is a suction cup, refusing to be withdrawn. Glenn doesn't fight it either. He wraps his arms around me, pressing my body into his and sneaks his moist, muscular tongue between my lips.

I must be out of my mind. Here I am, back with Glenn after I swore it was long over between us. My body simply can't fight it anymore. I guess if you go through enough stress, it can do crazy things to you. The alcohol doesn't help either. Nor does the vision of Marcus that filters over Glenn's outline in the darkness.

He flips me over onto the loveseat, laying atop me and groping to remove my clothes as he sucks on my lower lip. It's wet, sloppy, messy. But I don't care. All rational thought has vanished and I have succumbed to the need of my physical form. I look up at him but all I see are Marcus's features. His strong jaw, his rusty long hair, his sapphire blue eyes. *Am I with Glenn or Marcus?*

My consciousness comes and goes. At times, I don't even know where I am, whether I am awake or dreaming. All I know is that I can't put up a resistance to anything right now. My body is as rigid as a rag doll. I've never felt so weak in my entire life.

Suddenly, daggers strike my head when the power is turned back on and the light from the lamp is glaring right into my eyes. My back is arched over the arm of the loveseat, my body completely exposed. Glenn's cheek rests on my chest. He's passed out.

What have I done? Shame is too light a word to describe my feelings. I hate myself. No, I detest myself.

With a sense of urgency I push Glenn off me, and his limp body crashes to the floor, awakening him from his deep sleep. I scramble to find my clothes, trying to cover my intimate parts from Glenn's sight.

"Oh my god," Glenn says rubbing his exposed eye. "What did we . . . Polly I'm so sorry." The sincerity in his voice quells any resentment I hold towards him. This wasn't his fault. Not entirely anyway. It was all me this time. I started it. I'm to blame. A blanket of shame envelops me and I can't even find the words to respond.

I throw my clothes back on and pick up the empty bottles while Glenn dresses. My head throbs with each pulse of my heartbeat and every time I bend over and stand back up I nearly collapse with dizziness. Glenn tries to help me stand, but I just push him away and lean against Granby's desk. I can't stand to be touched by him right now.

Once the office is cleaned up and Glenn and I have straightened our clothing, we begin to exit the room. I stop him before he opens the door.

"This was a mistake," I say hardening my look into his eye.

"I know," Glenn replies.

My head is still in a drunken whirlwind, but I'm sober enough to know what we must do. If Marcus finds out what happened it will destroy him. "Marcus can't know," I command. "Nobody can."

"This will stay between us," Glenn assures. We have to lie. It's our only option.

Chapter 10

The moment I open the door Marcus snatches me into his arms and squeezes me so tight I'm afraid he'll choke the life out of me. "I heard what happened. I'm so sorry, Pollen. I swear I'll never do that to you again," he sobs. As he holds me, I can feel his muscles tense up; I imagine he's giving Glenn the evil eye. I begged Glenn not to come, that it would only upset Marcus, but he wouldn't listen. He refused to let me walk alone and insisted on escorting me up here himself.

Marcus releases me and reaches his hand out to Glenn, who is still waiting in the corridor. A brief moment of terror strikes me when Glenn takes his hand and Marcus wraps his other arm around Glenn's neck. But the anxiety fades when I see that Marcus is not attacking, but hugging Glenn.

"Thank you," says Marcus, fighting back the glistening tears that begin to flood his eyes. "Thank you for being there, Glenn. And for bringing her back to me." My stomach churns with rueful torrents of despair. If only he knew.

"Hey, no problem man," says Glenn, lowering his gaze. "Take care of her, okay?" Glenn begins to leave, but Marcus stops him.

"Glenn," he seems to be struggling internally to compose himself. "I was wrong about you. What you and the others did to me in that room . . . I don't think I will ever forget that. But, after today, after what you did for Pollen, I forgive you. I'm sorry for the way I treated you before. You're always welcome here." Glenn briefly nods and disappears down the corridor.

Marcus turns back to me and embraces me in his bear hug again. The dampness on his face rubs against my cheeks forcing my own tears to develop and fall. But mine are different. Mine are tears of guilt. Tears of lies and deception. Tears of infidelity.

"I was so worried. I could have lost you today," says Marcus.

I pull back, fearing that he will smell the stench of my betrayal. "I'm sorry," I say. I should never have..." But my words trail of in a flood of tears.

"It's my fault. I should have been there. You have nothing to be sorry for," says Marcus ignorantly. Yeah, right. *Nothing to be sorry for?* I have everything to be sorry for. I've done something he'll never forgive.

Marcus clamps my head in his hands and pulls my lips to his so hard our teeth collide. For the first time, I feel disgusted by his kiss. My stomach convulses with sickness caused by my own shameful actions. I abhor myself and don't deserve him. How can I cheat on him and then come home and kiss him as if nothing happened?

I allow Marcus to finish, so he doesn't suspect anything, and then I turn away, unable to look into those penetrating eyes.

"I need to take a shower," I say quietly.

"I'll start it for you," Marcus says, kissing me on the crown of my head before he goes into the bathroom.

"Are you okay Pollen?" says Timber, startling me. I didn't even realize she and Evie were sitting on the floor putting together a puzzle. Obviously Evie has no clue what has happened since she has barely even noticed me. That's good. She doesn't need to be frightened with that kind of information—another reason why I trust Timber and Marcus with her.

"I'll be fine," I say. "I just need some rest." And some major painkillers. And some happy pills, for that matter. Through the walls, I hear the gush of the shower water hitting the tile floor.

Timber's eyebrows remain wrinkled with worry. She can sense that something's wrong, but she knows that now is the wrong time to talk about it.

"Auntie Pollen, can you read me a story?" Evie asks with doe eyes. She's already dressed in her pink butterfly pajamas, ready for bed.

It breaks my heart to refuse, but I can't handle it right now. "Not tonight, sweetie. I'm really tired," I confess.

"I'll read to you," Timber jumps in, "right after we pick up our puzzle." She gives me a wink and squats down to help Evie put the pieces in the box.

Marcus reappears, followed by a white cloud of steam. "Shower's ready," he says. "I'll be right out here if you need me." I still can't bear to look into his eyes. It's just a painful reminder of the unadulterated love he has for me, the fact that I just wasted it for a few pleasurable minutes with my ex.

The water burns and stings my back and the steam causes my headache to inflate. I turn the knob to the blue side, forcing myself to endure the icy chill. I don't deserve comfort. Not now. Somehow I hope that the torture of the cold shower will help to ease my burden, but it doesn't. All it does is wash away the salty tears that just won't end.

I scrub myself with the shower sponge. I scrub hard, as if the scrubbing will wash away the damage that I caused, the knowledge of what I've done, the hurt that may one day be revealed. But I can't scrub it away. It's as permanent as the infinity fly on my temple. I'll have to live with it forever. Unless...

No, I can't. But maybe I can. The memory erasers in my tattoo are still active. If I can come into contact with the right amount of electromagnetic activity, I might be able to erase that moment. Just maybe . . .

That hope fizzles out. The moment I see Glenn again it will all come back. Maybe not right away. But under the right conditions it will. Just like it did before. Nothing is permanent.

I slide my back down the wall and come to rest in a fetal position on the shower floor. The spikes of water stabbing me have no effect any more. I just lay here and sob until Marcus knocks on the door.

"Are you okay, Pol?" his voice sounds muffled behind the gushing drone of the shower.

"I'll be out in a minute," I shout back. It's impossible to gauge how long I've been in here since I've only used cold water. I'm sure the hot water would have run out a while ago.

I'm not ready to face him. I'm not sure I ever will be. But the thought causes my stomach to convulse and I scramble over to the toilet on my hands and knees, unable to stifle the contents coming up.

I leave the water running while I stand in front of the mirror staring at the detestable image I see before me. Cupping my hand under the running faucet I rinse my mouth and guzzle down as much water as my spinning stomach can handle.

When I finally gather enough nerve to leave the bathroom I find Marcus already in bed, waiting for me.

"Timber left while you were in the shower," he says, "and Evie's asleep." I nod and climb into bed, still wearing my white robe, and face away from him as if looking at him would allow him to read my thoughts.

"I know you're upset with me," says Marcus. "I really am so, so sorry, Pollen. I was beyond selfish. I'll never let you go again." He eases closer to me under the covers and wraps his arm over me, spooning me.

"I'm not upset with you," I say. "I'm just tired." Marcus kisses the back of my head, turns the lights off and doesn't let me go for the rest of the night.

※

My headache has subsided to a very dull annoyance, but the noise and bright sunlight radiating in from the dome of the rotunda still aggravate me as I walk Evie to preschool in the morning. As we wait for the elevator by the main offices I hear two voices snap back and forth in a whisper. Myra and Marley, two of the head scientists, are in a heated discussion only a few feet away.

"What do you mean missing?" Myra asks.

"Missing, as in gone. Deleted. The data has disappeared. We can't find it," Marley replies in a hushed tone. She combs the dark curls out of her olive-toned face in frustration.

I've never seen Myra so stressed. She's always the calm reserved one, even in the face of danger. Yesterday, when the entire facility was in chaos, she held it together like she was going to a baby shower. Now, though, I can see the sweat glistening on her brow, her jaw clenched in anguish, even her posture is stiff and rigid.

"Marley, if they were stolen," she clasps her mouth shut aware of the everyday activity going on around her. She whispers, "Do you know what that means?" Marley nods nervously.

"And there's something else," Marley says. "The interior control panel has been tampered with."

"How?"

Marley looks around briefly and lowers her voice, "The circuit board has been destroyed and the nuclear capacitor is gone."

Before I can listen any further, Evie tugs at my arm. The elevator has arrived. After boarding, I turn back to find that Marley and Myra have gone rushing into the engineering deck.

⁂

"So, do you want to talk about it now?" Timber asks as we walk toward Arena Three several paces behind Yoric and Jansen.

It's been a few days since the incident and I've avoided training until today. General Granby granted me a reprieve from training for as long as I need, but I'm eager to get back in the field. Marcus insisted on training with me every day from now on, but I asked him to give me some space. If it were up to him I'd never leave his sight again. It's just so hard to be around him right now. The guilt eats away at my conscious every second I'm with him.

"There's nothing to talk about really." I say. "I was attacked. Glenn was there and saved me. That's it." I stare down at my feet while talking to her.

But Timber is too shrewd to buy into my apathetic response. She knows something is up. She also knows that it's too personal for me to share even with my best girl friend. She doesn't say anything, but I can feel the overwhelming concern in her energy. "Okay, there is something." I admit. "I just don't want to talk about it."

Timber smiles and nods as we proceed into the woods. The trees aren't quite as welcoming anymore. The crunching leaves beneath my feet emit a spooky resonance into the eerily silent atmosphere. The towering trees are tall prison bars waiting to trap me and send me back to Crimson.

We split up; Yoric and Jansen venture ahead while Timber and I stay back and count down until we are ready to pursue. We start off running at an even pace until we can no longer see the grassy field behind us. I slow my pace to a crawl and Timber changes direction to try and circle around the guys. My pistol is cupped in my hands, resting against my cheek, ready to take aim and fire at the slightest movement. Luckily, it's a calm, quiet day, without so much as a warm draft to disturb the tree limbs.

Each tree I approach becomes a temporary sanctuary to hide behind while I determine my next move. So far, the woods are so quiet I can only hear my own hushed breath. Even Timber has moved out of earshot. After checking for clearance, I carefully creep diagonally to another tree, resting my back against it once I am in its protective veil.

My ears perk up like a tiger on the hunt. I swear I just heard something. Or was the sound coming from me? It was too faint to be sure. I hold my breath, hoping to confirm my suspicions. There it is again. A tiny flutter, so obscure it could be the blinking of Yoric's eyelids. But I know I heard it. He must be close.

I wind my finger around the trigger of my gun and sprint out from behind the tree, looking left, right, left again. I move forward through the trees, looking all around, but nobody is here. My heart is racing. This situation is all too familiar and with Timber gone I am once again alone and vulnerable.

My breathing quickens as panic sets in. There's a loud thud behind me and before I can spin around Yoric has his arms around me and his gun pressed against the back of my head. My bloodcurdling screams resonate throughout the woods. In a desperate attempt to free myself I thrust my elbow, full strength, back into his chest and he cries out, hunched over. Still in full-blown self-preservation mode, I turn and crash my knee into his face. As he falls to the ground I aim my pistol at his right eye and begin to squeeze.

It's only when I take in the tragic sight that I realize what I have done and drop my gun. Yoric lies on the ground like a scared little boy, holding his chest while blood dribbles from his nose. He moans and cries out in pain. This was no training exercise. The strange similarity to the attack must have triggered a life-or-death response. PTSD, maybe? Something clicked in me and I truly feared for my life.

By the time Timber and Jansen reach us, I am huddled up against a tree, crying and unable to even look at Yoric, for fear that I will see the eyes of the blue and blood spattered bounty hunter. My entire body is quivering with hysteria. I never realized how traumatic that one event was for me. After all I've been through in the past few months, this must have been the final push over the edge.

How selfish I am. Again. Here I am feeling sorry for myself after I just walloped poor Yoric to a pulp. Timber comforts Yoric and speaks softly to him while Jansen approaches me. He speaks, but I cannot make out what he is saying. My mind simply can't comprehend. It's like the day I met Marcus and the car exploded in front of me. Everything is a blur and all sounds are muted. Jansen turns to Timber and says something, then helps me up and leads me out of the woods, with his arm around my shoulder, massaging the rock-hard tension that has built up there.

Out in the open field my mind begins to clear. "What have I done?" I say to myself. I'm still not sure if I am referring to my beating of Yoric or the affair with Glenn.

"It's okay, Pollen," Jansen says, in his soft soothing tone, which reminds me of a kitten purring. "You're still under a lot of stress. Do you mind if I asked what happened?"

I explain to him what happened the day of the attack and how Yoric grabbed me from behind, just as my attacker had. "I don't know what happened after that. I just . . . snapped. Do you think he'll be okay?"

"You bashed him pretty good," Jansen laughs. "I can't say he didn't deserve it, though. We all talked about this before we went out and agreed we'd take it easy on you. He should have known better."

"I should have waited," I say.

"Waited?" Jansen asks.

"To start training again. Or at least stayed at the range where I can't hurt anybody."

"That's probably a good idea," says Jansen.

After dropping our weapons off at the armory, Jansen walks me back to my apartment, where I remain for the next two days, curled up in my bed.

Chapter 11

Even though a week has come and gone, I haven't really spoken much to Marcus, despite his constant presence. His concern has turned to frustration, which I'm afraid will turn to suspicion if I do not alter my behavior soon. My distance was comprehensible right after I was attacked. But a week later, it seems odd and vexatious.

Everyone has pretty much kept their distance from me since the attack, except for Lana, who has been paging me incessantly for the past two mornings, wondering why Evie and I are not in class. Marcus has been handling it, telling her that Evie doesn't feel well and I am staying home to care for her. Obviously she doesn't buy it and her lack of compassion is evident by her constant prying.

Word about what I did to Yoric traveled around and Granby even paid me a short visit, encouraging me to train in the sparring arena for a while, where exercises are supervised and more controlled. Turns out I broke one of Yoric's ribs when I jabbed him with my elbow, so he won't be training for a few weeks. Won't be getting busy with Timber either. She insists that it's okay every time I try to apologize, but I'm sure she's just as upset about his injury as he is.

Much to my relief, Glenn has avoided direct contact with me since the attack, although I swear I can feel him watching me from a distance at times. Whether it's concern or desire I do not know. I'm just glad he's giving me space—it helps to fade the memories and emotions of that horrible day, making it easier for me to move on.

I insisted that Marcus continue going to work for the past couple days, but today he refuses. In fact, he even asked Timber to take Evie out for a few hours so that we could spend some time alone. Time that I have been nervously avoiding out of fear that I might let something slip and he'll find out about my betrayal.

I don't even want to get out of bed again today. Hiding under the security of my blanket seems to be the only comfort I find lately. Since Marcus can't coax me out of bed, he resigns to lying next to me, facing my back.

I'm frustrated that he's impeding my emotional barrier. It makes it that much harder for me to live with myself.

"You know, you'll have to leave the room at some point," he says, teasing me.

"I know," I say quietly. "I just need one more day." I close my eyes and try to let the whirring of the ceiling fan lull me back to sleep. Even when it fails, I still pretend I'm sleeping.

"Remember the day we met?" Marcus murmurs, breaking the silence.

"Which time?" I ask satirically. Marcus chuckles under closed lips. Not too many couples can say they fell in love twice without even knowing. But after Marcus and I escaped Crimson the first time we lost all memories of each other only to meet again in the woods. There was a vague familiarity when we met again, but no memories of our relationship.

"The second time," he confirms.

"How could I forget," I say. "You saved my life twice that day."

"And you saved mine twice that day," Marcus says. I never really considered myself a heroine. Oh, sure I planned the escape that ultimately extricated Evie, Marcus and I from Crimson. And I suppose I did rescue Marcus twice that day: first from the raging rapids and then I carried him to safety and sewed up his wound after he was shot in the leg. But I'm far from heroic. The thought makes me uncomfortable

"Pollen, look at me." My heart shivers with apprehension. Like a lazy cat on a hot day, I roll over to face Marcus, our noses nearly touching. His deep blue sapphire eyes sink into mine and I am trapped in his penetrating gaze as I have been many times before.

"We made it through that day because we had each other. Please stop pushing me away. I can't bear to see you like this." He brushes the wisps of hair out of my eyes as he did those early days after we found each other in the woods. For this brief moment in time, I forget about what I've done to him, to myself.

He inches closer to me and I allow his lips to caress mine. Uncontrolled, my body flinches at his touch, but rather than retreat, Marcus pushes on, crushing his lips firmly against mine. An emotional hurricane stirs within me; a combination of guilt, shame, lust and yearning. Tears dribble from my cheeks to his and he pulls away, wiping them from my face with his thumb.

"I'm sorry," I say, wedging my elbow beneath me. I reach out and wipe my tears off his face with the back of my hand. Before I can pull away, Marcus takes my hand and presses my palm against his face as a child would with her security blanket.

"No. I'm sorry," says Marcus. "I don't mean to push you. I just really miss you." His words kindle the whimpering flame in my heart. Perhaps if I share my passions once again with Marcus, I can bury the memories of what I've done forever.

Somewhere within me I find the strength to ignite the spark that drew us together in the first place. Marcus still holds my hand on his cheek. My other hand takes his other cheek and pulls him to me. My violent need to be free of the past overpowers my shameful sorrow.

Although Marcus is cautious in his handling of me, I part his silky lips with mine and thrust my tongue into the steamy abyss. His sandpaper face scratches mine as I sway my head side to side, being sure to caress every square inch of his mouth.

Marcus slides his hand up the back of my lacy camisole, tracing the arch of my vertebrae all the way up to my shoulders, sending electric shocks radiating down my spine. His bare chest presses against mine with nothing more than the delicate lace of the camisole between us. The thin fabric is an unwelcome barrier and I yearn to appease my craving for skin-to-skin contact. I raise my arms while Marcus eases the camisole over my head and releases my body from its modest confinement. His kisses leave my lips and travel down my neck, my shoulders, to my chest, where he teases me with his velvet tongue. My back arches in rapture and his hands follow my curves down to my hips, jerking them against his.

My hand glides down his waist to his stomach, tracing every sculpted abdominal muscle in detail, as it searches lower and lower.

As if there weren't a second to spare, Marcus slides on top of me, his kisses more intent and unyielding. He gazes into my eyes longingly as he undulates to the rhythm of a melodic sonata. Our eyes are locked, our souls entwined, and neither of us can look away. He pulls me in deeper and deeper with his mesmerizing gaze; I'm in a euphoric trance. Suddenly, his passionate tidal waves quicken to a heavy metal guitar riff and my hips rise up to meet his. The pressure builds deep within me, each pulse raising it up a notch. Just as Marcus takes his final plunge, my body erupts with an explosion of fireworks. I'm sure even the tips of my fingers are shooting sparks.

We lie together silently and intertwined until Timber brings Evie back home. There's no need for us to talk. We are one being again, one soul divided into two bodies. Ultimately connected through space and time. My illicit actions with Glenn are but a distant memory now.

An emphatic rap at the door awakens Marcus and me from our blissful respite, melted against each other among the sheets. We drag ourselves from the disheveled sheets, still damp with the sweat that poured from our ravenous bodies, and hastily get dressed.

"Did you hear?" Timber exclaims, marching in with Evie the moment I unlatch the door. Evie dashes off to her bedroom to find her favorite rag doll. Marcus stands behind me waiting to hear the juicy new gossip.

"Hear what?" I say, my eyebrow raised at a sharp peak. Timber tugs at my sleeve and guides me over to the couch where she sits me down. *Why is she insisting that I sit?*

"I know you've been, well, holed up for the past few days, so you probably don't know what's been going on. The shuttle's been damaged. Plans were stolen. Initially, they were thinking someone broke in to the complex, maybe while you were being attacked. But then they discovered it was an inside job." Timber's wide eyes tell me there is something deeper to this story.

My mind recalls the conversation I overheard between Marley and Myra. It seemed pretty serious, but I hadn't heard anything since. I assumed whatever it was, was taken care of. But the way Timber is staring at me frightens me. Deep down, I know what she is going to say, but I don't believe it. I can't believe it. My heart begins to climb until it lodges in my throat, suffocating me. *Please, don't say it.*

"Pollen, they arrested Glenn."

Chapter 12

I STORM INTO the main level offices and demand to see Chlamyra Rowan. I need to speak to someone in charge and since she's the first committee leader I met before we moved to Ceborec, and the one who essentially recruited Marcus and me, she seems like a good choice. There is no single leader or president here at COPS headquarters. The organization doesn't work like that—never did. There is a committee of high-ranked scientists, like Myra and Marley, military officers, such as General Granby and Sage, and various engineers. And none of them are politicians, which is probably why this place runs so smoothly.

Marley comes out of one of the back offices and gives me a friendly smile.

"Hello, Pollen. What can we do for you?"

"I need to speak to Myra," I demand.

Marley frowns, "Ms. Rowan is in a meeting at the moment. I can tell her you came by."

"Where's Glenn?" I ask, firm and resolute.

"Who?"

"You know who I'm talking about. Glenn Malek. The man you all accused of stealing the plans. Where is he?"

"Pollen, I can't give you that information," Marley replies. Her calm, haughty demeanor aggravates me further. I shift my weight side to side, searching myself for some way to reach Glenn.

"Fine, if you can't give me that information I'll get it myself."

I shove Marley aside, knocking her into the side of a desk, where a lamp tips over, and race past her toward the back of the office, to the conference room. As I approach the door, I hear Marley on the intercom calling for assistance. "Too late," I think to myself.

Looks of shock and distress paint the faces of the eleven men and women in the boardroom, as I burst through the door. The room is quiet and all eyes are on me. Only now, under their scrutinizing gaze, do I realize how stupid and impulsive this was. The red flush of embarrassment no doubt tints my cheeks.

"Can we help you, Ms. McRae?" Myra asks calmly, staying comfortably seated in her ornate mahogany chair.

I look around the room at all the faces staring at me awaiting an answer, and wonder if it's safe to announce my request or if I should speak with Myra in private.

"I need to speak with Glenn Malek."

Just as the words leave my mouth two Watchers come charging in. Each grabs one of my arms and they attempt to drag me out of the room against my will. General Granby stands and raises his hand in that elegant manner that he does.

"It's okay. Let her go." The Watchers stop and look up, bewildered at Granby. "You're dismissed." The Watchers leave as Marley slips into the room and approaches Myra.

"I'm sorry," she whispers. "I told her you were in a meeting, but she just pushed me aside."

Myra nods, "It's okay, Marley. Have a seat." Marley sits in the empty chair next to Myra. Myra turns and sternly looks at me, "Mr. Malek has been sent to a secure location to await interrogation. He is not permitted any visitors. I apologize for any complications this causes. Now, if you will excuse us, we have a meeting to finish."

Defeat. If only I had waited. If only I had spoken to her in private, maybe she could have given me just five minutes with him. That's all I need, really. My mind is swimming with a swarming concoction of anger, confusion, guilt, fear, and sadness. What will they do to him as punishment? Torture? My mind focuses on his empty eye socket and I shudder. Execution? Surely the COPS aren't that brutal, I convince myself. Or perhaps they'll go easy on him and settle for an interminable lifetime of imprisonment.

As I leave, I turn back once more, hoping for some peace of mind, and beg, "What will happen to him?"

"That is yet to be determined, Ms. McRae," Myra replies.

My walk back to the apartment is a snail's journey. Hopeless and defeated I don't want to see anybody. Not even Marcus or Evie. They'll be there now, waiting for me. Waiting to pummel me with cups of hot tea, soothing music, and anything else that might ease my misery.

I picture Marcus hugging Glenn. *"You're always welcome here."* Only after I betrayed him did Marcus finally open his arms to Glenn. And now, Glenn is accused of betraying us all. A flood of guilt washes over me when I realize deep down I am crying for Glenn. Part of me still loves him deeply. I don't believe he is responsible for what they say he did. I can't believe it.

I've just begun the lowly walk down the corridor towards my apartment when a placating voice stops me.

"Miss McRae, may I have a word please?" Granby's gentle tone soothes my aching heart so easily it's hard to believe he is a hard-as-nails commanding military general.

I turn to face him and he extends his arms to me, holding my arms snugly. "Are you alright?" he asks, eyebrows crinkled with worry.

It takes every ounce of tenacity to hold myself together, as I shake my head. "I'm sorry," I whisper, to keep my voice intact.

"You've nothing to be sorry for," Granby reaches into his pocket and retrieves a handkerchief to hand to me. I graciously accept and allow some of my tears to soak into it. I didn't know people still carried these things.

"I can't believe he did this," I say.

Granby stiffens and assumes his military stance. "I spoke with Ms. Rowan and the committee on your behalf." I gaze up at him, more attentive than ever.

"They agreed to a short visitation, before his sentence is to be carried out." My eyes light up, before darkening again.

"Sentence?"

"Mr. Malek is to be banished just before we are to go underground for the summer."

"Banished?" My mind is in a whirlwind and I can't seem to say anything other than one-word sentences.

"We cannot risk him returning here or to Crimson. He will be blindfolded and taken to an undisclosed location above ground. He will be forced to survive the elements on his own and seek out his own underground shelter."

Underground. Summer is almost upon us. The events of the past few weeks have distracted me and I've completely lost track of time. Glenn will be cast off to roam about the sweltering oven above ground. My mind searches for a way to change Granby's mind about the sentence, but the more I think about it they are already being unreasonably easy on him. They could have tortured or executed him, but that's not the kind of people they are. And I know keeping him here, even under guard, is a liability they just can't afford. At least he'll be alive.

"Thank you, sir," I murmur quietly. "When may I see him?"

"One week from today. Meet me on the main floor at eight and I will escort you," says Granby. I nod and return my dispirited shuffle back to my apartment.

My mind swims in and out of disturbing and threatening thoughts as I follow Granby down the winding corridors and staircases. Glenn is being held in a remote corner of the facility, previously unused since there were no criminals here. But now, he rests down there alone, guarded day and night. I don't know what to think. I don't even know what I am going to say to him. *Is he really a Crimson spy? Was he framed? Did he use me to gain access to the facility?*

Initially I was in denial. I didn't want to think Glenn would do those things. Convinced he had changed, I welcomed him back into my life. But now that I'd had a week to let it all sink in, it makes more sense. Of course he was a spy. He's the same conniving, sweet-talking Glenn he's always been. What a fool I was. I should have trusted Marcus; he was right all along.

My gut twists and turns in knots as we near the room where Glenn is being held. My heart is on a trampoline, reaching into my throat, making it difficult for me to breathe. My palms are sweaty and I'm constantly wiping them on the sides of my black leggings.

Ahead I see two Watchers standing guard and I know that we've reached our destination. My fingers begin to tremble, sending shivers up my arms. I've got to hold it together. The two Watchers step aside silently when they see Granby approach. He gives them a brief nod and unlocks the door with a silver key attached to a large key ring with at least fifty different keys attached.

"Miss McRae," he says, opening the door for me.

"Thank you," I whisper under my breath. He looks down at me with sorrowful eyes and it rips my heart to shreds. I can't cry now. I won't cry.

Stepping inside the room feels like I am back at Crimson. Cold, windowless, white walls surround a nearly empty room. Glenn sits in the center of the room, cuffed by his wrists and ankles to a cushioned armchair. He's nodded off. His head hangs lazily over his left shoulder and his full, pouty lips are slightly parted.

Seeing him here, being this close to him, transports me back to that regretful day in Granby's office. Ire floods my veins. *Was that part of his master plan? To get me drunk and take advantage of me?* Maybe he even planned the attack; hired some pathetic bounty hunter to carry it out, leaving him to rescue me. The idea sickens me.

The slap that jolts Glenn from his slumber stings my palm with a thousand razor sharp needles.

"Argh!" he groans. Glenn shakes his head, trying to work out where he is and what just happened. My hand left a rosy imprint on his left cheek—a perfect target for the tight-knuckled fist that follows. His head jerks back as I try to shake the pain out of my hand.

"Pollen?" Glenn says, dazed. I glare at him with narrowed eyes and his own eye widens.

"I hate you."

"Pollen, please tell me you don't believe them. That I did what they say I did."

I pace the floor like a tiger eying its prey. "I don't know what to believe anymore," I growl, my voice flat and breathy.

"I didn't do it. You have to believe me," Glenn pleads, begging me with his sharp green-flecked copper eye.

"You've betrayed me before, Glenn. I didn't want to believe then either! How could you? Was this all a ploy? Using my trust to gain access to the facility? And I suppose getting back into my pants was just an added benefit, hmm?" I stand there glowering at him, arms crossed, body rigid with tension. My skin is flushed scarlet and my body feels explosive. Glenn looks down at the floor, devastated, shaking his head.

"Pollen, you know I didn't mean—"

"No, I don't know!" I shout back at him releasing a smidgen of the tension that has built up inside me. "I don't know anything about you anymore, Glenn. I risked myself, put myself out there for you. Because you made me believe you'd changed."

"I *have* changed, Polly. You have no idea," he mutters. An almost indiscernible tear streaks the side of his face. Even his eye patch has a stain of moisture seeping through. For a brief moment my heart flutters and I want to run to him and wipe the tear away. *No. I must stand my ground.* Glenn is a conspirator, conniving and evil to the core.

I kneel down in front of Glenn, hardening my stare, shooting icy daggers into his soul. "You will never change, Glenn. I *know* that now." I want to sink my claws into his face so badly, my hand quivers. But gazing into his eye, my reflection staring back at me through his pupil, I still see the boy I fell in love with all those years ago and I can't bring myself to do it. I feel the tears pushing against the dam behind my eyes and my bottom lip quivers. I have to get out before the floodgates burst open. I withdraw from him and look to the door for my escape, inhaling sharply to stifle the sob. As I reach out and turn the handle, Glenn interrupts sharply, "Pollen I need to tell you something. It's really important." He emphasizes the last three words with a staccato articulation.

"I don't care. I'm done here," I say, my voice breaking up as I choke back tears. As I open the door, the Watchers enter the room, followed by Granby.

"It's about your brother!" Glenn shouts, craning his head around the men to get a glimpse of me. My head whips back around just before the door slams shut. *What? What could he possibly have to tell me about my brother?* He died a year ago. No. This is just another attempt to win me back. I can't let him take over my emotions. Muffled sounds filter through the door from the room and I hear Glenn's voice once more.

"Drake's not dead!"

CHAPTER 13

I FEEL LIKE I've just been slugged in the gut. My stomach clenches. My breath shortens. *Drake's not dead?* This can't be true. Can it? Two different voices are battling it out in my head as I attempt to come to grips with the words Glenn just spoke.

I reach for the doorknob and twist, but it's locked. Pressing my ear against the cold steel door, I hear General Granby speaking in his harsh military modulation, but I can't make out what he's saying. A minute later, the door opens.

I stand back to allow Granby through and stare as the Watchers drag Glenn out, gagged, blindfolded, his wrists and ankles shackled. I follow nervously, lagging behind, as they escort him down the hall, then they vanish down another corridor.

My mind has simply shut down. The sheer stress of all of this information I've had to process lately has just become too much. I return to my apartment where Marcus awaits my return and curl up in the bed for three more days.

"I'd expected you to arrive on time your first day back from your little vacation," Lana snaps at me, arms crossed, tapping her toe.

She's lucky to have me at all today. I feel so run down and exhausted despite all the rest I've had. But I had to come in to work. I've missed too much already, and Evie's been missing her friends. If there were any other way around it I'd avoid Lana for another week. But I suppose I'd have to come back and face her eventually.

"I'm glad to be back," I sigh, giving Evie a brief smile across the room.

Lana shoves a stack of coloring pages in my hands. "I need you to make copies of these. When you're finished, you're on potty duty. I've got to adjust the plans for tomorrow."

Tomorrow we go down south. Underground, that is. The entire facility has been on eggshells about this event. It's the first summer since the virus was released that we will be underground. In the past we've been accustomed to traveling via the Web, the underground circuit of tunnels that mimics the roads above ground. But with the remaining population of local survivors centered at either Crimson or Ceborec, the Web will be as empty and void as in the dead of winter. I'm worried that our restriction from the Web and the inability to go above ground will result in cabin fever.

I enter Lana's drab office and set the pages down on the copier. Her office is no bigger than a bathroom stall, but she insists on filling her desk with all sorts of useless junk: figurines, coffee mugs, small toys. I'm sure this all has some sentimental value to her; but really, does she need this much crap on her tiny desk?

I slide the pages into the paper feeder and press start. While the copies are printing I pick up a figurine of a little dark haired girl from the desk and study it. It looks like cheap, imported porcelain, and crudely painted, like something you'd buy at a dollar store. On the bottom, in tiny handwriting, is "To Mommy, Love Rainn."

"Put. That. Down." Lana stands in the doorway scowling at me. My eyes soften. I didn't realize she was a mother. I've always seen her alone. Her daughter must have succumbed to the virus. That would explain her testy attitude.

I gently return the figurine to her desk. "Sorry, Lana. I didn't know you had a daughter."

Lana's lip quivers, but the scowl remains. "I asked you to make copies. Don't touch my desk. The children are ready for the bathroom." Lana turns away and raises her hand to her face, pinching the bridge of her nose. It seems I just found Lana's weakness. As tempting as it may be, given the way she treats me, I decide not to exploit it. Not yet anyway.

Lana sits in her office while I organize the six children into a line outside the preschool bathroom.

One at a time, I guide each child in, standing just outside the ajar door in case they need assistance. Fortunately most of the kids are potty-trained, but accidents happen often and practically all of them need some wiping assistance.

Beau is the first to use the bathroom and he is in and out in virtually no time.

"Wash your hands Beau." He grins at me. "With soap," I order.

Alyssa is next. She takes several minutes, indicating that she needs help. Holding my breath I slip inside and help her finish. Lana always makes me do the dirty jobs.

Waiting outside the bathroom door, I can smell Lana's breakfast all the way from across the room: an omelet with onions and mushrooms. Her breakfasts are usually not this pungent. I must be overly sensitive to the smell this morning. I didn't eat breakfast myself because I haven't had much of an appetite since seeing Glenn. But my stomach begins to do somersaults and my throat tightens as I stand here inhaling that awful odor. Maybe I'm really not well.

"Auntie Pollen, come with me," Evie asks, her featherweight hand grasping mine.

"Evie do the best you can and I'll come help you when you are done." Evie goes into the bathroom and I wait, resting my head on my forearm against the doorjamb.

"Auntie Pollen!" Evie calls to me from inside and I enter as a wave of heat bears down on me. I help Evie wipe and pull up her pants but the dizzying sensation takes over.

"Go wash your hands," I say and after she leaves the bathroom, I slam the door behind her, lean over the toilet and unleash the monsters in my belly. Then again. And again.

A rapping at the door snaps me back to attention. "Pollen? Are you okay?" Lana asks sounding unusually concerned.

I dab my chin with toilet paper and flush the contents before coming out to face her. "I must have caught Evie's stomach bug," I say, shielding the painfully bright overhead lights from my eyes. I just want to go lie down in a dark, quiet room, away from any strong sensory stimuli.

"I think you should go," says Lana, catching me by surprise. "I don't need any of these kids getting sick in here."

"Okay," I say, taking Evie's hand. "Thank you, Lana." She nods almost imperceptibly and I go home.

"Nap time, Evie," I say, shepherding her into her bedroom decorated with pink and yellow butterflies. She turns around and punches her hands on her four-year-old hips.

"I'm not tired. No nap!" she snaps at me.

"Evie. Auntie Pollen is very tired and I don't feel good. My tummy hurts. I need you to take your nap so that I can lie down and take a nap too."

Evie shakes her head, over exaggerating each turn. "Uh, uh."

"Evie. When I say it is nap time, it is nap time." I say sternly. I hate to admit it, but caring for Evie has given me a newfound appreciation for my parents. I don't know how they could have put up with Drake and me. We were such brats. I just wish they were around now so I could tell them how much they mean to me and how sorry I am for giving them a hard time.

"No!" Evie lowers her brows and glowers at me while crossing her arms in defiance.

I throw my hands up in the air, exasperated and too weak and sick to put up a fight. "Fine! Just stay in your room and play then."

I charge off to my bedroom, leaving Evie behind in hers and collapse onto the bed, ignoring the blankets. *Why am I so tired?* I drift in and out of consciousness, thinking about Glenn and what he said about Drake. *Could Drake really be alive?* It was a closed casket funeral. They said he was blown to bits by a landmine. But what if that really didn't happen? What if we just buried an empty coffin? But I can't trust Glenn. I've already established that. Or can I? Maybe he was telling the truth all along. But then, who else could have sabotaged the shuttle and stolen the plans. He's the only outsider here. My confusion frustrates me to no end. I shouldn't think about this right now. I feel too sick.

There's a knock at the door. I glance over at the clock. It's two o'clock. *Already? Where has the time gone?* Timber's here to watch Evie while I go to train with Marcus. I can't go today—not feeling like this. But I would enjoy her company.

I open the door and lean against it.

"Oh, Pollen, you don't look well," Timber says, pressing her hand against my forehead.

"I don't feel well," I say. "I'm not training today."

"Do you want me to go?" she asks.

"No, come in," I say, opening the door wider.

"Where's Evie?" Timber asks, looking around the living room.

"In her bedroom."

Timber tiptoes over to Evie's room and peeks inside, closing the door gingerly before she turns back to me. "She's out. Sprawled across her bed wearing her finest pink dress and princess crown."

I smile. "I told her to take a nap earlier, but she refused. So I just let her play in there while I rested."

"Can I make you some tea?" Timber asks. I nod. Tea might help to ease my stomach.

Timber shuffles around the tiny kitchen nook, filling a kettle with water and placing it on the single burner range. The kitchen is only a kitchen in that there's a little countertop to prepare food, two cabinets and a mini fridge for storage, and a single burner range and microwave for cooking. Marcus unplugged the microwave as soon as we moved in for fear that the radiation might trigger memory loss from the chemical in the tattoos we were imprinted with from Crimson. Usually, though, we just eat in the food court.

I curl up on the couch, laying my head on the arm cushion. After a few minutes, Timber brings me my cup of black tea with a splash of hazelnut milk.

"Thank you, Timber."

"What's up, Pollen?" she asks as I carefully sip the hot tea. It burns my upper lip so I blow on it gently before attempting another sip.

"Nothing. I'm just tired. And a little nauseated. I'll be okay after I get a good rest."

"Something's different about you," says Timber, narrowing her eyes. She sits next to me and leans her elbow against the back of the couch, resting her cheek on her fist. "Ever since you were attacked, you've been really distant and . . . unhappy. Look, I don't want to push you, Pollen. You know that. But you *can* talk to me."

"I know," I gaze off into space, debating whether to tell her about my affair with Glenn. Maybe it would help, to get this off my chest. I don't think she would tell Marcus. But I don't want her to look down on me either. Timber has a kind heart. She'll understand.

"Timber I've done something horrible," I start, and, from out of nowhere, high tide rushes in. Timber leans over me and, taking a tissue from the box, wipes the tears from my cheeks. The tissue saturates quickly so she leans over and pulls out three more for me.

"What is it, sweetie?"

"It's Glenn," I say, gulping air between my sobs. "After I was attacked, we were locked in Granby's office—when the power went out. Glenn found some small bottles of liquor in Granby's desk. Of course we drank them, after what had happened and all. Then, I don't even know how it happened."

Timber's eyes widen. "You didn't . . ."

"When I woke up, our clothes were on the floor and we were laying together on the loveseat." I can barely breathe now, my wailing too strong to control. Hiccups interrupt every few words. "I didn't want that to happen. I can't believe I did that to Marcus."

"Oh, honey," Timber reaches across and takes me in her arms. As she presses against my breast I feel a sharp pain as if she's just jabbed a sensitive bruise, and I flinch back, grabbing my chest. Timber arches her brow, bewildered and deep in thought.

"You said you were tired and nauseated?" I nod. "Do your breasts hurt?" I nod again.

"Oh my god, Pollen. You're pregnant."

Chapter 14

"I'M PREGNANT?"

Timber stands back in the corner of the medical examination room covering her mouth to hide her shock, while Dr. Yipolis peruses my medical history. I feel numb; like this isn't really happening. Perhaps it's just a dream. A really bad dream. *Wake up, Pollen. Wake up!*

"It would appear so, Ms. McRae," says the hideously handsome young doctor. He shakes the ebony bangs from his brow, in a move only models could perfect, and looks up at me through his long dark lashes with his brilliant ultramarine eyes.

"From the look on your face I presume you were not trying?" His voice is unnaturally gentle, like hot melted caramel flowing from his perfectly chiseled lips. It helps to ease the tension that seems to be permanently constructed in my muscles.

"No," I whisper, looking down at the floor. I can't look him in the eyes—they remind me of Marcus.

"And you cannot remember the date of your last menstruation?" I shake my head in shame. Why would I bother with that? There's just been too much going on to even care.

"We'll do an ultrasound to determine how far along you are, and then I'll give you further instructions. Would you excuse me?" Dr. Yipolis and Timber leave the room and Timber gives me a reassuring glance and soft smile just before she closes the door. I shift uncomfortably on the table wearing my white paper gown, which leaves little to be discovered.

The imaginary ticking in my head begins. *Tick. Tock. Tick. Tock. What could be taking them so long?* I take deep penetrating breaths to try and calm myself down, but they are futile. *What am I going to tell Marcus?* He's infertile—he'll know I betrayed him. What else could he think? I envision that twisted, angry look on his face when we were at Crimson and he'd thought I'd joined the Enforcers. That fatal look would be butterflies and roses in comparison to learning this.

The door handle clicks and I wrap my arms around my paper gown, as Timber rolls in the ultrasound machine on a cart, kicking the door shut behind her.

"You okay?" she asks, plugging in the machine.

"For now," I reply, still shaken.

Timber flips a switch and the machine hums as it starts up. She places one hand on my knee and the other behind my shoulder. "I'm here for you, Pollen. No matter what happens."

I nod sadly. "We both know what will happen."

"You don't know that." She shakes her head. "Besides, there's no rush to tell him. If it is Glenn's, you're still very early. There's still a chance . . ."

Timber falls silent. Pain clouds her eyes before she looks away and presses some buttons on the machine.

"Lie back," she says, holding my back and gently lowering me down on the paper-lined medical bed complete with paper pillowcase.

"Miscarriage," I say. Timber nearly drops me. She looks petrified.

"What?" Timber's eyes widen, as if she'd just seen a ghost doing the hokey pokey with a zombie.

"That's what you were going to say, isn't it? There's still a chance I could have a miscarriage."

Timber shakes her head, trying to rid herself of some horrible thought. "Yes, you could. But nobody should ever wish for that. I'll go get Dr. Yipolis."

I want to press her for more information. There's something she's not telling me. Did she have a miscarriage before? That would explain her strange reaction. But I decide to bite my tongue instead. She'll tell me eventually.

Timber leaves and strolls back in about thirty seconds later with Dr. Yipolis. My body tenses as he instructs me to place my feet in the stirrups at the end of the bed, exposing my pride and joy to his gorgeous deep blue eyes.

Timber picks up a wand-like device from a rack on the side of the machine, rolls a condom onto it, and squeezes a translucent cyan jelly onto the tip. She hands it to Dr. Yipolis, who sits on a rolling stool between my legs. *Why, oh why, did the OB/GYN have to be a hot doctor? Why couldn't it be some fat, wrinkly old lady?* Dr. Yipolis is actually the OB/GYN, internist, and sometimes a surgeon, though it's not really his specialty. There are only two other doctors here and neither of them is adept in women's health.

"Relax," he says, gently inserting the warm wand inside me. "Just some pressure." I wince from the sensation. If I weren't so worried about Marcus right now, I'd probably be squirming with discomfort. But the fear of facing him tugs my attention from my physical body.

I close my eyes as the hot doctor maneuvers the wand inside me, leaning left, then right, and then circling it around. A chill bites my legs as the air conditioner kicks on and I reflexively shiver.

"There it is," says Dr. Yipolis. I open my eyes and focus on the ultrasound monitor, but all I see is an indistinct monochromatic blob of flesh.

"That's it?" I ask incredulously.

Timber fiddles with the ultrasound machine, taking some measurements.

"Looks like your fetus is very young. You're only about four weeks along."

Four weeks! It's only been just over two since Glenn and I . . . this has to be Marcus's baby! But how will he react when I tell him? Will he be happy or suspicious? It doesn't matter. My fears have dissipated and now I can relax and enjoy my pregnancy. I close my eyes and feel my upturned lips emanating relief.

When I open my eyes, Timber looks hard at me, shaking her head, as I exhale sharply. What's she trying to tell me?

Dr. Yipolis finishes his exam and holds out his hand to help me sit up. His hand is unnaturally soft, like that of a child's. I'm glad he's got some feature that turns me off, despite his dashing good looks.

"Miss McRae, the fetus looks healthy and normal for this stage of the pregnancy. I would like to offer my congratulations, however, you are the first pregnancy we've had since the virus." My smile melts away. What is he getting at?

"We don't know how exposure to the virus might affect the fetus. I'd expect if your fetus has the double mutation, it would be immune, just as you are. But since we have no record to compare it to . . . well, to be honest we just don't know.

"I'd like you to take it easy over the next eight weeks. This pregnancy could be unpredictable, but it's important. You may give birth to the first post-virus child. That's nothing to be taken lightly. I'd like you to come in weekly for testing, so we can monitor the progress and take note of any developments. Would you be okay with that?"

Overwhelmed with all this information, my mind has entered a void, and I'm speechless. I simply nod.

"Good," says Dr. Yipolis. "You can get dressed and I'll see you next week." Just before he leaves, the kind doctor turns back to me, "And Miss McRae, congratulations again."

Timber remains in the room with me, turning off the machine and preparing to take it away. Then she places her hand on my knee again.

"Pollen, are you alright?"

I shake myself out of my trance and glance up at Timber, with a grin that stretches eye to eye.

"It's not Glenn's," I murmur, eyes glistening with happy tears. "Four weeks. It can't be his."

Timber's shoulders slump and she looks down, disheartened. Moving behind me, she hops up onto the paper-lined bed and gently massages my shoulders.

"Pollen," she sighs wistfully, "pregnancy always starts on the date of your last period. That's how doctors determine the due date and how far along you are. I know it's confusing, but the first two weeks don't really count. Conception would have taken place two weeks ago."

My heart shrivels up and turns to dust. The smile that donned my cheeks just a few seconds ago has died and my shoulders tense up under Timber's fingers. I had forgotten all about that. I should have remembered how they calculate the date. After all, I had been pregnant before.

"So it could still be Glenn's," I mutter breathlessly.

"It would appear so," Timber says, rubbing her thumbs into the solid mass surrounding my neck. "But it could be Marcus's, right?" she asks with a hint of optimism.

I turn to face Timber. She drops her hands in reaction to the desolate expression on my face.

"He can't have children," I say solemnly. "That's why his first wife left him. He's infertile."

Timber's face droops and she wraps her arms around me, allowing me to cry into her shoulder. *How could this happen? Why me? Why now?* I was so happy with Marcus and Evie. We were going to be a family. Spend our lives together. Now with one horrible mistake I've destroyed that possibility.

"We need to unpack, Pollen. We're going to be here for a few months, might as well get comfortable," Marcus says, adjusting the mirror he just hung on the ecru tinted wall and eying the reflection of the boxes that sit stacked in the corner of our temporary underground apartment. On the far wall hangs a virtual window—a light box that emits manufactured sunlight, mimicking the sunrise and sunset, so it feels like we are above ground.

The apartment is much smaller than our first home—a studio apartment with a double bed and pull out sofa for Evie. Marcus and I don't have the privacy we're used to, but it doesn't matter too much. I haven't been in the mood to fool around with him ever since I discovered my pregnancy. It hurts too much to know how this will affect him.

I keep waiting for the right time to tell him. *Who am I kidding? There will never be a right time.* Deep down I've been praying for a miscarriage. It's the only way out. I guess I'm just scared. And I want to hold on to him as long as I can before his love for me turns into spite.

"I will," I say as I lie face down on the bed reading the Ceborec newsletter. They distribute the newsletters once a month. Usually it just lists updates on the shuttle, upcoming events, and a list of birthdays, as if those really matter anymore.

"When I'm feeling better," I sigh.

Marcus sits on the edge of the bed and sweeps his hand across my brow, brushing the hair out of my face.

"Still feel like crap, huh?" I nod. "The doctor still doesn't know what it is?" Not only have I been hiding the truth from Marcus, but I've been flat out lying to him as well. I don't really feel that sick anymore, just incredibly tired. I don't want to unpack because I know he'll throw me out as soon as I tell him I'm pregnant. He thinks I've been seeing the doctor for some mysterious illness when I go in for my weekly tests. That's what I've been telling him anyway.

It's been three weeks now, since that fateful day in the medical clinic. I know I'll have to tell him soon. I've been holding off in case I have a miscarriage. Part of me wants to lose the baby. That would make things so much simpler. But it would also remind me of losing Lex, the baby I lost almost three years ago, which could possibly rip me to shreds.

"Pollen, is there something else going on?" Marcus asks, rubbing my stiff neck with one hand.

Oh no. I was afraid my behavior would raise his suspicions. *What do I do? What should I say? Play stupid. Yes, that's it.*

"What do you mean?"

"I mean, you've been really distant with me for, like, the last month, babe. You don't want me to touch you. You're always tired. You don't talk to me anymore. I can tell something's up."

"I told you, Marcus. I'm just not feeling well," I affirm, turning away from him to hide my lying eyes.

"For a month, Pollen? Come on. Whatever it is, you can tell me," Marcus pleads. *Yeah, right. I don't think this is what you have in mind, Marcus.* I feel the tears beginning to well up.

"Could you leave me alone, please?" I ask, trying to push him away so I can cry in private.

"No, Pollen," he snaps. "You have to stop this. Stop hiding from me." Marcus leans over me, turning my head back to gaze into my eyes. I can't hold it back any longer. Salty streams start to glide down my cheeks and drip onto my pillow. "See, I know something's going on."

"Leave me alone Marcus," I say, snapping my face back. I can feel the crushing of his ego as he stands and moves away from me.

"Come on Evie. Let's leave Auntie Pollen alone," says Marcus. I can hear their footsteps tapping toward the door. "I guess she just doesn't want some of us around anymore." As the door slams, the mirror jumps off the wall, shattering to millions of pieces.

I lift my head heavily from my warm indented pillow in response to a rap at the door. *Who could that be? Did I fall asleep again? What time is it?* As I drag myself out of bed I see the spiky shards of glass on the floor, reminding me of Marcus. He's really mad at me. Maybe I should just go ahead and tell him my secret and get it over with. I'm only prolonging the agony.

Sidestepping the shattered mirror, I open the door and find Timber there. She's still wearing her scrubs: dark blue with a bumblebee pattern.

"Pollen, Dr. Sexy sent me to give you your lab results," she says handing me a large brown paper envelope. "Everything looks good so far."

Timber glances over my shoulder and sees the glass sprawled across the floor. Then she studies my face, which is probably still stained with tears from earlier. Her eyes widen.

"Pollen, did you tell Marcus about the baby?"

A crash sounds from behind Timber in the corridor. She turns and we both rest our startled gaze on Marcus, who has just dropped a vase full of white daisies.

"What baby?"

Chapter 15

The glass from the vase shattered and the floor is littered with the broken pieces intermingled with white daisy petals. Evie tiptoes over the remains and into the apartment behind me.

Marcus's eyes are fixed on mine. I can't read him, though. He looks utterly confused. His eyes slowly descend to my belly, which I hadn't realized I was grasping with my left hand, then back to my eyes in understanding. The edges of his lips curl up and for a split second I think everything is going to be all right. He's happy.

But suddenly his face distorts into a twisted grimace that conveys to me his worst nightmare. It doesn't even look like Marcus anymore. The color drains from his blue eyes and they look empty, hollow. Then he's gone, tramping down the corridor in a fury.

"Marcus!" I call out, but he doesn't even turn back. "Marcus, please don't go!" I collapse to the floor unable to contain my gushing tears. *I've lost him. I've really lost him.* I knew he would leave. He didn't even give me a chance to explain. The heartache is indescribable; like my heart is being squashed like a spider and painfully stretched on a rack simultaneously. The only time I can remember that I felt worse than this was when I discovered Lex, dead in his crib and held his lifeless blue body in my arms. As horrible as I feel, I remind myself that this is nothing more than a rainy day compared to that gruesome memory.

I broke down and took Evie to the Ceborec daycare center this afternoon. It was so hard to let her go into the care of virtual strangers, but I need to get back to my training and clear my head. I haven't seen Marcus since yesterday when he stormed off—he never came home. It was a long, agonizing, sleepless night.

The first underground level of the training facility is almost exactly the same as the above ground facility, with the armory, sparring arena, and shooting range. There are four lower levels that serve as group training arenas, which mimic the Web, in case of a summer season assault.

I meet Timber at the armory where I pick up my usual weapon, the DS-42 pistol.

"Marcus come home yet?" Timber asks.

I sigh. "No."

"I'm sure he will, Pollen." Timber flashes her reassuring smile, but I cannot find the strength to return it.

"He'll probably come back to pack up his things," I say dejected. What's the point of hoping for the impossible? This will never turn out as I hope. Might as well get used to disappointment.

"I have a feeling it will all turn out okay, Pollen. Be optimistic for a change." I can't stifle the caustic laugh that pops out.

"Optimistic, huh? I suppose it can't get any worse at this point."

"There you go," Timber encourages, wrapping her arm around me and squeezing my triceps.

"Afternoon, ladies," Harrison smiles as we approach. He winks at me. "Haven't seen you in awhile—have you been cheating on me?" I stiffen and my pulse races. *Does he know?*

"Pollen's not been well," Timber pipes in. "But she's feeling better today, right?"

"Right," I say, clearing my throat. I have to remind myself of Harrison's sarcastic demeanor. Of course he doesn't know about Glenn and me. How could he?

"It's good to see you Pollen," he says politely for a change, sensing my discomfort. He hands us each our five magazines. As we turn to leave, I notice that he hasn't given me the extra bullets like he usually does and I glance back raising an eyebrow.

"Sorry, Pollen. Security's been jacked up since the incident yesterday," he says, holding his hands up in the air.

"Incident?"

"Yeah, you didn't hear?" he asks as if I've been living in a hole for two years.

I shake my head and then turn to Timber, who looks just as clueless as I do. I've been so wrapped up in my own miseries I probably wouldn't have noticed anyway.

Harrison beckons us with his finger and leans forward, peering around to make sure nobody's within earshot. "There's been another security breech," he says in a hushed tone. "Parts of the shuttle were damaged and some components missing again."

It takes me a minute to comprehend what he's saying. Glenn was banished over three weeks ago. All access points to the underground facility are heavily guarded, so he couldn't have broken in.

"Wait a minute. You're saying this just happened this week?" I ask. Harrison nods. "Are there any suspects?"

"Not that I'm aware of. That's why they're cracking down on us." Harrison waves his head back toward the corner of the ceiling behind him where a security camera has been installed. I've noticed cameras before all over the building, but never thought anything of them. Maybe they weren't in use before.

"Can't they just look at the security footage?"

"That's what I said," Harrison says shaking his head. "Maybe the perp had a really clever disguise. Or maybe the cameras just weren't working. I don't know."

I can't believe it. All this time I believed Glenn had betrayed us. I was wrong. We were all wrong. Now he's out there somewhere in the wilderness, in the scorching heat of summer. I hope he's found a way underground. I can't bear to think of him up there, alone, with no food, limited water. I could have saved him, if only I'd believed him. Stood up for him. How selfish I've been.

Suddenly I'm not so eager to train today.

<hr>

My muscles are screaming for a soak in the hot bath after an engaging training session that was weeks overdue. I really need to get back in the arena consistently again. I resolve to pick up Evie after my bath and a quick nap.

A disturbing thought comes to mind as I walk down the gloomy corridor to my apartment. I've been thinking about what Harrison said, about the security breech. Last time that happened was the day I was attacked. Marcus and I had a fight the night before and weren't speaking that day. Then Glenn was blamed for the incident. Then it happened again yesterday, when Marcus stormed off and never came home. What if Marcus is responsible? *But why?* The first time it happened he was probably trying to get rid of Glenn. That makes sense. He felt threatened by Glenn's presence so he could have framed him. But what about now? What could motivate him to do this and who would he frame? *Me. He wants to get rid of me.*

Wait, what am I thinking? Marcus isn't a spy. He has no ties to Crimson. It couldn't be Marcus, could it? Surely he wouldn't do anything like this.

Ominous dread blankets me as I approach the apartment. I wonder if Marcus came back. Will he be here now? What will I say to him? Or maybe he's already packed his things and left, leaving an empty shell of a room. My stomach clenches and coils in anticipation. I take a deep breath and open the door.

On the small kitchen countertop is a new vase full of fresh daisies and yellow roses. Their sweet fragrance fills the tiny apartment. A new mirror hangs on the wall where Marcus hung the other one that broke yesterday.

Marcus looks up from the corner of the room, where he is unpacking a box full of my clothes and sorting them into drawers. His expression is sorrowful, nothing like the scowl from yesterday.

I stand in the open doorway paralyzed, not knowing what to say.

"Pollen," Marcus starts. He trots across the floor to me and before I can say anything his arms are wrapped around me in a warm embrace. "Pollen, I'm so sorry."

Sorry? Sorry for what? I should be the one apologizing. I betrayed you and then I got pregnant. Oh Marcus, you're too good for me.

"I should never have abandoned you like that. I was so stupid, so naïve. I can't believe I actually thought you'd slept with your ex." Of course you thought that. It's the only thing that makes sense. And it's true.

"Where were you?" I gulp.

Marcus pulls me in from the doorway and shuts the door behind us.

"I stayed with Nicron last night. Jansen was there, too. We had some drinks and talked. Then I spoke to Timber this morning and then Dr. Yipolis."

"Why?"

"Because after I talked to Jansen, I realized that there was no way you would go back to Glenn. And Timber's your best friend here. I know you confide in her, so that's why I went to see her. That's when she told me I might not be one hundred percent infertile. So I saw the doc to get confirmation. It's a long shot, like one in a million, but turns out I can have children if I find a compatible partner." Marcus slides behind me and clasps his hands around my belly.

"You can have children," I say, emphasizing the 'can,' trying to convince myself of my own words. Still holding my stomach, Marcus nudges my head to the side with his and gently kisses my neck where it meets my shoulder at the clavicle.

Marcus believes this is his baby. It *could* be his baby. He's so happy. I refuse to say anything that will take that away from him.

Finally, relief sweeps over me. Marcus never has to know. Glenn is out of the picture. We can move on with our lives. But a lingering sense of guilt stings me when I imagine Glenn, falsely accused of committing treason and wrongly banished for it. I love Marcus with all my heart and soul. So why do I still feel so torn?

"I can't wait to be a father," he whispers longingly into my ear. My skin tingles with tiny pinpricks and I remember why I fell in love with this man. He's going to be a wonderful father.

Marcus reaches over and pulls a white daisy from the vase, still keeping his other hand firmly on my belly, and draws it in front of my eyes.

"These remind me of you."

I twist my head around to look at him, puzzled. A daisy? Of all the flowers in the world an ordinary daisy reminds him of me? He combs his fingers through my hair.

"When I was a kid there were wild daisies that grew in the meadow down the street from us. I had to climb over a fence to get to them because they were on farmer Gus's property and he didn't like trespassers. It was dangerous and I was nearly caught a few times, but it didn't matter to me. It was worth it to see the look on my mom's face when I came home with a fistful of daisies for her." Marcus pauses and inhales sharply. He really did care for his mother and misses her dearly.

"They remind me of you, because of their simple, natural beauty. And because of the danger I put myself in just to claim them." I can feel Marcus smile against my cheek, and I smile too, remembering how he put his life on the line many times to rescue me.

I sigh gently, recalling a more depressing meaning associated with the innocent flowers.

"They remind me of death," I mutter. Marcus hold on me tightens.

"Why?"

"Remember when we were at my house? When I went into the garden and found my parents graves, I planted some daisies in them. Kind of like my way of saying goodbye."

"Oh, Pollen, I didn't—"

"No, it's okay!" I interrupt. "Of course you didn't know. But I like your story. I don't want to spend the rest of my life being reminded of death every time I see a daisy. I'd like to think of them as signaling a new beginning. My life with you."

Taking me by surprise, Marcus spins me around and his tractor beams draw me in to his brilliantly glowing blue eyes again. His eyes are so deep, beautiful, and full of love. Love for me. He takes his hands off my hips and reaches into his pocket with one hand, gently holding my left hand with the other.

"Pollen, you are my world. Last night, being without you, it was the worst night of my existence. I don't ever want us to be apart again." Marcus pulls his hand out of his pocket revealing an antique silver ring with a large diamond set in an intricate knotwork frame. I gasp. My stomach plummets to the floor and my legs nearly turn to jelly.

"Pollen, marry me."

Chapter 16

"Your maid of honor?"

Timber's jaw drops and she grabs me and hugs me, swaying widely from side to side. Her freshly cut hair prickles my cheeks.

"Pollen! Of course I'll be your maid of honor!" She squeezes the breath out of me again. I knew she'd be happy for me, but wow. I didn't expect this. Gapes and stares from the dance floor make me flush magenta under the violet lights. The new nightclub, aptly named The Snake Hole, just opened a few weeks ago and this is the first chance I've had to come down and let my hair loose.

We sit at the bar and Timber orders some fruity girlie drink with an umbrella in it. I resign to drinking sparkling water with a splash of lemon. I wish I could celebrate with a real drink.

"So have you two set a date yet?" Timber asks, stirring the pink liquid with a narrow straw.

"We were thinking maybe in a couple weeks," I say, sliding my finger along the condensation building up on the outside of the glass.

"So soon?"

"Well, it's not like we have a ton of people to invite. Or a venue to shop for. I mean, all we have to do is arrange a time with the minister, reserve the chapel, and send out some invites."

Timber looks at me regretfully, but I smile back. I always dreamed of having a big outdoor autumn sunset wedding with all my friends and family in attendance. My dad, wiping away tears as he steps in time with me down the aisle. My mother weeping silently in the front row, trying not to smudge her mascara. For a second I allow my heart to break silently for that lost dream. But truth be told, after all the stress I've undergone in the past few weeks, I'm just happy to be where I am now. I'd marry Marcus in the back of a dumpster for all I care and I'd still be gleaming joy.

Speaking of which, I've been meaning to ask Timber what she said to Marcus. Whatever it was, after they talked, he didn't believe I'd cheated on him. She must have told him something pretty special to get that thought out of his mind.

"Timber, after Marcus left he said he went to see you. What did you tell him?" Timber's face contorts and she looks serious.

"I told him you'd never do anything to hurt him. That whatever he suspected was unfounded." She looks down dejectedly. "Pollen, I don't like to lie to people. It's not me, it's against my nature. But you're my best friend and I don't like to see you hurt. And I didn't like seeing Marcus like that either. You two belong together and I felt it was my responsibility to keep it that way."

I knew she was my best friend for a good reason. I reach over, still sitting, and give her a heartfelt hug.

"Thank you," I say, wiping the moisture from my eyes. "You're the best."

"Anything for you, babe," she says.

"So how are things with Yoric?"

"Good," says Timber, averting her eyes and looking at her drink as she swirls the ice around with her straw.

"Really?"

"No. Not really. He can be such an adolescent sometimes, you know? Ever since we moved in together we're always fighting about stupid shit, like where to hang a picture, or how long I take in the bathroom. I can't stand being around him anymore."

"Timber, all couples have problems. Give it some time."

"Problem is, I don't know how much time it's going to take for him to grow up. Sometimes I think it's just hopeless. Maybe we're not meant to be."

"So why don't you just leave?"

"Because the make-up sex is out of this world," Timber smiles. I frown. "No, really. I do love him. Very much. And I know he feels the same. It's just that living together is so new for both of us and. . . I guess this is just the adjustment period."

Marcus and I never needed an "adjustment period." We've lived together since the day we arrived and we've always gotten along for the most part. Yes, a few squabbles here and there, but nothing that really drove me crazy. I guess our schedules don't allow us to spend enough time together to annoy each other.

I think back to my secret conversation with Yoric and I feel confident now that I gave him some good advice. Maybe they *should* live together first, before marrying, to see if they are compatible.

"You'll be okay. You just need to make sure you guys spend some time apart."

"Yeah, I think you're right. We kind of rushed things in the beginning. I'd always accompany him to work and we'd eat breakfast together. Lunch together. Train together, when I'm not with you. Dinner together. Not to mention the rest of the evening and night. This is really good for me Pollen, we should have girls night out more often."

I chuckle, "I'll enjoy it more when I can actually drink!"

"Not for eight more months, babe!" Timber says, tossing back the rest of her drink and throwing her hand in the air, signaling to the bartender for another one. He whips up that fruity concoction and lays it in front of her with a wink.

"So who's the best man gonna be?" she asks.

"I don't know. Nicron maybe? Or Jansen? Marcus hasn't said. I was thinking about asking Lynx to be in the wedding party too, but I haven't seen her lately. We're meeting for dinner tomorrow night so I'll tell her then."

"Anyone going to walk you down the aisle?" Timber asks, sipping through her straw.

"I was thinking about asking General Granby. He's so sweet and reminds me of my dad. I think he'd do it."

"That's a great idea, Pollen. Hey, you should invite everybody, you know, the whole facility and have a huge wedding!"

I cringe. I don't even know half the people here yet. It would be really weird getting married in front of a crowd of strangers.

"I don't know. That might be a little over the top, don't you think?"

"Pollen. This is not only the first wedding since the virus, but the first happy event in general. People need an excuse to celebrate. Something positive, you know? This would be great for everybody."

People have been looking rather morose lately. Especially since we're underground now. I decide to swirl the idea around in my head for a while.

"I'll discuss it with Marcus. And slow down!" I say as Timber whips back her head and slurps down her drink.

The food court is abuzz with commotion as usual. Once again, Lynx is running late for our dinner. We ought to just agree to meet twenty minutes later, so I don't have to wait so long. But then, I might not be fortunate enough to find an empty table if I come later.

I find myself daydreaming about the upcoming wedding. I found a gorgeous gown at the Ladies Boutique earlier today. That's the shop that specializes in ladies formal wear, separate from the casual ladies wear shop. It's an ivory strapless, form-fitting satin gown with ivory lace and bronze bead accents and a train that could sweep the dust off a six-lane highway. I won't wear a traditional veil, but I haven't decided on my hairpiece yet. Obviously Evie will be the flower girl. We found a cute, yellow empire dress for her. It's a little too big, but Timber said she could tailor it. I don't know if we'll have a ring bearer. I suppose I could ask one of the boys from Evie's class.

I've become so wrapped up in my wedding plans that I nearly forget where I am or how long I've been waiting. *What is taking Lynx so long?* It's common for her to be late, but I've been waiting for nearly an hour.

The crowd in the food court is starting to disperse; yet I still can't see Lynx anywhere. Should I be worried? Maybe I'll just go to her office and see if she's still there. We'll just have to meet up another day this week. I've already eaten anyway.

The aerospace engineering department is just below the main floor on the west side of the facility—the highest floor in the underground lair. It's quite a trek to get there, but I need the exercise anyway. I've been getting way too lazy these past few weeks.

As I pass by the glass windows that border the engineering department I get the strange feeling something is wrong. People are inside, working, but there's a thick shroud of tension lingering in the air. I peer inside, but I don't see Lynx. Perhaps she's been tied up in a meeting.

The receptionist is a sweet young man named Luke. He's got one of those boyish faces that never seems to age, yet he's a few years older than me. His blond hair hangs over his eyes, so that when he looks up at me, I almost miss the look of alarm behind them.

"Hi Luke, is Lynx still around?"

"Lynx?" he gulps.

"Yes. She was supposed to meet me for dinner, but she didn't show. I thought maybe she might be stuck in a meeting."

Luke remains silent, gawking at me. Something's wrong. I hope she hasn't been hurt or worse. My muscles tense at the thought and a storm begins to brew deep in my stomach.

"Luke? Where's Lynx?"

Luke inhales deeply and looks down at some papers on his desk. "Pollen—" He pauses. "Lynx was arrested this afternoon. For conspiracy to commit treason against the COPS."

"No," I whisper. Not Lynx, too. That can't be. Someone must have framed her. And if they framed her, they could also come after me. Or Marcus. No this isn't right. My hands begin to tremble.

"No. No, she couldn't. She wanted to get away from Crimson just as much as I did. There's *no way* she could have done this." First Glenn. Now Lynx. *Who can I trust anymore?*

"Pollen, she confessed. Lynx was a spy for Crimson."

I gasp, but can't seem to catch my breath. The room spins around me and the floor wavers from side to side. I try to grasp on to Luke's desk, but the dizziness overcomes me and I collapse.

The faint, muffled sounds of talking men filter into the bleak white room where Lynx sits, cuffed to the very chair that held Glenn only a month ago. Granby let me in to see her as a personal favor, in the hope that I could get some information out of her. I doubt I'll get much.

Lynx can barely look at me. Her bloodshot eyes are puffy and her cheeks stained and sticky with tears. She looks like she hasn't slept in a week. I'd almost feel sorry for her, if I hadn't known her betrayal.

"Why?" I ask, staring down at her. Just one simple word, the only reason I came to see her. At first she remains silent and I wonder if she's taken a vow of silence, then she speaks.

"I didn't want to," she mutters.

"Why!" I say more forcefully and she jumps in her seat.

"They threatened me." Lynx raises her eyelids to look at me briefly then returns her gaze downward. "I was captured by the Crimson Enforcers after we escaped. I didn't know what was going on. I couldn't remember. They explained the mission to me and said that if I didn't cooperate they would take me back to Crimson. I agreed because I wanted my freedom."

"So you got your freedom. You're here. Why would you sabotage our efforts and relay the plans to Crimson? It's not like they can just walk in here and take you back."

"I didn't actually intend to carry out the plans until . . ." Her voice fades away.

"Until what?" I kneel down to catch her gaze.

"Until they tested the implant."

"Implant?"

Lynx nods. "Before they set me free to join the COPS, they implanted a chip, just under the infinity fly." I move in closer to get a better look at the tattoo on her temple. Just under the skin, below the hairline, is a small cylindrical lump I had never noticed before.

"When they activate it, it sends out a pulse to the auriculo-temporal nerve, which causes severe pain and nerve damage. It also contains a one-way communicator, so they can relay instructions, and tracking device, so they always know my whereabouts." I feel a twinge of sorrow for Lynx. I honestly don't know what I'd do in her situation. Perhaps I would have done the same.

"So how did you get the plans to them?" I ask. It's not like she can just hail down the postal service and send a package.

"There's a place out on the perimeter, a hole where a tree used to be before it rotted away, where I left the stolen plans and components. A Crimson agent was supposed to pick them up. That's where I left them the first day when . . ." Lynx's voice goes silent again, but I already know what she was going to say.

"The day I was attacked," I finish.

"I'm so sorry, Pollen. I had no idea they would try and hurt anyone, I swear." Tears stream down her face again. As angry as I am, I believe her. I know she didn't intend any harm to come to me. But the fact that her espionage caused all of my problems from the last few weeks boils my blood. If it weren't for her I never would have been trapped in that room with Glenn. Never would have gotten drunk and slept with him. Probably wouldn't be pregnant. But deep down I wonder; if I weren't pregnant, would I still be marrying Marcus?

I shake the distracting thoughts away and focus my attention back on Lynx.

"But . . . Glenn killed the guy that attacked me. So the plans must—"

"There were two of them," Lynx interrupts. "The plans made it back to Crimson safely." She lowers her head again. The shame in her face does little to placate me.

"So why did you do it again, destroy the shuttle?"

"It was part of my assignment—to slow down the construction of the shuttle. So that they can reach A1D3 first and establish a stronghold there."

So the Trinity are building a shuttle too. That explains why they stole the plans. It wasn't enough for them to destroy the planet we call home. Now they are going to abandon the mess they made.

Chapter 17

*K*EEP YOUR HEAD UP. *Ears open. Focus Pollen.*

Darkness envelops me in a silent, open cocoon. If I were to drop a hair right now it would cause an echo to ring out through the corridors. You would think that I'd be used to the eerie silence by now having experienced it so many times, but one never really gets used to the deathly stillness when you grow up accustomed to background noise.

Training Arena Two looks just as the Web did a few months ago when Marcus, Evie, and I escaped from Crimson. Dreary blackness lit only with the dim yellow emergency lights. It sends shivers into my bones when I remember the ominous clap of Sage's footsteps and having to crawl to safety after I injured my ankle from the impact with the train. Fortunately it was a clean break—and it only took a few weeks to heal completely with the osteogenic injection they gave me. I still get shooting pains in my ankle and calf now and then, but nothing I can't shake off.

I lean against the wall, slowing and quieting my breath. Closing my eyes, I allow my other senses to open up. The air is still and comfortably chilly down here. It smells of new paint—they just finished renovating the floor a few weeks ago and the odor hasn't dissipated yet. Without my eyesight, my ears are more attuned to the microscopic sounds. Yes, there it is. The faint swish of fabric sliding against its own friction.

It's difficult to anticipate where it the sound is coming from. Footsteps are inaudible here. We are wearing shoes with soles made from an organic material called Hemlex that makes virtually no sound despite its tightly gripping surface.

I hear a whoosh behind me and open my eyes to catch an obscure shadow dart past. Holding my pistol in readiness I take a step. Stop. Another step. Stop. I squint my eyes, but still see nothing. A few steps later I am standing at an intersection. I look right then left, but still see nothing. I close my eyes once again to strengthen my hearing. I hear nothing when he grabs me from behind.

"You're mine," he whispers delicately. His steaming breath tickles my ear. I holster my gun and press my body back against his.

"After tomorrow you'll be stuck with me forever," I say, twisting my ring around my finger.

In one fell swoop, Marcus twists me and drives me down to the floor on my back, laying atop me and resting his forearm beneath my head. He gently caresses the wisps of hair from my eyes.

"That's what I've wanted since the day I met you," Marcus says, playing with my long braided hair. He leans forward until his lips are a hair away from mine and I can taste his breath. Then he hovers. I expect him to kiss me at any moment, but to my surprise, he doesn't. *Why?*

"What's wrong?" I ask.

"I was just remembering the last time we were in a dark tunnel together. If I remember correctly, we had an audience."

"Evie."

"Mm hmm. But now we're all alone," Marcus says, poking his fingers into my braid to unravel it.

"Hmm. I wouldn't be so sure about that," I say. Marcus keeps unraveling my braid but raises his eyebrows.

"Why?"

"You know they've got security cameras all over the facility. And *I know* they've been using them recently. I'm sure they have some in here too, we just can't see them because it's so dark."

Marcus pauses and lifts his head, staring down into the corridor.

"Screw it," he says and plants his lips on mine, diving his tongue between my lips and entwining it with mine. Marcus's fingers comb through my hair and mine climb the rocky terrain of his triceps up to his back and into his shaggy auburn locks. His kisses leave my lips and trail along my jaw line, gently nipping my skin as I raise my chin higher. He continues down my neck, his hands tracing the figure of my body.

Marcus tugs at the hem of my shirt when I stop him. The idea of being watched makes me nervous enough as it is, I don't want to be caught making the first official COPS porno.

"Stop," I say. Marcus chuckles.

"Sorry, I guess I got carried away." He falls over next to me and we lie facing each other inches apart. My finger traces a line from his collarbone down to his belly button.

"I can't wait to be Mrs. Marcus Stygma," I whisper.

Marcus glides his hand over my belly, just under my shirt. "And I can't wait to be a daddy."

I close my eyes, disheartened. Is this the only reason he's marrying me? This may not even be your baby, Marcus. But I can't tell you that.

"Marcus, would you have asked me if I wasn't, you know, pregnant?"

Marcus's face softens as he brushes his knuckles across my cheeks. His eyebrows draw together.

"Is that what you think? That I proposed because you're knocked up?" I remain silent, awaiting his answer.

"Pollen, I told you. I wanted to marry you from the moment I met you. I just didn't want to scare you off by moving too fast. If I thought you'd say yes, I'd have asked you ages ago." I wish he had.

I lean over and chastely kiss him on the corner of his lips, brushing mine against his bristly goatee. Then I fall to my back, holding my left hand in the air and gaze up at the ring. The diamond reflects tiny glints of yellow sparkles from the dim lights.

"That was my mother's," Marcus says. "And her mother's. It's been in the family for generations. I'd been carrying it around with me ever since she passed away. You have no idea how many times I've been tempted to give it to you." I smile, my heart full of a haunting concoction of love and regret.

"I love you, Marcus."

"I love *you*, Pollen. More than you'll ever know."

"You're dressed already?" I yawn, twisting into the disheveled blankets on our bed. Marcus is already draped in his tuxedo. His crisp white button-up shirt is partially open at the top, revealing the cleavage of his pectoralis major muscles coated a fine net of auburn hair. Evie's bed lies empty.

"I didn't want to be late to my wedding. You know, I'm marrying my soulmate today." He smiles and winks.

"Where's Evie?" I ask.

"Timber came by early to get her so they can get ready together. She wanted to let you sleep in."

"What time is it?"

"Almost nine thirty. Why?"

I jump out of bed and slip into a simple yellow sundress. I had made an appointment at the medical clinic this morning. It's my wedding gift to Marcus. I remember when Drake got married, he and Ivy were supposed to give each other gifts, but he had such a hard time choosing one for her. I helped him pick out a gold bracelet engraved with the words "My heart is yours."

I wasn't sure what to get Marcus. Options are limited these days and he's not really into material possessions. I thought of some kind of jewelry, but in his line of work he can't really wear it anyway. I wanted to get him something really special, something unforgettable.

"I have to give you your wedding gift," I say as Marcus squints at me enigmatically.

"Now?" he asks, as if he's in a rush to leave.

I slip on some sandals and grab his hand, heading for the door. "Leave your tie here. You can finish dressing when we get back."

A short, stout nurse named Orla leads us to the ochre-painted examination room. Her brown, beady eyes narrow suspiciously at Marcus under her jet-black bangs as she hands me my paper blanket.

"He's the baby's father," I say. "I want him here." She nods, but frowns as she leaves the room.

Marcus eyes the paper blanket curiously.

"What's that for?" he asks.

"For modesty," I say, reaching under my dress to remove my panties. Marcus grabs my hand.

"Allow me," he says. A sly one-sided smirk stretches into his cheek and I pull up the skirt of my dress.

Marcus kneels down and his warm, rough hands cup each side of my hips. He sweetly kisses my belly button and a tingling electric shock dissipates into my limbs. Slowly, he slides my panties down and pulls behind each of my knees to remove them from my ankles.

"Oh, what I would love to do to you on this table," Marcus whispers.

"It will have to wait," I say, pulling him back up. He tucks my panties into his back pocket.

"I think I'll hold on to these for a while," his impish grin growing wider.

Almost on cue, Orla abruptly enters, carting the ultrasound machine behind her. Her eyes dart to Marcus, still grinning devilishly.

I scoot onto the table, while Marcus stands by my side opposite the machine. Marcus unfolds the paper blanket and lays it across my lap. There's a knock at the door and it opens.

"Good morning Miss McRae," says Dr. Yipolis, and he nods briefly to Marcus, who returns a slight nod. "Looks like you've got a busy day today, so let's get right to it."

I lay back on the table while Dr. Yipolis wheels his stool between my legs. Marcus shifts uncomfortably next to me. I can tell he doesn't like what is going on. I don't think he ever realized he had to share the vision of my lady parts with somebody else, especially a smoking hot doctor. I take his hand and squeeze reassuringly. He glances back at me, but the tension in his eyes doesn't fade.

Orla squeezes the blue goo onto the ultrasound wand and hands it to the doctor, who carefully inserts it. I watch Marcus as he squints at the screen.

"There it is," says Dr. Yipolis. "See that little flutter in the center? That's the heartbeat." The little blob has grown a little into an elongated peanut shape.

In the center, the flesh ripples much faster than a typical heartbeat.

Marcus's eyes glisten as he gazes in awe at the monitor. The tension that clouded them a moment ago has vanished, leaving only the essence of unconditional love. He can't take his eyes off the screen.

Marcus shakes out of his trance when the doctor removes the wand, leaving only a blank screen. After handing the wand back to Orla, he takes another smooth, palm-sized contraption from the bottom shelf of the cart and squeezes the blue gel on it.

"It might be a little early, but let's see if we can hear the heartbeat."

He gently slides the hem of my dress off my belly, resting it just below my breasts, revealing the beginning of my slight baby bump. Marcus holds the paper blanket in place, more for his comfort than mine. The gooey gel is warm, wet, and soothing, like aloe vera gel after a charred sunburn. Dr. Yipolis glides the device around slowly, then stops when the static is broken by a quick, pulsating thump.

Marcus inhales sharply. A single tear escapes from his eye as he gazes lovingly into my eyes. The musical beat of our baby's living heart draws our souls together.

"Oh, and Pollen, we have the results back from the amnio. Would you like to know the sex of the baby?"

Keeping my eyes fixed on Marcus, I nod.

"It's a boy."

Marcus gasps and more tears rush down over his cheeks.

"Thank you," he says. "This is the best wedding gift I could ever hope for."

Chapter 18

*T*AKE A DEEP BREATH, Pollen. This is it.

Evie, Timber, and General Granby accompany me in a small office opposite the assembly hall. We could have used the chapel for the wedding, but Marcus and I liked Timber's idea of making it a huge ceremony to cheer everyone up in the wake of our underground hibernation. She even put the announcement in the Ceborec newsletter to ensure everyone knew about it. The assembly hall is really the only place that can accommodate such a huge gathering.

Evie peeks out the door while Timber adjusts my dress. The fabric skims my body, hugging every curve with alluring grace. It's snug around my belly, which is already beginning to protrude. In the past, I would have been embarrassed and probably found a larger size dress to disguise it. But after this morning, I'm proud to wear my tiny baby bump. Marcus will love it. Timber ties a bronze colored cord around my waist and attaches Marcus's wedding ring, a silver knotwork band that matches my ring, in the knot, allowing the loose ends of the cord to fall gently between my thighs.

On my wrists I wear a pair of bronze cuffs, which intricately swirl up my forearms. A matching bronze choker wraps my neck with the same intricate design falling down my décolletage. My hair is swept up in about a dozen braids and pinned tightly to my head, with a few wispy tendrils framing my face. Tiny daisies tucked into the braids finish the look.

"Everyone's waiting," Evie whispers. She looks darling in her sunshine yellow empire waist dress. Her hair is swept up like mine and she wears a crown of daisies and tiny red tea roses, to match the ones in her white basket.

"Showtime," Timber smiles. I look over at General Granby, who looks solemn, but content in his traditional black tuxedo, and I wonder if he's thinking about his own daughter, who he'll never get to walk down the aisle. He smiles gently and places his hands on my shoulders.

"Thank you, Pollen." I think that's the first time he's ever addressed me by my first name. Granby's not an emotional man, but he really seems touched.

"For what?"

"For asking me to do this. You don't know how much it means to me. You and Marcus—you are like family to me. I could see from the moment you two entered Ceborec you are meant for each other. And I wish you all the happiness this life can bring you." Oh no, I can feel it coming. The pressure building up behind my eyes.

"Granby, stop it. You're going to make me cry," I say, pulling my earlobe adorned with simple bronze studs.

Granby gently kisses my forehead and says, "Are you ready?"

I take a deep steadying breath. "I've been waiting for this day my whole life. Yes. I'm ready."

Timber opens the door and I follow her out, admiring her shimmering yellow gown. It's simple, but elegant, and looks absolutely fantastic on her petite frame.

Suddenly, I hear crashing footsteps tromping down the corridor towards us. It's one of the Watchers who stand post at the entrance to the Web. I can't remember his name, but I've seen him before.

"Granby," he calls out and we all stop and stare at him, one of the very few people not attending the wedding. "Granby, there's a situation down below. We need you to come."

"Excuse me," he says to me and pulls the Watcher aside, speaking too quietly for me to hear. Granby frowns and looks my way; a veil of regret hangs over his eyes.

"Pollen. I'm so sorry, but I have to deal with this. Can you do this without me?"

No, I can't. My heart is broken. I really was looking forward to sharing this with Granby, the only father figure I know here. I nod, disappointed, but not willing to let anything ruin this day.

"I'll try to be back for the reception. Excuse me." Then he and the Watcher jog down the corridor. I nervously watch as they shrink and disappear. I wonder what could be going on that the Watchers can't handle on their own. No doubt we'll find out later. But for now, I have a wedding to get to.

I turn back, but Timber is missing. *Where did she go?* Evie stands and waits patiently, sniffing the daisies in her basket. A heartbeat later, Timber returns from the assembly hall, with Harrison, who is smartly dressed in a black suit, with red paisley tie. His streaked hair is neatly tied back, giving him the appearance of a cultured artist rather than an unkempt ammunitions dealer. I didn't realize he could clean up so well. Even his piercings and the tattoos that peek up out of his collar look chic.

"I hear you need someone to walk you down the aisle?" he asks.

"You would do that for me?"

"Well, I'm still jealous that Marcus got to you first. But to be honest, there's no one else I'd rather lose you to."

I smile and wrap my arms around him. He even smells good, like cinnamon and clove.

"Oh Harrison, thank you. You know you've always been like a brother to me."

Harrison makes an exaggerated gesture, grasping his heart and falling back. "Brother! Oh man. Well, you know if it doesn't work out with Marcus, we could always pursue an incestuous relationship."

My jaw plummets in shock. "Harrison, stop!" I playfully slap him away.

"If you two are done, I've got a wedding to start," Timber says, preparing to open the doors of the assembly hall. We recompose ourselves and stand in readiness.

I hear the music begin to play. It's a hauntingly beautiful piano nocturne played by our resident concert pianist, Hamric Benstarro. Timber probably treated him in the medical unit—that's how she knows most residents here. In fact she has such a huge social circle that she insisted on planning a whole lavish wedding for me, a task I found entirely too daunting.

Timber takes Evie's hand and together they walk down the aisle side by side. Evie tosses the tiny daisies and red rose petals leaving a trail resembling a field of wildflowers.

As I approach the entrance to the assembly hall I am enthralled. Timber went all out with her planning. I don't even recognize the room. Guests are seated at round tables, each draped with white tablecloth and holding a centerpiece of white daisies and red roses encircling a large white candle dotted with bronze studs. Each table seats at least ten guests and I can't even fathom how many tables there are at each side of the red carpet that leads to the dais at the end of the hall. Even the chairs themselves are draped with white slipcovers and tied back with wide shiny red ribbons, which hold a large daisy at the knot.

The ambiance of this once cold and unfeeling hall is out of this world. It is dimly lit with tiny lights dangling from the ceiling. I gaze up to find that, much to my surprise, the tiny lights are actually shaped like infinity flies. *Oh Timber, you are so clever.* A symbol of our undying love.

As Harrison slowly guides me down the aisle my eyes are drawn to the left side of the room, where the banquet is set up. A cake larger than Mount Baerstynn takes up most of the space with five lacy tiers, adorned with daisies and red roses, dotted with bronze beads, and topped with a golden sugar infinity fly. And just in case that is not enough to feed the crowd, two more three tiered cakes flank the sides.

Continuing my journey down the aisle I can see that the entire facility is in attendance, except for the few Watchers standing guard at the entrances. And Granby, of course. I smile politely as I pass Dr. Yipolis and a lovely young lady I've never met, whom I can only assume is his girlfriend since she can't keep her hands off him. Further up I spot Jansen and Yoric with some of the guys they usually hang out with. I snicker at the fact the Yoric is the only face in the room not staring at me now. He can't take his eyes off Timber. In the front are the elites, the officers of the committee, Myra, Marley, and the others that are in charge here. Myra smiles and winks at me.

Now, for the first time, I look up at the raised platform where Marcus stands gazing down at me. The backdrop is completely covered with foliage, giving it a lush, outdoor appearance. It even smells woodsy. Marcus stands under a white ivy-lined arbor, in his black tuxedo with an ivory vest. Behind him stands Nicron in a matching tuxedo, looking fit and happy as ever. Timber and Evie stand off to the side as I approach the arbor.

As I turn to face him, Marcus drops his gaze to the ring dangling over my belly.

"Ring-bearer?" he whispers. I nod and his eyes glaze over with tears. I've never seen him look so happy, apart from this morning during the ultrasound.

I can't believe it. I'm finally here. I'm going to marry the love of my life and we're going to be a real family with a child of our own. My life is perfect. I only wish my parents and Drake could be here to share this with me.

From behind the arbor the minister, who I didn't even know was there, steps forward. I've never met him before, since I never attend mass at the chapel. He's a short stout man with combed over hair that is either blond or gray or a mix of both. It's hard to see in the dim light. He wears all black with a purple scarf draped over his neck. As he recites some lines from a small leather bound book he carries, my attention is fully focused on Marcus. He's trapped me in his penetrating gaze once again, and whatever the minister says goes straight through the tunnel in my head unabsorbed. Finally he announces that it is time for our vows, which Marcus and I agreed to write ourselves.

Marcus takes both my hands in his, never taking eyes off mine. I take a moment to try to compose myself. Now I suddenly become aware of the crushing density of people in the hall, all eyes pressing down on me. My nerves are brittle and I can't seem to find my voice.

Marcus jumps in to save the day. Smiling down at me, he begins his vows. I was supposed to go first, so I'm relieved when he begins to speak. His voice flows so smoothly, like warm honey.

"Pollen, you are the sun my life revolves around, the air I breathe, the torch that lights my way. I vow to be your loving husband, your rock, your shadow. Wherever you go, I will be right there with you. We've been through a lot together and we made it out because we had each other. Like the infinity fly, my love for you will always survive the most treacherous times. I love you, Pollen."

That's it. The dam behind my eyes has burst and tears gush down my cheeks. Marcus reaches into his jacket and pulls out a silver band. Taking my hand in his, he begins to slide it on.

My nerves relax a bit, enough I think to allow me to say my vows and finish this.

Suddenly the doors to the assembly hall burst open in a thundering explosion that startles everyone in the room. My shoulders tense and Marcus jumps back in alarm. He still holds my hand, but the ring on my finger remains firmly in his grasp. Glenn storms down the aisle, his face beaten and bloodied, his clothes soiled and ragged.

No. This can't be happening. It must be a nightmare. I pinch myself and will myself to wake up, but my surroundings remain. All of a sudden I feel sick. Really sick. I grasp my belly trying to contain my illness.

Glenn's gaze lowers to the hand that rests on my protruding belly and back to my eyes. Then his eyes seem to play a game of ping-pong. *Belly. Eyes. Belly. Eyes.* The look on his face says it all. *No Glenn, please. Don't say it.*

"So it's true," he whispers, but the room is so silent, it seems to bounce off the walls. "You're pregnant." Marcus grips my hand tighter, crushing my fingers together, still looking down at Glenn, almost as if he's waiting for confirmation of his suspicions. Glenn takes a few steps forward until he is standing at the bottom of the steps and looks intently at my stomach.

"That's my baby."

Chapter 18

THE LOOK IN Marcus's eyes is stark, empty, like looking into a bottomless well. He still grasps my hand when he tears off his mother's ring. He yanks it so forcefully I thought he might break my finger.

Everything that happens is a blur, and yet my awareness is magnified. Maybe it all happens so fast that it just feels like a blur, like when we rode the high-speed COPS train here and the yellow emergency lights of the Web melted into the darkness. I find myself permanently etching the images in my mind. This is a day I will never forget.

Marcus lunges off the platform, hurling himself at Glenn like a lion to its prey. They have it out, throwing punches and kicks, spraying blood and sweat. I want to stop it, to stand between them and let them hit me instead. But I'm frozen to this spot, helpless to do anything.

Nicron leaps off the platform and thrusts his arms around Marcus, who is pummeling Glenn on the floor. But Marcus jerks back and sends Nicron flying into the table of elites. Myra and Marley jump up and flee to safety.

Finally Jansen, Yoric and some other men at their table step in and hold Marcus back as Glenn curls his body up on the floor, his face bloody and torn. Granby charges in with two Watchers behind him. They grab Glenn, who is now too weak to even walk on his own. If the fight had continued, Glenn wouldn't have stood a chance against Marcus.

Marcus shakes from his captors and paces back and forth, his chest heaving violently as he catches his breath. His black tuxedo jacket lays crumpled on the floor, the white boutonnière shredded to tiny white flakes. His sweat-laced shirt is gaping open, revealing the curled hairs of his upper chest. His neatly combed back rusty hair now hangs in tangles and sweat over his fiery eyes.

I still haven't moved since Glenn arrived. My feet have grown roots into the dais, unable to move given the emotional toil that was thrust upon me. No. That I thrust upon myself. I should have known this was coming. How could I think I could betray Marcus and get away with it?

After Glenn is dragged out, Granby and Marcus exchange a few words among the chaotic crowd of gossiping onlookers. They are audible, but I'm still too stunned to discern what they are saying. Marcus is full of ire, obviously. But Granby is back to his role as hardcore military commander. He shouts down to Marcus and Marcus shouts back. I've never seen Granby like this, but I suppose it suits his position more aptly than the caring patriarch.

Marcus begins to leave and then turns back to me. A spark of hope rises when our eyes meet. Maybe Granby said something to calm him, to make him change his mind. But his jaw clenches and there's nothing but hatred in his eyes as he looks up at me from the base of the steps.

"You're nothing to me now," is all he says before he storms down the aisle and out the double doors. Every stomp down that red carpet, away from me, pounds a nail into my aching heart.

Finally, the roots give way, dizziness consumes me, and my legs give out, collapsing my body to the floor like the rickety frame of a marionette. My breathing grows heavy, labored.

A hand brushes my arm, Timber's hand, and a switch is flicked on. All the emotion that has built up inside me comes pouring out and I find my legs can move again. I grope Timber's tiny body, using it to climb back to my feet. I fly down the steps onto the red carpet and out the doors, kicking my shoes off so that I can run faster. In the corridor I look left then right. Marcus is leaning his forehead against a wall, punching it furiously. His blows resonate down the corridor, reverberating within my soul.

I approach Marcus apprehensively. He's so angry; I should be frightened, but he's never hurt me before. I have to take a chance. Maybe if I explain what happened he'd understand, eventually. It's a long shot, but I have to try.

"Marcus?" I murmur. I don't know if he heard me or if he's just ignoring me, since he continues to strike the wall fervently. His knuckles are bloody, black and violet and the skin is peeling off. His face has turned a shade of red I didn't know could exist in human skin.

I reach out to touch his arm before he throws it forward again, but he swings around, yanking it away from me, propelling me into the floor. Agonizing pain fills my insides—not from the fall, but from the torturous heartbreak. He really, truly hates me.

"Don't touch me," Marcus growls.

"Marcus, please just listen. It's not what you think." I lift myself up off the floor, but remain distanced.

"What I think? What I think is that you slept with your ex, got pregnant, and allowed me to believe it was my child! Tell me, am I wrong?" His eyes are clouded with tangled webs of torment. All because of me.

"I didn't mean to," I cry.

"Didn't mean to what? Bed him or lie to me?"

"Neither. I mean . . . I didn't know what I was doing. And I couldn't tell you because I knew how much it would hurt you."

A sardonic chuckle escapes from him before he glowers at me again.

"Didn't know what you were doing? So, what, you have no control over yourself now?"

"Marcus, we were drunk," I say.

"Oh, well, that makes it all okay," he shouts sarcastically. Then he turns and strikes the wall three more times.

"It was a mistake. I never meant to hurt you."

He stops and turns back to me, shooting bolts of lightening into me. I cower in his fury.

"Mistake? You knew what that would do to me, Pollen. And you did it anyway. Drunk or not. It's your problem now." He looks into my eyes, then down at my belly, as if he just fell into a cesspool of vomit and feces. "I'm done with you. Stay away from me."

I collapse onto the floor as he tromps away, without even a glance back. I bury my face in my arms and what little semblance of an emotional shield I had put up ruptures. Tears spew out of me from every orifice. I could drown in my own salty tears if I lie here long enough. I don't care. The powerful bond that Marcus and I shared has been eternally severed. How could I ever expect him to forgive me? I can't even forgive myself.

I hear voices around me but I pay them no heed. I just want to be left alone. Alone with my suffering. Left alone to die on this cold, unrelenting floor. I'm lying in a dark and lonely abyss at the precipice of a black hole, ready to be sucked in to nonexistence. *Just leave me alone.*

The floor falls out from beneath me and soon I feel the warmth of somebody carrying me. I don't bother to open my eyes to see who it is; I couldn't see through the veil of tears anyway. From the smell, citrus and cedar, I'd guess it was Granby. I lean my head into his chest and allow my tears to soak into the fabric. I am once again a child in my father's arms. Only I'm not crying over a skinned knee, but my shattered heart, my irreparably broken dreams.

I don't remember being brought back to my apartment. I drift in and out of consciousness, seeing the alternating faces of Jansen and General Granby who seem to be afraid to leave me alone. Perhaps they view me as suicidal now. I can't say for sure that I'm not.

In those moments when I sleep long enough to dream, my head is filled with nightmares. But they're not the fantastic nightmares of my youth. No, these are reality. I relive the moment Glenn burst through the door. Marcus attacking him. I feel the pain of Marcus's scorching eyes. And the worst memory of all—that moment when he ripped the ring off my finger. I wish he'd just taken my finger with it.

At some point I fall into a deep slumber. But it is anything but restful.

The scorching heat threatens to devour every ounce of moisture from my body. I stand in a dark room engulfed in vivid yellow-orange flames that dance around me like glowing ribbons rising from the floor. My tattered ivory wedding gown disintegrates into rags on my body.

In the distance a scream rattles me. But I cannot move. My feet have been nailed to the floor—literally. I look down at the enormous nail heads at the apexes of my feet. I try to pull and twist them out, but they won't budge.

Marcus appears before me, his tuxedo in rags. His eyes are no longer the oceanic blue I come to love. Now they are almost pure black, reflecting only the scarlet flames that surround us. The hatred in his eyes burns a hole into my chest. The stinging is almost unbearable. I open my mouth but before I can say anything his hair turns to flames then his body disappears in a pile of black ash.

My heartbeat drums louder as it strives to pump the thickened blood throughout my veins. Suddenly I can't breathe. Paralyzed and suffocating, I try to lie down, to surrender to my imminent death. A voice rings out, awakening me.

"Auntie Pollen!" *Evie?*

"Auntie Pollen, help me!" Evie's screams are the bloodcurdling push I need to rise up and face my fate. I can't lie here and wave the white flag yet. She needs me.

"Evie, I'm coming!"

I jolt up in my bed, surrounded by stark darkness. Sweat seeps from every crevice of my body as if the fiery torment of my nightmare had actually happened. It takes me a moment to catch my racing breath. Then I fall back on to my pillow and cry myself back to sleep.

Chapter 19

I STARE AT THE LITTLE PEANUT on the ultrasound printout, remembering how just yesterday Marcus and I shared a moment of utter bliss, listening to the pattering of our little boy's heartbeat. The flimsy photo paper has become creased and wrinkled from over handling, and smudged on the bottom edge where my tears seeped into it. In the course of only a few hours I experienced the happiest moment of my life, and the darkest moment.

I've been bedridden since they brought me back here yesterday. I'm still wearing my wedding dress, though now it is wrinkled and soiled. Marcus's wedding band is still tied to my waist. I slip in on to my index finger and twist it around, trying to find some source of comfort. But there is none to be found.

A knock at the door forces me to abandon my cozy nest of blankets and pillows that still smell of Marcus. It's probably Timber, bringing Evie back. In all the hoopla, I vaguely remember Timber saying she'd keep Evie for the night, to give me some rest. I suppose that's why Granby and Jansen were here instead of her. She knew I'd never let Evie stay with anyone else.

I drag myself to the door, stopping to glance wistfully at the mirror on the way. I could pass for a pretty decent zombie right now. My skin is a ghostly shade of white and the makeup I wore yesterday is smeared with gray mascara lines drawn down my cheeks. My hair is still pinned up, but it's barely hanging on. I quickly pull out the pins and comb my fingers through the braids to give it that wavy 'just got back from the beach' look. It'll have to do for now.

By the time the knock sounds again I am already opening the door. Glenn stands outside with his fist still raised. His left cheek is swollen, painted with varying shades of violet, and his bottom lip has crusted over where it was split yesterday. The look in his eye could make even a heartless shrew swoon.

"Don't," I mumble, looking down at the floor, anywhere but his face.

"Don't what?"

"Pity me."

"Can I come in Pollen? I just want to talk." His voice is soft and gentle, like velvet.

"Why not? I don't think there's any more damage you can do," I grumble, opening the door and slithering back to my bed.

Glenn steps aside into the kitchen nook and I hear the water running for a few seconds. Then he kneels down by the bed, and gently washes the smudges from my cheeks with a damp cloth.

"I'm sorry, Pollen. I don't know what came over me yesterday. I swear to you, I didn't mean to crash your wedding like that. That wasn't my intention at all. I want you to be happy. I really do, even if it is with someone else. But after what they told me, I had to see for myself."

"After who told you what?"

"One of the Watchers. He told me you were pregnant. I remembered what you'd said about Marcus—how he can't have kids, and I knew it had to be mine. I'm so sorry for what I did—it just took me by surprise and, I don't know, something just came over me, like I was possessed or something. I grossly overreacted."

A sharp, acerbic half laugh escapes my mouth.

"I think you took everyone by surprise." I shake my head while exhaling sharply. "Marcus left me. He won't see me anymore." I'm sure Glenn's happy to hear that. After all, he must have had *some* selfish intentions for crashing the wedding. But his expression isn't exactly one of triumph. It's more concerned.

"Give him some time Pollen. Maybe he'll come around." Glenn's attempt to cheer me up falls flat. He doesn't know Marcus like I do.

"No, Glenn. He won't. You didn't see how happy he was when we heard the baby's heartbeat. He was crying. The doctor told him he could still be the father. He really believed that."

Glenn slides over onto the bed and lies behind me propped up by his elbow. Before I can protest that he is overstepping his boundaries, he leans over and wipes my tears with a handkerchief. Then he places one of the blankets over my shoulder and gently strokes my arm. I don't know what his intentions are, but I relax and allow him to console me.

"How far along are you?" he asks quietly.

I have to think for a minute before I can respond. "Ten weeks. I think."

"Are you still having morning sickness?"

I almost ask him how he knows, but then I remember—we've been through this before. The first time, when I was pregnant with Lex, he was the only person I confided in during the first trimester. I was so young and scared; I couldn't tell my parents until it was impossible to hide the bump even under baggy clothes and an armful of books. Glenn eased me through the nausea and fatigue of those first few weeks, not like a panicking teenage boy, but as a warm-hearted father-to-be.

"Yes. No. I was, but I think it's just my emotions making me sick now."

"You should eat."

"I'm not hungry."

"Pollen, when was the last time you ate?"

I didn't eat anything yesterday because of the wedding. My dress was already tight around my belly and I didn't want to add any more inches. I figured I'd eat at the reception. And of course I couldn't even think of food without reflexively gagging after Marcus renounced me.

"It's been a couple days," I murmur.

"Damn Polly, you've got to eat something. It's not just about you anymore. Why don't you get dressed and I'll take you down to the food court," Glenn commands, standing back up.

"No!" I sit up and grab his arm. "I don't want to see anyone right now. And if Marcus sees us together—"

"Okay. I understand. Look I'll go get you something and bring it up, okay?"

I nod just to get him to leave. I probably won't eat whatever he brings up anyway.

Glenn returns about half an hour later and slinks into the bed at my feet where I hadn't budged since he left. The savory scent of teriyaki fills my nostrils and awakens me from my trance. My first instinct is to rummage the kitchenette for a bowl to vomit into.

"I wasn't sure what you wanted, so I got this," Glenn says hooking his fingers under the flap of one of the two takeout boxes he brought and handing it to me. I peek under the lid. Fragrant peppers, mushrooms, and peas sail through swirls of wispy rice noodles. I can't believe he remembered. When I was pregnant with Lex, I used to call Glenn at all hours of the night and beg him to bring me this dish. It was all I craved for nine months.

I peer up at Glenn through my lashes. I don't have to say anything. He deciphers the look on my face as one could only do through an unspoken connection.

"You think I'd forget the noodles? You pestered me for months about that." He laughs.

A sad smile stretches my lips.

"Sometimes I imagine how different things might have been if Lex hadn't died," Glenn sighs. "He probably would've survived the virus too. We'd have been a family. A real family."

My smile diminishes. "If I hadn't killed him."

"Polly, stop that." Glenn snaps. "It wasn't your fault. Stop blaming yourself."

I fumble with the lid, attempting to close it, but Glenn stops me. "Eat," he commands.

"But Glenn, I really can't—"

"Please, eat," he pleads in a gentler tone.

I really don't want to. My mouth sours and my throat tightens as I imagine the taste and texture of the noodles in my mouth. I can't really handle anything stronger than water right now. Perhaps my past craving has turned into a pregnancy aversion. But to appease him I pinch the fork he offers me and twirl it around in noodles, taking birdlike nips.

Glenn studies me as I attempt to keep the sparse food from regurgitating. I can feel the warmth of his gaze burn into me, making me squirm with discomfort.

"Do you have to watch me?" I blurt out.

He laughs. "I'm sorry. I just want to make sure you actually eat something. Plus I like watching you. It brings me comfort after the past month."

After a few more nibbles, the nausea fades and with regretful awareness, I have to admit to myself that Glenn was right about eating. I actually feel better—physically anyway.

"Glenn, how did you get back here?"

Glenn shifts on the bed so that he is leaning against the bars of the footboard, facing me, with one folded leg on the bed. He jabs his fork into his takeout box, and swirls it around.

"I was wandering the Web and found my way back. I knew it was risky, but I hoped that after all this time they'd realized I wasn't the culprit and let me back in."

"So they just let you in?"

"No." Glenn spears a large hunk of chicken and brings it to his mouth, chewing thoroughly before speaking again. "The guys at the south entrance held me at gunpoint for a while. Then Granby came. He escorted me inside and explained what happened—

with Lynx. When I asked to see you, he told me about the wedding.

"That's when that one Watcher said you were pregnant. I just snapped. They refused to take me to the hall, so we got into a scuffle, and, well, you know the rest."

My tears well up again at the memories of the wedding. I need to stay off that subject, keep the attention on Glenn for now.

"How did you even get into the Web?"

"It was about a week after they banished me. At first I didn't know where I was. They dropped me off in some remote wooded area and I wandered around for a day or two. I found a cave to shelter in—turns out they dropped me by a mountain. Initially, I thought it was Mount Baerstynn, but it wasn't. I guess that would have been too close to Crimson.

"Anyway, the heat was rising exponentially every day, but the cave seemed to remain cool so I was preparing to stay there for a while. I needed food. I found a road and followed it. That led me to an abandoned a general store. Lucky for me, because it was so remote it hadn't been looted. But instead of transporting the food back to the cave, I thought I'd check the bunker. I stayed there for a few weeks, then when I thought enough time had passed I used a key I found to unlock the padlock to the Web. It took about three weeks for me to find my way back."

"I'm sorry . . . about what happened to you," I whisper, although I'm more sorry he came back.

"Pollen, it wasn't your fault. You know that. And it's not your fault what happened between us. But it happened and now we have to deal with the fallout."

I sigh. I hate it when he's right. I wish I could turn back the clock and undo the last couple of months.

Sitting in silence, poking at my noodles, a memory creeps into my head. My head shoots up at Glenn.

"Glenn. Before you were banished you said something about Drake; that he was alive."

Glenn tenses and scratches his neck while he speaks as if he wants desperately to avoid the question. "Yeah, I did, didn't I?"

"Well?" I prod.

Glenn exhales softly and rubs his eyes. I can see he's anticipating my reaction. "He's at Crimson. In solitary. D321."

My heartbeat races and my lungs deflate. *How can that be?* They told us he was killed by a landmine. Why would they take him to Crimson and tell us he's dead? My mind whirls in confusion.

"How do you know?"

Glenn hesitates, then reluctantly continues, "They brought him to the interrogation room. I'm sorry I didn't tell you before. I didn't want you to do anything rash. He asked about you."

The interrogation room. Thanks to Marcus, I know what they do there. I look up at Glenn's eye patch and shudder at the thought of what they might have done to my brother—what Glenn might have done to him.

"Did *you* torture him?"

Glenn stands up and turns his back to me, cupping his hand over his forehead, giving me my answer. But I have to hear it for myself.

"Glenn. Answer me!" I demand.

"Yes," he breathes. I gasp, trying to control my breath but my body is going into full panic mode.

"Get out," I growl through gritted teeth.

Glenn turns back to me, begging with his lonely eye. "Pollen, that's not me anymore I—"

"Get out!" I scream and hurl my box of noodles at him. They slither down his shirt like elongated worms. Glenn hangs his head and traipses to the door.

"I really am sorry," he says as he closes the door and the room is quiet once again with only the sound of my heaving breath to keep me company.

All the painful memories of my shattered wedding are superficial scratches compared to this. My brother is alive. Imprisoned and tortured, but alive. How can I lie here and wallow in depression when I know he's suffering there all alone. Evie needs him. She needs her real father. I never thought I'd say this again.

I have to return to Crimson.

Chapter 20

AFTER A FEW MORE DAYS of moping and staring at the peeling paint on the ceiling, I renounce the sanctuary of my apartment and make an appearance in public. Much to my chagrin, daily life has gone relatively unchanged. My world was flipped upside down, like a bucket of sand at the beach, discarding pieces of me into a pile of dust, and I'd naively expected that the drama would have extended to the other residents here. Sadly, they have been going about their days, enjoying their happy lives, sending me the occasional sidelong glances. Only Marcus, Evie, and I have felt any change.

The week drags by endlessly. Lana has been oddly supportive and friendly to me at the preschool. I guess she feels sorry for me. I never thought she could be capable of compassion. Evie sometimes gets upset that Marcus is not around. She misses him. I haven't seen him myself. He never even came home to pick up his things. It's almost as if he's purposely adjusted his schedule to be furthest away from me at all times. I feel so empty without him.

I've seen Glenn a few times over the past couple weeks. Each time gets a little easier, but I still want to scratch his other eye out for what he did to Drake. I know he's sorry—he says it every time he sees me. It's just so hard to forgive him after how much he's hurt me and the people I love. Timber's been taking care of me when she can. I've lost a few pounds because I still can't eat very much without my stomach turning back flips.

Timber's been begging me to go to The Snake Hole with her, but I don't want to leave my room. Every night she comes by, trying to lure me out of my little hole in the wall. I don't want to be around all those people. The same people who watched me fall apart after Glenn revealed my infidelity. And I don't want to see others dancing happily and having fun. I want everyone to be just as heartbroken and miserable as I am.

"Please Pollen," Timber pleads. "You've got to come out and live your life."

"I don't want to live my life. I want to curl up into a ball and die."

"You've been trying to do that for a week. Obviously that's not working for you. Come on. I won't take no for an answer."

Timber opens the bureau drawer, pulls out a cute mint green tank top and a black skirt, and tosses them on the bed.

"Get dressed."

Before I can object she tells Evie that she'll be going to daycare for a few hours. Evie jumps up and down like a pogo stick. I don't like the idea of sending her there, but forcing her to stay with 'grumpy Auntie Pollen' is starting to bring her down. I suppose I should let her go—she enjoys being around the other kids. And I do need to get out. Holing myself up here is just prolonging the devastation.

Down at The Snake Hole the music is blaring and conversations are screaming. The noise pollution is making me almost as sick as food does. I convince Timber to let us sit on the outer edge of the bar, furthest away from the speakers.

With my sparkling water and lime in hand I peer around the room, looking for Marcus. I really miss him, but in a way I'm scared to face him. Not seeing him for so l long I can't gauge what his feelings are toward me right now.

"Stop looking," Timber says.

"I wasn't," I lie. "I was just seeing if there's anyone else I know here."

"I know who you are looking for and don't. Trust me. You need to give him some more time. He's not ready yet." I turn back to Timber, discerning.

"Have you seen him?" I ask. She reluctantly nods.

"How is he?"

Timber stirs her straw around in her drink as she struggles with finding the right words to answer.

"He's . . . keeping busy."

"What, working?"

"Yes," Timber replies in one extended syllable. I sense there's some deeper meaning to that single word. Sometimes she can be so easy to read when she's lying. I suppose that's why she doesn't like to lie.

"What else?"

Timber sighs deeply. "He's been training a lot—with Granby." No wonder she didn't want to tell me. Timber knows I didn't want Marcus to join the militia. It was one of the very few arguments we had before the incident with Glenn. I was so worried something would happen to him. Now he's gone and done it. Did he really want to or is he just being defiant so he can throw it in my face?

Suddenly, my eyes are drawn up by some magnetic force across the room. It's as if they are being tugged and no matter how much I struggle, there's no resistance. All I see are those piercing sapphire eyes, looking dead and unfeeling at me.

"Marcus," I whisper. I charge across the dance floor before Timber can react to stop me. Arms flail and legs kick me as I squeeze and coil my way through the crowd of partiers. I'm not one for dancing—I come from the two-left-feet variety. I never really understood the pleasure people gain from it. I feel the dirty looks burning holes into me, though I look straight ahead, as if I don't notice.

By the time I reach the other side of the lounge, Marcus has disappeared. I spin around and twist back again, scrutinizing every face under the dim scarlet and gold hued lights. He couldn't have left already. I trace the perimeter and finally my gaze meets his again. He is leaning back against a wall in a shadowed corner holding a beer bottle down by his side. Nicron stands close by, looking warily at me.

Marcus speaks no words, yet he tells me to go away. His face mirrors the expression he gave me that last time I saw him, after the wedding. For a moment I consider a dashing escape to protect my fragile ego from being crushed again. But I can't pull myself away from him. I need him. I approach cautiously, and Nicron steps forward to greet me.

"Pollen, you should go," he says.

"I need to speak to Marcus."

"He doesn't want to talk to you. Just go home and take care of yourself."

"No," I say, shoving him out of the way. Nicron doesn't put up a fight. He steps away, giving us some privacy as I step closer to Marcus.

"Marcus," I utter, not quite loud enough to carry over the pounding bass. Marcus simply shakes his head at me, taking a long swig of beer.

"Marcus, I miss you," I say, slightly louder.

"Don't," he barks. Under the red-hued lights, his furrowed brow and scowl resemble a devil from hell. He frightens me, and yet, I can't leave.

"Please give me a chance to talk," I plead, tears beginning to fill my lower eyelids. Marcus tips his head back, chugging the rest of his beer in one shot.

"I have to go," he snarls. He drops the bottle to the floor where it shatters into a mass of dark brown specks and pushes by me as he disappears into the dancing mob.

I collapse into a chair at the empty table next to me and bury my face into my clammy hands. My shoulders quake as I vainly attempt to stifle my cries. I should have listened to Timber. He doesn't even want to see me. I understand how badly I hurt him, but has he grown so cold and completely devoid of emotion?

A hand drops on my shoulder and awakens me from my whimpering. A drunk woman has used me as a crutch but tries to play it off as compassion.

"Are you okay sweetie?" she shouts, shooting spittle at my face. Her alcohol-laced breath causes my stomach to clench into a knot. I flash her an artificial smile and nod. One good thing about the lighting at The Snake Hole; it's too dark to decipher tears from sweat.

I'm about to return to my cocoon of melancholy when I see someone has already sat down at the table with me. I swiftly wipe my cheeks and raise my head to meet Glenn's gaze. He's brought two glasses of clear bubbly liquid with a wedge of lime in each. He pushes one to me. I sniff it first to make sure it's not alcoholic and then let the icy liquid roll over my lips.

"Timber said this is what you were drinking," he says, projecting his voice over the drumming music. I narrow my eyes at the glass resting between his fingers.

"Sparkling water," he shouts. I continue to stare incredulously at him. Glenn never drinks water in an establishment that serves alcohol. "Don't believe me? Here, I'll trade you." He slides the glass to me and I reluctantly draw it to my mouth, taking a tiny sip. He *is* drinking water. The look on my face can't hide the shock I'm feeling. Glenn has always been the first to crack open the contents of a liquor cabinet.

"When did you stop drinking?" I ask, noting that if I weren't pregnant I'd have died of alcohol poisoning by now.

"The day after . . ." he voice drifts off. I raise my eyebrows and tilt my head slightly. "Well, you saw me the last time I drank."

"Oh," I murmur in quiet awareness. Glenn has pulled some stupid stunts in the past under the influence. Once he toilet-papered a police officer's house for giving him a ticket. Another time he drove a backhoe off a construction site and parked it at a donut shop. He actually got caught and arrested for that one—his father bailed him out. The day he was released from jail, he was back to the bottle. Even that couldn't convince him to quit drinking.

But here he is now, clean and sober. Is he doing this for me? Trying to win me back? If that's the case I need to make it perfectly clear that we are not getting back together. I'm still in love with Marcus and I'm not ready to give up on him yet.

"Why are you here?" I ask. If he's not drinking and he's not with anyone else then he's obviously here for me. Maybe he's been following me. That's disturbing.

"I just wanted to check this place out. It wasn't here before I was ousted." Glenn sips his water, taking in a large ice cube with it. "Plus a coworker called me and said he saw you here. I wanted to see how you were. I'm glad you're getting out now."

"Timber dragged me here," I whine. "I was okay, until I saw Marcus. He still won't speak to me."

Glenn looks down dejected.

"Pollen, do you want me to take you home?" It's almost like he read my mind. I've wanted to go home since before I arrived. I nod, eagerly.

Outside the club I can still hear the thumping bass all the way to the elevator. The corridors are nearly empty. There's only an inebriated couple leaning against the wall, trying to swallow each other from the inside out. Glenn's fumbling hands tell me that he wants to either hold my hand or my waist or shoulder, but he's being the unlikely gentleman, maintaining his distance. Maybe I don't have to set boundaries after all.

We step into the empty elevator. When he's certain we're alone, he finally speaks.

"Pollen, I'm going to be honest with you." *Oh no.* "I'm still madly in love with you."

Glenn gazes down at me, smoldering. *Oh god, no. Not in the elevator. There's no escape for me here!* I avert my eyes to cool down the atmosphere.

"I know you don't return my feelings after all the shit I've done. And I know your feelings lie with Marcus." *Phew, at least we're clear on that.* "Fact is, I care about you and I don't like seeing you like this. I know we've had our share of problems. I want you to know I've changed. I'm not the selfish jerk I used to be. And it's all because of you. This is one thing you really can blame yourself for."

What am I supposed to say to that? First he declares his love for me and then acknowledges my feelings for Marcus. Now he's giving me credit for something I had nothing to do with. What game is he playing?

"Glenn I didn't do anything," I whisper.

"No, you didn't. But I changed because I didn't want you to see me as the monster I was. I wanted to be worthy of you. I know now that I will never be worthy of your love. But maybe I can still have your friendship?"

"Oh Glenn, who am I to say who's worthy of what? I've done my fair share of deplorable acts. We all have. I don't know whether you are worthy or not. But I will accept your friendship if you accept that I can't be with you *that way* again."

Glenn wears a pained smile.

"That's more than I deserve," Glenn says, satisfied. There's a sparkle in his eye. He really has changed and I can see it now. I should be feeling lost and abandoned after seeing Marcus tonight, but instead I feel strangely at peace. Is it Glenn? Is he making me feel this way?

When the elevator stops, Glenn continues to walk me all the way to my apartment, stopping at the door.

"Pollen, I hope this isn't asking too much—"

Glenn looks down, reluctant to speak his mind.

"What is it?"

"Can I give you a hug?"

"You're asking me if you can give me a hug?" A smile creeps onto my face. I'm flummoxed by his request. This definitely isn't the straightforward, no holds barred Glenn I know from my past. The old Glenn wouldn't even give me the opportunity to push him away.

"I just don't want to cross the line," he affirms. His single eye softens.

"Of course," I say.

Glenn curls his arms around my shoulders as I lean in and rest my head against the valley of his chest. I stand there in the comfort of his embrace longer than I had anticipated. The warmth and the gentleness of his body feels so good, I'm almost tempted to invite him in. But that might give him the wrong impression. Plus, Evie—

"Evie!" I shoot back out of his arms in a panic. "I forgot about Evie!"

"Shh. Where is she?" Glenn asks, his hands still resting on my shoulders.

"We took her to the daycare before we went to The Snake Hole. I can't believe I forgot." After all these months of never letting her leave my sight because I didn't trust anyone; now *I'm* the one that can't be trusted. *I'm* the one who forgot her. How could I be any more irresponsible? And now I'm having a baby of my own?

"I'll go get her and bring her back, okay? You go inside and rest," Glenn says.

"You can't. Only authorized guardians can pick up the kids. Your name isn't on the list."

"I'll walk with you," Glenn says.

Initially I think to object. But I'm enjoying his company too much to let him go so soon. I'll get rid of him after I get Evie.

The daycare is only one floor down from us, so we skip the elevator and take the stairs.

"Are Evie and Marcus close?" Glenn asks curiously.

"Yes, very. He's like a father to her," I say. Then I remember that Evie's real father is alive and in that dungeon at Crimson. My heart sinks. I still haven't thought up a decent plan to break into Crimson and get him out, but I'm determined to figure something out. After all, I *have* escaped *twice*.

"So how is she reacting to him being gone?"

"She's upset, but taking it well for a kid her age I guess. She misses him."

We round the corner and approach the window-lined wall of the daycare center. I screech to a halt, pressing my palms up to the glass, gaping inside. Glenn continues walking but turns back when he sees me frozen to the spot.

In the daycare center, Marcus sits on the floor and helps Evie put together a puzzle. He's actually grinning, something I thought he'd forgotten how to do. His smile is sad. It breaks my heart to think of how he must feel—losing Evie *and* the baby he thought was his. Suddenly that magnetic radiation begins to surface and his eyes rise to meet mine. The smile folds into a grimace and suddenly I'm aware that Glenn is standing right next to me.

Chapter 21

"Glenn, you have to go. Now."

"I'm in room forty-seven on level J if you need me," he says with quiet deliberation. I nod and he wheels around, disappearing into the stairwell.

I turn back to the window. Marcus is whispering to Evie. Then she clings to him as he stands up. He tries to peel her hands away, but every time he does, she hurls herself back at him like a yoyo.

Walking into the daycare lobby I barely notice the other kids reading books and playing with toys on the floor. As I close in on Marcus and Evie, a glint of light reflects off of Marcus's cheek. A tear. Was it Evie's reaction? Seeing me? Or maybe both?

"Evie, it's time to go sweetie," I say, trying to sound calm and masking the pain of seeing Marcus in my broken voice.

Evie doesn't even look at me.

"Come home, Marcus. Please," she cries. Marcus unwinds her hands from around his legs and squats down so that he's eye level with her.

"I wish I could Evie," he says quietly. The pain in his voice rips yet another hole in my shattered heart. "But right now I need to spend some time on my own."

"But I want you to come back. I miss you."

"I miss you too, darling. We'll still see each other. I promise. Now you take good care of your auntie, okay?" He kisses her forehead. I'm taken aback. He actually acknowledged me, and not in a detestable way. I'm not *nothing* after all. It's a positive step in the right direction, even if he won't acknowledge me. At least I'm still human, I hope.

Marcus stands and combs his fingers through his mussed up hair. He looks at me briefly before charging past. There was something different in his eyes tonight. Not so much anger, but pain—immense, torturous pain. I twist to watch him leave and as he does, he hangs his head low, rubbing his face with the back of his forearm.

Evie sits on the floor with her arms and legs crossed, scowling at me. She reminds me of a glowering gargoyle garden statue—stiff and indignant.

"Evie." I crouch down to meet her gaze. "I know you're upset. But let's talk about this at home, okay?"

"I don't want to go home," she pouts. "I want to go with Marcus."

"I know. But Marcus has to live somewhere else for right now."

"Why?" Another piece of my heart chips away. How can I tell her that he left because of me? She'll hate me. The ferocity of the four-year-old that means the world to me is not something I think I can cope with right now. But I can't lie to her either. That's not how I want to raise her.

"Marcus and I had an argument. He needs to be away from us for a little while."

Evie's eyes soften and glisten with fresh tears. "Will he ever come back home?" My wishful thinking says yes, but reality slithers in, smashing my hopes to pieces with a sledgehammer. The decision to remain positive or to be honest volleys back and forth in a seemingly endless tennis match. For right now, positive wins out.

"Maybe," I lift my voice to try to sound hopeful. It's the best I can do for now.

Evie's eyes brighten softly. "When?"

"I don't know. Just be patient and give him some time. Hey, I have an idea."

"What?" Evie stands and leans in toward me.

"How about we go upstairs and draw an 'I miss you' card for Marcus?" I feel a little devious, playing on Evie's yearning for Marcus and love of crayons.

"Yes, yes!" Evie hops on her toes. I make a quick stop by the front desk to sign Evie out on the handprint identifier, and we take the short walk upstairs.

Today is Leisure Day. The one day of the week when virtually nobody has to work or train. Marcus and I used to spend the mornings sleeping in late while Evie watched cartoons on her tablet. Today, though, I sleep in alone.

Evie is already awake. In the background I can hear the pings and animal noises from her favorite game, "Word Zoo." It teaches kids letters and simple words using the interface of a zoo. Evie's love of animals made it a conspicuous favorite.

Evie's cereal trickles to the floor as I mindlessly try to pour it and hold the kettle under the running faucet at the same time. I huff at my clumsiness. Maybe I should have slept in a little longer. Timber says it's 'pregnancy brain,' but I'm in denial. I still won't acknowledge the existence of the tiny being in my belly. I don't want it to be there. It's caused too many problems already.

There's a knock at the door and I glance up at the plain black and white mechanical clock on the wall. Ten forty-five. I didn't realized I'd slept in this late.

"You're not dressed," Glenn says as I open the door, wearing my red plaid flannel pajama bottoms and white camisole. His astounded look confuses me. Why should he care if I'm dressed or not?

"Yeah, I just woke up. Am I going somewhere?"

Glenn eyes me incredulously. "Preggo brain again?" I squint, cocking my head to the side. *What is he talking about?*

"The assembly?" he continues. I vaguely remember reading about a mandatory assembly in the newsletter. And then there was a door hanger on my doorknob earlier this week, a reminder, but I didn't give it a second look.

"That's today?" I'm not sure if it was a question or statement, but I flip around and scramble through my drawers finding something decent to put on in a hurry. Glenn steps in and closes the door.

"Hi Uncle Glenn," says Evie as she dances over to him happily. She's already dressed in a pair of denim shorts and a yellow blouse with puffy short sleeves and lacy collar.

I throw on a plain black tee shirt over my white camisole and change into a pair of snug knee-length shorts, fumbling with the button to get it to fit over my bulging belly.

"I think it might be time to start looking in the maternity section," Glenn laughs. I give him a hard stare and he stops abruptly, which forces a short, staged coughing reaction. Frustrated, I grab a hair elastic, and wrap it around the button, through the buttonhole, and back around the button. *See? No maternity clothes needed.*

I look at the clock again—ten fifty.

"Evie, eat some cereal quickly before we go," I say as I'm sliding a sneaker onto my foot.

"I already did. You were sleeping."

I glance up at the cereal I had poured for her, most of it on the floor. I'm astounded that at her age she's already doing things for herself. She shouldn't have to fend for herself so young. I'm doing the best I can, but maybe it's inevitable, with the desolate mine field this world has become, and both her parents dead. Or one of them anyway. Who knows whether my brother will make it out of Crimson alive? Yes, she'll need to learn to take care of herself. Perhaps it's better this way. I may not always be around to protect her.

I finish tying my shoes and join Glenn and Evie by the door.

"That would be record time for you," Glenn bites, hinting at the hours I used to spend in the bathroom preparing for our dates. I glare at him as we leave.

I can't stay mad at him for long. We've really developed a close friendship since Marcus left me. We'll never have the relationship we once shared, but this is better. This is stronger and more authentic. I like this Glenn a lot.

I get chills as we step in through the double doors of the assembly hall, the hall where my wedding took place, or should have anyway. I take a deep breath to settle the shivers running through my bones.

The two-story room looks completely different now—cold, with bright, glaring lights raining down. The back wall is paneled wood and the side walls are painted tan. Rows upon rows of folding metal chairs sweep across the hall with a few aisles to break them up.

On the platform are General Granby, Myra, Sage, and a wall of militiamen to back them up. Marcus stands among them, rigid and unfeeling, staring straight ahead, as if looking at something in the distance. Or looking at nothing at all.

We are among the last to arrive, only finding seats in the back row. Evie whines that she can't see, so Glenn lifts her onto his shoulders where she can get a better view.

I lean over to Glenn, and whisper, "Do you know what this is about?"

He doesn't look at me. "Not exactly. But I have a feeling it's related to some . . . intel . . . I told Granby."

"What?" I ask, but Myra takes the podium and Glenn doesn't answer me, despite the hard stare I give him.

"Good morning and thank you all for joining us here today," she starts. Myra goes on conveying news from around the complex: accomplishments and setbacks regarding the Earth mission; the status of crops in the greenhouses; openings, closings, and delays; and other announcements that are of interest to the residents. Then she steps aside and passes the podium to Granby, who makes a special announcement.

Granby coughs and clears his throat before he begins.

"There have been some developments in our relations with the Trinity. As you all are aware, the Crimson Survivor Refuge is their stronghold. An inside source has revealed to us that they are beginning to develop a shuttle which is on course to colonize A1D3."

He glances down at the podium briefly, I assume to look at his notes, then looks back up.

"We will not allow that to happen." Several people in the room erupt in cheers and some others clap. Granby pushes his hand down, signaling the crowd to maintain composure.

"I know that many of you are in support of our plans to travel to A1D3 and start a 'clean' colony. I know many more of you are in support of eliminating the Trinity—"

The crowd roars with cheers even louder than the first. Evie wraps her arms around her ears and squeezes her eyes shut.

"Yes, yes I know," Granby says, lifting his voice above the commotion. "So today I want to announce that we are planning a mission to Crimson."

Granby pauses expectantly while the patriotic residents of Ceborec explode with ovation. He waits patiently for the applause to die down before continuing.

"The primary objectives of this mission will be to take back the plans that were stolen from us in addition to their own plans and destroy the vessel that they are building. Commencing immediately after the assembly, we will be having open sign ups for the militia. You will be required to complete three rigorous weeks' basic training, and five weeks' specialized training based on your placement. Details of the mission will be forthcoming only to members of the militia. I hope to see many of you soon."

Granby quickly departs the podium and speaks a few silent words to Sage before taking his rigid stance on the platform.

My mind is whirling. Myra takes the podium again and concludes the assembly, but the words are merely background noise to my thoughts. This is the opportunity I've been waiting for. This is my chance to save Drake.

The possibilities are coming into focus now. Energy pulses through my bloodstream as I visualize the daring rescue mission that releases Drake from his abysmal captivity. I've been unable to formulate any kind of coherent plan since Glenn revealed to me that he was alive. But now, everything is coming together. The gears are spinning and there is no stopping them.

It's only now that I happen to notice the tables flanking each side of the platform. After Myra concludes her final words, she and the others on the platform divide in half and each takes their place sitting behind the tables.

Then they are shielded from my vision as the crowd of onlookers rise. Some stumble out the double doors, happily going back to their leisurely activities. Some stand around chattering about the latest gossip. But most of them flock to the front of the assembly hall claiming their spaces in line. I turn to Glenn, but he's gone and only Evie stands beside me holding my hand. I have to get in that line.

My eyes scan the assembly hall for a friendly face I know. The only face I recognize can hardly be classified as 'friendly,' but Lana knows Evie well enough and I think I can trust her.

"Lana!" I shout over the cluster of women gossiping between us. She looks my way briefly as I filter through the group. I've never really seen Lana outside the classroom before. She looks strange, dressed in blue jeans and a plain tee shirt. Somehow, she looks less intimidating.

"Lana," I say approaching her. "I need you to watch Evie for a few minutes. I'll be right back."

"But, Pollen!" she cries out. It's too late. I've already dashed away and I'm not turning back now. She wouldn't abandon Evie in a place like this.

The sign-up lines for the militia stretch all the way into the aisles, but they move fairly quickly. I assume we only need to give them our names since they have every other shred of information about us on file. I peer around and spot Glenn already at the table on the other side of the platform. I should have known that's where he'd be. Always the eager soldier—just as he was at Crimson.

As I draw closer to the table, I spot Marcus and I instantly regret coming to this table. For a second, I consider switching to the other side. But the line is moving so swiftly I don't have time to change my mind.

The man in front of me leaves and I approach the table, where a lanky brunette woman gawks at me.

"I'm Pollen McRae. I'd like to sign up please," I state firmly.

She remains silent, looking down at my well-disguised belly. I don't really look that big with my black tee shirt covering it. But I guess it's no secret to anyone here that I'm pregnant. Not after the wedding fiasco.

"I, I don't think you can join," she says cautiously.

"It's my body, my decision. I want to join the militia," I scold. My eyes burn into her.

"I'll need to check with General Granby first. Excuse me." She stands up and I watch her as she walks across the platform toward the other table.

"What the *hell* do you think you're doing?"

I turn back and Marcus is standing across the table glaring at me, leaning in as if he's ready to pounce.

I'm speechless for a second. My heartbeat thickens, and a tiny sliver of my heart mends itself. This is the first time he's taken the initiative to talk to me. Despite the circumstances, I'm actually a little flattered.

But the look in his icy blue eyes frightens me. It's not so different from the look he gave me at The Snake Hole and after the wedding, while he was beating down the wall with his fist. I can't let him see the fear lurking behind my eyes. I must remain strong.

"I'm joining the militia," I say firmly, trying to stiffen my muscles to look taller.

"No, you're not," he growls.

I place my hands on the table and lean in, mirroring his stance.

"This has nothing to do with you, Marcus."

"No, it doesn't. You are not putting the life of that baby in danger. Now. Go. Home."

"No!" I shout, a little too loudly. A few people nearby stop and stare at me before going back to their business. "I don't care about the damn baby anymore." I wince at the sound of those words. I can't believe I just said that.

"What the hell is wrong with you?" Marcus sneers. "Why are you doing this?"

"Because my brother is still alive," I bark.

Marcus's eyes widen. Before he can say anything else, the brunette returns to her seat, followed by Granby. I look up at his regretful eyes.

"Pollen, I appreciate your tenacity. The militia would greatly benefit from your talents," he says optimistically. My posture straightens as I smile proudly.

"But I cannot allow you to join at this time."

My body suddenly feels weak. The smile dissipates and my ego is crushed. I glance down at the brunette, who looks smug.

"It's simply not safe for your unborn child. You need to stay here and take care of yourself," Granby says.

I glance over to Marcus who is still frowning, but seems to carry an air of satisfaction as he sits back down. I turn and walk dejectedly back to the double doors, where Glenn and Evie are waiting.

"You didn't," Glenn snarls at me. The anger is evident in his single narrowed eye.

"And you did," I narrow my eyes back at him.

"I'm not the one carrying our child," he snaps. "Pollen, you can't be selfish now. You wouldn't drag Evie into this, would you?"

"Selfish? You think I'm being selfish? For wanting to rescue my only brother—Evie's father?" As the words come out of my mouth I instantly regret saying them.

"Daddy?" Evie squeals. The last thing I wanted to do was give her false hope, in case Drake doesn't make it out alive.

"We'll talk about this later, Evie," I snap at her. Taking her hand I pull her out of the assembly hall, making my way down the corridor as Glenn stomps alongside us. We continue arguing all the way back to our apartment, despite the fact I was rejected from joining.

"Why did you join? Why, when you have a baby on the way, too?" I ask with tears filling up my eyes. One escapes, plummeting down my cheek and on to my shirt, leaving a black stain darker than the fabric. Glenn reaches up and wipes the trail from my cheek with his thumb.

"Because I want what's best for you. This mission is necessary for our survival. If the Trinity have the ability to leave, do you really think they'll just leave in peace? Hell no! They will weave a tapestry of death and destruction and revel in it. That's the kind of people they are. I can't sit back and watch it happen. Pollen, I'm not scared for myself anymore like I was in the beginning. I'm scared for you."

"But if you go, who will stay here with us?"

"You won't need anyone to stay with you. Granby is on top of things. The Watchers will still be here to protect Ceborec."

Something stirs deep within me. A feeling that scares me more than being attacked in the woods. More than being captured and imprisoned at Crimson. And more than the thought of losing my baby.

"I don't want you to go."

Before he can move his hand away I cup it in mine, holding it to my cheek. Then, as if we were saying our final goodbyes, I clamp my arms around his broad shoulders, resting my face in the crook of his neck. Glenn's arms cross around the back of my waist, pulling me in tighter. I *want* to be in his arms.

"Don't worry, Pollen. Everything will be okay. And I will get Drake out. I promise."

CHAPTER 22

I SAW VERY LITTLE of Marcus and Glenn over the past few weeks. Their training schedules kept them busy most days. Glenn and I would hang out every Leisure Day, when he had the day off. He would talk about how grueling their schedule was—twelve to fourteen hour days with only two short breaks for lunch and dinner.

The militia have their own training arenas and armory on two floors that span the entire facility. Sometimes, Glenn said, when they began training they would use the holographic room that normally housed beef and poultry, temporarily herding the animals to another part of the facility for a day. In there, they could simulate the outdoors, since the heat above ground had reached temperatures too dangerous to train. Recently, though, as the temperatures have been dropping, they've been granted approval to train outdoors to prepare them for the attack, which will take place on Liberation Day, the day we used to celebrate our release from the underground bunkers. I have a feeling this year it will take on a whole new meaning.

I asked how Marcus was, but of course Glenn always kept his distance from Marcus, so he could never really tell me much.

The soldiers are due to be shipped out on their Crimson mission next week. I spent most of the day today with Glenn, while I gave Marcus some alone time with Evie. He still won't see me. It upsets me but the sting isn't as bad as it used to be. I've almost accepted his rejection and the fact that we can't be together anymore.

Glenn and I watched an old black and white movie in the cinema and he made me dinner in my tiny kitchen—pasta with fresh pesto. Then we just sat around and talked; Glenn mostly told stories about the other soldiers—particularly the new recruits, who had a difficult time adjusting to the rigorous training.

As the hours pass and my internal clock winds down, I expect Glenn to leave, but he doesn't. I hate to have to ask him. It seems so rude after the lovely day we had.

"Glenn, it's getting late," I say, hoping he'll get the hint.

"There's one more thing I want to do with you, before I leave next week."

Uh oh. I had a wonderful time with him, I admit, but I'm still not eager to rekindle our relationship. What do soldiers want with women right before they go into battle? I'm sure it's not sharing a glass of lemonade.

"Glenn," I whine, shaking my head. He laughs at my demeanor.

"What?" I demand.

"What did you think I was going to ask you for? Sex?" He laughs again.

I toss a pillow at his face, but his amusement continues.

"Well, what *do* you want?"

"Come with me," he says as he takes my hand and lifts me up from the side of my bed. Before we leave, he takes the blanket from my bed and tosses it over his shoulder.

"What's that for?" I ask.

"You'll see." His devilish smirk brings a smile to my face.

Glenn leads me down the corridors and up several flights of stairs.

"Why don't we just take the elevator?" I ask.

"Because we can't."

"Why?"

He pauses to gather his words.

"This way is more discreet."

The stairs end at the top level of the underground facility. Glenn opens the door and drags me down through the maze of corridors again. I have no idea where we are going. How can he become so familiar with this place so quickly? I barely even know how to traverse my own floor.

We approach a door at the end of the corridor where a Watcher stands guard. Glenn slips something into his hand, and he unbolts the door, allowing us to enter the staircase to the upper level.

As we ascend the stairs, I hold back, afraid to go any further.

"What's wrong?" Glenn asks, turning back to me.

"We can't go up there, Glenn. It's too hot."

"It's dusk, Polly. And summer's almost over. It's only about ninety-eight degrees. Don't you want to get some fresh air?"

I nod reluctantly. Fresh air is exactly what I need. It's bad enough to be caged underground all summer, but to have to endure the angry scowls from Marcus and the desperate loneliness is just asphyxiating.

As we burst through the doors that lead outside, I am overcome with the sweltering heat. True, it's not as bad as I had expected, but it's still too hot for comfortable living.

Glenn lays the blanket out on the hill next to Ceborec and sits down behind me so that I can lean back against him comfortably—my belly is getting larger and finding a comfortable position to sit in is getting more difficult.

"Polly, do you remember the day we met?"

My mind drifts back to my mid-teenage years. My friend, Kendra, and I went to the Liberation Day bonfire at Macville Park in my hometown of Endmore. It was the first time my parents let me go without them. I had just turned fifteen. Kendra knew some of the kids from the senior class, so we hung out with them. Glenn was among them. He couldn't take his eyes off me all night.

"Of course I do," I reply.

"Back then, I was young, immature, stupid. A bully."

"Yes, you were," I smiled. He used to get into a lot of trouble in those days. Without Glenn's mother, his father did the best he could raising Glenn, but sorely neglected him. Glenn channeled his anger and frustration in negative ways: starting fights, skipping school and picking on weaker kids. But his behavior improved after we began to date.

"I got one thing right that night."

"What?"

"I fell in love with you."

My body stiffens. I still don't know how to respond to that. I love him dearly, but Marcus—
No. Marcus doesn't want me anymore. He's made that abundantly clear. Maybe I *should* move on. Although it feels more like a regression with Glenn.

"You don't have to return my feelings, Pollen." My muscles loosen. "I just want you to know that I'll always be here for you. No matter what."

I turn around, shifting my body between his legs to face him.

"I love you too, Glenn. But it can never be the way it was."

"I know," he says, curling his lips up at one side.

He clasps my hand, weaving his fingers between mine and then kisses me gently on the forehead. Sparks rush down my spine and I lean in closer, gazing into his eye. I don't want this to happen and yet, simultaneously, I do. Maybe it's loneliness, lack of affection. I want to kiss him. No. I want to kiss Marcus. But Marcus isn't here.

Glenn's other hand wraps around the side of my head, holding it in place but not pulling. I lean my face in further, closing my eyes as my lips approach his. I think about the early days with Marcus after we had lost our memories of each other, and how he pushed me away because I was vulnerable. Glenn does not do that. He takes the opportunity presented to him and kisses me back. Here we remain, holding each other under the hazy crimson moonlight, until it's time for Evie to return.

When we arrive back at the apartment I'm stunned to see Nicron standing with Evie outside the door. What, Marcus couldn't bring her himself?

"Hi, Pollen," Nicron says sadly, eying Glenn suspiciously.

"Hey, Nicron. Where's Marcus?'

"He asked me to bring Evie back."

"Of course," I reply, rolling my eyes. "Thanks."

Nicron gives a quick nod and descends the corridor.

"Well, let's get to bed, shall we?" I say to Evie as I open the door. I take her inside and help her change into her pink pajamas. Glenn hovers in the doorway.

"I guess I should be heading home. Good night Pollen."

"Wait!" I call out. I tuck Evie into bed and kiss her goodnight, then nervously approach the doorway, where Glenn is leaning patiently.

That kiss did something strange to me tonight. It reminded me of Marcus and all those nights I spent with him that I took for granted. I hate being alone.

"I don't want you to go," I whisper. I can't seem to look him in the eye. He tips my chin up with his finger, forcing my eyes to meet his.

"I've got to train in the morning, Pollen. I need to get some rest. And you do too."

"Stay with me tonight. Please?"

Glenn cocks his head to the side curiously.

"You want me to sleep with you?"

"Yes . . . No! I mean, I want you to spend the night. Just sleep though, nothing else." I hope that my intentions are clear, but his chuckle indicates that he understands.

"Okay, Polly. But I have to get up early."

Glenn lies behind me in the double bed I used to share with Marcus. It feels like I'm betraying him further by allowing Glenn to sleep here. But Glenn wraps his arm around me and as I drift off to sleep I pretend it is Marcus. And all feels right with the world.

Tomorrow morning the soldiers are setting off on their mission. Today will be my last chance to speak to him before he leaves. Maybe even forever. I'm determined to make him listen.

I've been hounding Glenn for details of the mission for weeks. He's refused to tell me because it's classified, and because he doesn't want to risk being banished again. But every now and then I manage to eke out little bits and pieces from him. I think I've figured out the gist of the plan.

They are going to travel above ground and attack Crimson on Liberation Day, three days from today, to catch the Enforcers by surprise. While they are attacking from the outside, three specialized groups will enter from the Web. I'm not sure how they intend to get through security measures, but of course they've got some kind of feasible plan in place. One group will steal the plans, another will plant bombs on the shuttle which will be set to detonate after they leave, and the third will break into the greenhouses and release an infinity fly, which will wreak havoc on their food supply. Glenn has assured me that he is in one of these three groups and that he will break out Drake and bring him back. I wish I could go myself. But there's no use in wishful thinking.

I stand under the steaming shower, gently circling my soapy hand over my ballooning belly. The reality of pregnancy still hasn't quite hit me despite my bulging midsection. I know I'm pregnant. I can see the physical evidence of it. I think I can even feel him moving sometimes. But I haven't made the emotional connection since Marcus left me. Sometimes it just feels like a dream that I'll eventually wake from.

I don't want this child to be born. I know that sounds hideous. Maybe part of me wanted to join the militia so that something would happen to make me lose the baby. I can't bear the thought of giving birth and falling in love with this child, only to lose him like I did Lex. I'm not ready to be a mother again. I can barely handle taking care of Evie on my own. How am I going to care for a newborn? And to have that constant reminder of my affair with Glenn, I don't know if I could love that child the way a mother should.

I finish rinsing off and twist a towel around me before gazing at my image in the foggy mirror. I wipe the condensation away with a dry washcloth and stare at the remnants of the scar on my face as the condensation slowly reforms, fogging the mirror again. If only the scars inside me were so visible.

I've laid out a flowy white skirt with an elastic waistband, and a silk chartreuse sleeveless top that covers up my belly nicely. By the time I finish dressing the mirror has cleared and I return to primp my hair and face. I want to look my best today.

Evie is also dressed in her favorite, a white chiffon dress with pink sash, and a pink hat with silk flowers in the front. Together we head down to the assembly hall, where they are holding the sending off ceremony for the soldiers.

The hall is crowded, as I'd expected. The soldiers are all dressed in a lightweight green and gray camouflage getup. Despite the breathable fabric, they are sure to roast when they go outdoors tomorrow. The temperature has dropped to tolerable levels for bathing suits and tanks, but not full uniform.

I peer around the room trying to find Marcus or Glenn, but there are so many people obstructing my view. I resign to just meander through the crevices betweens the small clusters of friends saying their goodbyes.

Up ahead, I spot Timber's ashen hair. She hugs a tall soldier with very short blond hair. I don't recognize him from here. Timber initially joined the militia, but decided to stay behind to keep me company and help take care of Evie and me. A short distance away is Jansen, who also joined the militia, shaking friendly hands with an older, gray-haired man. I think he's Jansen's boss at the factory.

"Pollen," Jansen says in his soft angelic voice. I reach over and give him a one-armed hug, while still holding Evie's hand.

"You take care of yourself, Jan," I say, releasing him.

"And you take care of yourself." He emphasizes the last word as if he's referring to the whole package: Evie, the baby, and me. I smile softly.

"I will." I glance over at Timber who has just released her hold on the mysterious man. Only then do I recognize Yoric. Of course, who else would she be hugging like that? He looks so different with his hair buzzed off. So . . . grown up. Jansen walks me over to them.

"Be good, Yoric," I say in a motherly tone. "And don't screw up because you've got a good woman to come back to."

Yoric laughs. "Yeah, I know," he says rubbing the back of his neck nervously.

"Seriously, take care," I say, wrapping one arm behind him.

"Thanks, Pollen, I will."

"Have you seen Marcus yet?" Timber asks, interrupting our hug. I pull back and look around.

"No, I haven't. Do you know where he is?"

"I saw him over there earlier," she says, pointing toward the back corner of the assembly hall.

"Thanks. I'll see you later Timber."

I continue my journey into the labyrinth of smiles and tears, tugging Evie behind me. I wonder whether Marcus will even see me. He's avoided me for the past couple months like I have some incurable communicable disease. I'm not sure how I will react if he won't talk to me now. This mission is beyond dangerous. There's a chance he may not come back alive. I couldn't live with myself he's killed in action.

A hand falls on my shoulder and I spin around hopefully. Glenn frowns, seeing the disappointment in my face, but I try to smile, weakly.

It's not that I'm not happy to see him. Of course I am. But I've spent so much time with him recently, and after he spent the night last week, I made my peace with his leaving.

Glenn leans over and encases me in his bulky arms. He's really worked himself into great shape these past few months. He's lost his love handles and gained an eight-pack of steel. I'm sure the old me, the me that existed before the virus hit, would have swooned. He continues to embrace me tightly and his breath tickles my ear as he whispers into it.

"Get plenty of rest. And, please, don't forget to eat."

"I'll be okay," I say, pulling back. I look deeply into his eye. "Are you sure you have to do this?" The possibility of losing Marcus is bad enough, but Glenn has become a best friend to me recently. He's the only person here who knew me before the virus, and since coming back he's been my rock. I don't think I could bear to lose both of them.

"Yes." I reach back up and grab him again, squeezing him closer to me this time.

"I'll miss you," I whisper, barely containing the tears that threaten to break through.

"I'll always love you, Pollen. No matter what." Glenn squeezes his arms tighter, and then releases me. I try to keep my eyes down, to avoid looking at his face because I know it will make me cry, but he gently tugs at my chin, drawing my face up. His eye burns into mine. His gaze drops to my lips and I'm sure he's about to kiss me, but he holds back. He knows I still don't feel the same about him, despite what happened last week.

"I'll bring back Drake. I promise."

I bite the inside of my cheek. I don't want to cry now. Not before I see Marcus.

"Thank you, Glenn," I whisper, then rising on my toes, I lean in and chastely kiss his cheek. He returns the kiss on my forehead as I lower.

As Glenn squats down to say goodbye to Evie, my eyes lock on Marcus. No wonder I didn't see him before. His hair has been cut short, just like Yoric's, and he's almost unrecognizable. He's standing close to the double doors. There's a woman with him—a brunette like me—who is a soldier also. She smiles shyly and plays with her freshly cropped hair as if she's trying to twirl it around her fingers, but he doesn't seem to notice how crazy she is about him. He flashes a friendly grin, but it's the kiss she plants on him that sends a stinging pain of jealousy into my heart.

"We need to say goodbye to Marcus," I say as Glenn stands back up.

"Of course," he murmurs sadly.

"We'll come back and see you off if we have time," I say quickly. Unfortunately Glenn doesn't have many friends here, what with him being banished and destroying my wedding. Everyone just sort of steers clear of him. It makes me sad to think Evie and I are the only connections he has here.

As soon as he is in her line of vision, Evie bolts toward Marcus.

"Marcus!" she screams, holding her arms out wide for a hug.

"Evie doll!" Marcus smiles as he picks her up and swirls her around, causing her to lose her hat in the process. I pick it up and stand back, giving them their moment. Finally he puts her down and our eyes lock. I guess I was expecting that angry fire, but it's not there anymore. The look is more impassive, with a hint of sadness. He knows that this is his last chance to see me, to talk to me. He may not get another.

I had hoped when I appeared to Marcus the other woman would shove off and give us some privacy, but she just stands by and pretends not to pay attention, though it's obvious she's listening.

"Can we talk?" I ask apprehensively.

"Yes," he nods.

"Somewhere else," I whisper, eyeing the brunette. Although she's looking away, she stiffens, a sure sign that she's received the icy stare I've sent into the back of her head.

Marcus leads Evie and me out the double doors and into the corridor. I get a flashback of the last time we spoke here, right after the wedding. It sends a jolt of pain up my spine.

"Marcus . . ."

My mind goes blank. Oh great. *Now is not the time to be speechless, Pollen.* In lieu of words, I throw myself onto Marcus, releasing the tears that I've kept bottled up. I can feel my protruding belly press against his rocky abs and I wonder if it's too much, if he'll push me away. He hesitates, but finally rests his arms softly against my back.

"Please don't go," I cry.

"I have to," he whispers.

"No. You don't. Stay here. I'll do anything, I swear." I can't believe that I've turned into a pitiful, sniveling crybaby, one of those pathetic schoolgirls whose life revolves around some boy. I was so fierce and self-secure when Marcus and I were together. But when he left me he ripped that part of me away.

Marcus pushes me back cautiously, keeping his hands on my shoulders to keep me from leaning back in on him. "This isn't about you, Pollen. It isn't about us. Not anymore."

"I'm so sorry," I sob. His eyes soften and his brows curl up. "I never meant to hurt you."

"I know," he says, his face rigid and wrinkled with emotional turmoil. I sense that he's not fully over it, that he just wants me to have some resolution before he leaves, just in case he doesn't come back.

"You've moved on," I whisper knowingly, unable to look him in the eyes. He inhales sharply and leans his back against the wall, sighing.

"Pollen, I've done nothing but train for the past two months. I haven't had time for a personal life. There's nothing for me to move on to right now."

"That woman was getting pretty friendly with you." I say bitterly as I nod my head in the direction of the assembly hall.

"Kharma's nobody. She's on my squad."

"She really likes you."

"Is this what you really want to talk about?"

"No," I mumble. We stand for a moment and it seems the silence grows louder than the racket coming from the assembly hall.

"I should go," Marcus says, using his foot to propel his body away from the wall.

"No, wait." I grab his arm just as he's walking past me. "I need you to know, Marcus—I never stopped loving you. And I never will."

Marcus's face reddens, making his auburn hair appear flat brown. His expression deepens on his face and I can see a glistening in his eyes. He caresses my cheek with his knuckles, the way he always used to. My cheek burns where he brushes it. A good kind of burn, like lifting my face to accept the sun's scorching rays. Marcus abruptly drops his hand shaking his head, as if denying the emotion, and then he's gone and I stare at the wall in disbelief. I don't know if he went back into the hall or down some corridor. All I know is that was the last time I'll see him before he leaves.

Chapter 23

OUR FOOTSTEPS ECHO eerily down the empty corridors as Evie and I walk somberly back to our apartment. I told Glenn that I'd come back if there was still time, but I just couldn't. I'm too confused, too upset. How am I supposed to interpret that final gesture from Marcus? He still loves me—I know he does. Or was he just trying to convince himself in a last ditch effort? Perhaps he just wanted me to have some closure, in case he doesn't come back. If I'm being honest with myself, that would be the most plausible explanation.

I lay Evie down on her bed, leaving her in her dress. She begged to wear it to bed and tonight that's not a battle I want to wage with her. Just as her eyes flutter closed, there's a light tapping at the door. She doesn't wake. I guess the evening was just as exhausting for her as it was for me.

I don't know why I'm so surprised to see Glenn. I almost expected it to be him when I opened the door. I suppose I was hoping it would be Marcus, coming to tell me he's had a change of heart and he forgives me. Yeah, only in my dreams. Either way, neither of them should be here now. They're supposed to be sleeping in the upper levels tonight with the rest of the soldiers. They've got an early start tomorrow and they'll be heading straight out the main entrance first thing in the morning.

"Glenn, aren't you supposed to be upstairs?" I ask, wearily.

"They're still in the assembly hall. And I wanted to say goodbye one last time. Without an audience." I step out of the way, inviting him in. "I can't stay long."

I lean into his arms where he embraces me softly and leans his back against the wall, stroking my hair.

"Did you find Marcus?" he whispers.

"Yes."

"How did it go?"

"I don't know."

"Pollen, don't beat yourself up over him. We've all made mistakes. It's his loss."

"I know. I just hate that it has to end like this."

Glenn straightens and tips my chin up, looking pointedly at me.

"Pollen, don't talk like that. This isn't the end. For any of us."

"But you are going into battle. Some are going to fall. It's inevitable."

"Not Marcus. And not me. Don't believe for a second that either one of us is not coming back."

A buzzing noise emanates from Glenn's hip and he looks down to turn his pager off.

"I have to go now." I nod reluctantly and turn to open the door. Glenn stops me. "Can I have one more kiss? For good luck?" He smiles.

Since we are alone I offer a little something more. I reach up fanning my fingers behind his head and pull him down until his lips meet mine. Despite his dominant personality, he allows me to take the lead. My lips slowly glide along his and he submissively returns this kiss. I release his head, slowly sliding my fingers down the back of his jaw to his neck, finally resting on his bloated pectoralis muscles.

"Thank you," he whispers, leaning his forehead against mine. After a moment he takes my left hand and kisses it. I watch him intently as he walks down the corridor and out of my sight, committing him to my memory, just in case the worst happens. Which it probably will. Most of the people I love die. I'm a death magnet.

I turn out the lights and settle into bed. Lying under the mess of covers, I stare out at the white line of light slipping under the door from the corridor, imagining a pair of shoes stopping and another knock at the door. But I know better. Marcus has already said his goodbye to me. He won't be coming back. Not for me anyway.

"Auntie Pollen?" I didn't realize Evie was awake.

"Go to sleep Evie," I mumble, curling my hands into the blanket at my neck.

"Is my daddy alive?"

I've been evading this conversation for months now. I always seemed to find ways around it. I didn't want to get her hopes up. But now I'm simply too tired to come up with any excuses.

"Maybe," I say.

"Where is he?" Evie's voice sounds so tiny in the dark, like the diminutive squeaking of a mouse.

"Uncle Glenn thinks he's at Crimson."

"Why didn't I see him when we were there?"

"Because they had him in a special place."

"Why?"

Because they captured him during war, sent home another man's mangled body parts, and put him in solitary confinement. Oh yeah, and Uncle Glenn tortured the shit out of him. My bones shiver and I pull the blanket tightly over me, as if that would cease the tremors.

"I don't know, Evie. Just go to sleep," I yawn.

"Auntie Pollen?"

"Yes?"

"Are Marcus and Uncle Glenn coming back?"

"I hope so."

I hate waiting rooms. All my life I avoided going to see the doctor whenever I could out of the acute repugnance for these atrocious rooms of terror. That's probably where I developed my internal ticking clock. I always used to play off my illnesses as if they were nothing just so that my mom wouldn't drag me to the doctor's office so I could sit in nervous anticipation for thirty minutes and be seen by the doctor for five. The waiting was always a hundred times worse than the actual exam.

I've already studied the dark gray walls of the lobby and the patterns in the striped chairs that are welded together to form rows. I've been here countless times in the past few months. At least once every two weeks, sometimes more often. I keep telling myself to go check out a book at the library, but I never get around to doing it. I've never been much of a reader. My mind wanders even while I'm reading my textbooks, which I finished weeks ago, due to my abundance of time spent alone.

The white door swings open and Timber pops her face out.

"Hey, Pollen. You ready?" I smile and nod, pushing myself up off the seat as if I were eight months pregnant instead of almost five.

Once we're in the privacy of my stark white examination room, she explodes with excitement.

"Did you hear?" she bubbles, excitedly.

"Hear what?"

"They're going to let us move up early. They're even opening up the training arenas outside today!" Now I get why she looks like a Liberation Day fireworks display. We haven't seen the sun in months. I never did tell Timber about my tryst with Glenn under the moon. So technically I *haven't* seen the sun in months.

"Seriously?" I ask suspiciously and she silently nods. "I'm totally going up today. Can you watch Evie?"

Timber's smile melts a little bit. She was probably hoping we could train together. But without

Marcus and Glenn here, I really don't want to leave Evie in daycare. She needs familiar faces to watch over her.

"Sure," she frowns. "Are you going to be okay by yourself? You know, Glenn and Marcus both asked me to babysit you."

The words she said were almost like gibberish when I heard 'Marcus' come out of her mouth. His name sounded like the coo of a dove after a tumultuous explosion.

"Marcus?"

"Yes, Marcus. He's still pissed at you Pollen, there's no doubt about that. He's hurt, deeply. But despite his attitude, he still loves you."

Another piece of my heart is stitched back together. There is hope after all. He still cares about me. I shake my head to disperse my random thoughts.

"Wait did you say they asked you to *babysit* me?"

"Yeah, they're both worried about you. Afraid you might go and do something stupid, I think. Like training by yourself," Timber says in a mocking tone.

"Timber, you said yourself they're letting us up early. There won't be anyone up there. Everyone who isn't at Ceborec is still bunkered up. I'll be perfectly safe. Plus, they wouldn't let us out before doing a thorough sweep of the property, right?"

"You have a good point, Pollen. Okay, I'll watch Evie today, but I'm going up tomorrow." Timber tosses me my paper blanket. "You'd better hurry up. Dr. Sexy will be here any minute." We both share a quick laugh as she leaves.

My day has just gotten remarkably brighter. Marcus still loves me and I get to bask in the glimmering rays of sunshine. There's no better way for me to vent my fears and frustrations than running in the woods and shooting inanimate objects with paint bullets.

Above ground, the air feels like a convection oven, extremely dry and hot, but the gusty wind keeps it reasonably comfortable. I swear out of the corner of my eye I see steam rising from the ground. Serves me right for choosing to train during the hottest time of the day. I dressed light, wearing a simple henna tank top and knee-length khaki shorts. I'm wearing my Hemlex shoes, even though they are only meant for indoor training. I'm curious to see whether they'll keep my footsteps silent on the rough, outdoor terrain. Plus, they're extremely comfortable for running.

I was surprised to find that Harrison wasn't at his usual post today. At first I thought maybe he was still tending the underground armory, but the new guy at the ammunitions station said he'd joined the militia. Has it really been that long since I've seen him? I thought they'd just pulled him aside to work the soldiers' armory. I didn't even see him at the assembly hall—I would have said goodbye if I had. Then again, just like Yoric and Marcus, it would have been very difficult to spot him without his trademark long striped hair.

For a period of time that flies by unnoticed, I simply lie out in the field just outside the woods and soak up the copper rays that filter through the rusty haze in the sky. I wonder what kind of pollution could have given the air that unusual tint. I've never seen that color in the sky before, at least not outside a major city.

A huge gusty wind interrupts my reverie and I decide it's time to shoot something. I feel slightly awkward and out of balance running with this dome on my front side. It feels enormous to me, even though I know it will grow much bigger in the coming months. After a few minutes, though, I get into the rhythm. I used to love running when I was younger; I even placed in our high school's track meets. Now I know why. The freedom, the thrill, the pulsing of electrical currents through my veins. This is when I truly feel alive.

I dash into the woods, maneuvering between the pines and the poplars and the sycamores, shooting at distant trees as I move. This has always been my greatest weakness and I'm determined to see it through. I don't really know what exactly I'm looking for, but as soon as I spot a tree that could serve as a potential target I shoot, trying to simulate a real life or death situation where I don't have time to react.

I miss every shot from my first magazine. It's been almost a week since I've been to the shooting range so I stop and choose a distant tree to become the victim of some stationary shooting. I use up two more magazines while I readjust to the motions of shooting again. I can't believe how out of practice I've become in just one week. Maybe I'm just a pound or two off balance.

Once again, I'm back on the move, this time slower, allowing myself more time to aim as I squeeze the trigger. I hit my target three out of eight times. I load my last magazine and pick up speed, hitting five out of eight times. An adrenaline rush pulses through me. The combination of running and hitting most of my targets has just put me in the mood for a more intense thrill. Something . . . stupid.

Timber's voice echoes in my mind, "Don't do anything stupid, Pollen. Don't even think of following them." She spoke those words as I left her with Evie. Sure, I thought about going out on my own, following the militia and doing my part to contribute to the mission. But that really would be stupid—even for me. If I were discovered, they'd just send me back and they would be short a soldier or two. And even if they didn't see me, I couldn't do anything crazy like that on my own. Not with paint bullets.

No, Marcus cared enough to ask Timber to watch over me, so I'll respect his wishes. I won't do anything that will put me in danger. I wonder what kind of thrill seeking adventure I can find out here that's not *too* dangerous.

I stop to look around and I realize I have no idea where I am. I must have run pretty far to be this lost. Even beyond the haze I can see the sun is straight above me in the sky, and I've been zigzagging through the trees, so I can't tell which way is which at this point. I contemplate briefly whether I should keep moving or stay put and wait for the sun to move. It'd take too long if I wait and Timber and Evie will be expecting me. I choose to keep walking. I'll eventually hit the perimeter at some point and run into a Watcher standing guard.

I continue to walk for about twenty more minutes, then, ahead in a clearing, I see a uniformed Watcher facing me. *That's funny, I thought they were supposed to be facing the other way.*

"Halt, ma'am," says the husky Watcher. His hair looks mussed and he glares at me through his black sunglasses. "This is private property."

"I'm Pollen McRae. I live here." I turn my head from side to side, trying to figure out how I got outside the perimeter. I must've been so lost in my thoughts that I just simply wasn't paying attention. "How did I get out here?" I ask myself aloud.

"Miss McRae?" The Watcher lowers his gaze to my belly than back up. "I'm sorry. We're a little understaffed today, you must have slipped through and circled around. I'll be happy to escort you back." The Watcher offers his hand, but I decline as politely as I can.

"It's okay, I'll go on my own. I wouldn't want you to get into trouble for leaving your post."

"Oh, don't you worry about me. You seem pretty lost. I'd feel much better if I saw you safely back."

I press my lips together in a hard line and force the edges to curl up while I nod. I don't know this man, and even if he is here to protect me I don't like the idea of him accompanying me on my long walk back. I just want to be alone with my thoughts.

After we've walked what seems like two miles something in my gut feels wrong. I still don't recognize this stretch of woods. And this guy is emitting some creepy silent vibes. As I study him from the corner of my eye, my foot catches on a protruding tree root and I manage to land on my hands before my belly touches down.

The Watcher scrambles to help me up, losing his sunglasses to gravity in the process. He stares at me, a fulfilling satisfaction glowing in his pupils, as the terror takes hold of me. The white of his eye bears the triangle tattoo with a black dot in the center. The mark of the Trinity. He is not a Watcher. He is a bounty hunter.

Fear grips both of my lungs in a double fisted chokehold. My heart balloons into my throat as the panic sets in. I barely have a chance to gasp, when just out of my vision his hand comes down behind me. A striking pain hits me like lightning, inducing the blackness that dissolves me.

CHAPTER 24

MY HEAD IS in agonizing pain—like someone is rhythmically stabbing it at the base where it meets my neck. I try to turn it from side to side, but that just sends more pain shooting throughout my skull. I swear I hear a crackling when I shift my head. Did he break my skull? Maybe it's whatever I'm lying on. A plastic bag, or something.

My eyelids are heavy as lead, and I crack them open just enough to see the blackness framed with broken yellow lines. *Are we in the Web?* I can't be in a train if I'm seeing the ceiling, but I'm moving fast—

I can feel the air whipping loose strands of hair into my face.

I hear a groan and when I see the dark outline of the bounty hunter look down at me I know the sound came from my own lungs. I shut my eyes quickly, but it's too late. Another blow lands on the side of my skull, sending me into another deep darkness.

<hr>

"Ahh." This time I moan quietly before I even open my eyes. I'm stationary now. No wind splashing my face. No movement rippling my body around. No jarring vibrations to send my screaming skull into a death wish, although the hard surface underneath my head earns a close second place. Something is vaguely familiar about my position despite my refusal to open my eyes. The musty smell. The cold, hard surface I'm lying on. The restraints that bind my ankles and hold my wrists in place by my sides. The vise holding my aching head upright. I'm back at Crimson.

I squeeze my eyelids tighter together, willing myself to go back to sleep. An eternal sleep. I just can't take anymore. It's not worth it. At least Evie is safe. She'll be safe with Timber. Timber will make a good mother to her. And if Drake or Glenn or Marcus makes it back alive, she'll have a father, too. She doesn't need me anymore. I can rest with my parents now. I'm ready.

But it's hopeless. I can't will myself to die any more than I can will the restraints to open and set me free. As much as I try, it's impossible.

With anchors of apprehension weighing down my eyelids, I weakly heave them open. I'm stunned to find that I am not in the medical exam room like I was the first time I was brought back and buckled to the table. Instead, I'm in a darkened sepulchral room.

Since my head is secured in place, I can't see anything other than the still shadows that paint the dark gray ceiling above. There are no overhead lights, so I'm not sure what is illuminating the room. There's a strange vibration to the dim light that reminds me of when my dad used to fall asleep on the couch watching TV. I'd sometimes get up in the middle of the night for a drink and that eerie vibrating glow from the living room would freak me out.

I lie here, listening to the thumping of my throbbing heart keeping time with the painful stabbing in the back and side of my head. Every pulse ripples through my skull like the enthusiastic wave of fans at a stadium. Who needs a clock when I've got my own personal ticker of pain to count down the seconds?

I close my eyes again and focus more intensely on the pain, hoping it will harden me, making whatever future torture they have planned for me more bearable. It hurts, yes, but I try to make peace with it. I press my head back harder into the steel table, intensifying the pain. I wince and then push it back again. I continue the pattern, each time lasting a few seconds longer. Eventually, a pleasurable numbness takes over and the pain is hardly noticeable.

The hammering in my head comes back with a vengeance when a buzzing rips the silence and the table begins to tilt forward. My eyes shoot open and daggers pierce through them into the back of my skull.

As I tilt up, the wall and floor in front of me rise up into my field of vision. Three huge rectangular screens buzz with an iridescent glow on the curved wall. I hadn't noticed it when I was staring at the ceiling, but the room is round and nearly empty with just some chairs stacked around the perimeter, all of them empty apart from one. One chair holds a stack of clothing. My clothing. I try to look down to see what I'm wearing, but my head won't budge. However, the chilly draft suggests I'm in a hideous medical gown, open and tied in the front.

A single Enforcer stands against the wall. He is a bulky man clad in the infamous blue uniform, but it's different than what I remember when I was here before. The jumpsuit looks the same, but now there's a helmet with a translucent blue visor. A tiny red light shines from the left side where the visor meets the helmet. I wonder if it's some sort of technological gizmo and what purpose it serves. The Enforcer seems to be listening intently. Perhaps a communication device?

"Affirmative." The gruff voice bounces off the walls in the chamber, and the Enforcer moves behind me, out of my range of vision. I hear some clicks and the screens in front of me flicker to life.

Each of the screens displays the bust of a different person. On the right, a woman in her fifties. Her tightly pulled back ginger hair is thinning and her face appears gaunt, but she has clearly made an attempt to look healthy with too much makeup. On the left screen is a middle-aged man with a strong, square jaw. His hair has been buzzed almost to the scalp, leaving only a dark shadow on his head. His thick eyebrows form a straight line dividing his face from his forehead and his beady eyes seem to poke deep holes into me.

And I recognize the face of the white-haired man in the center screen—the face of Crimson—Edgar Wisecraft, oil tycoon. He looks thinner and sicklier than he did in the video introduction they showed us when I arrived at Crimson. I assume the other two are Marge Rosenfritz, queen of the biotech industry, and Frasier Trident, head of the largest weapons manufacturing firm in the world. They must still be hiding out in their bunkers, living off of stockpiled canned food.

I shudder when the awareness punches me in the gut. I am being directly addressed by the Trinity—

the powerful trio who programmed the release of the virus that devastated my world. The three people who murdered billions of innocents, including my own parents, and sentenced my brother to a life of torment in an underground dungeon.

I notice a tiny red light between each of the screens—cameras focused on me. The three sets of eyes bear down on me, and what little confidence I had when I awoke has diminished. I feel like the kid who skipped school, and now I have to answer to the truant authorities, only this is much more formidable.

"Welcome back to Crimson Miss McRae," Wisecraft starts, in a gleefully satisfied tone, making me think they've been searching for me since our escape. *Why me?* I'm nobody. Certainly I'm no more valuable to them than any other survivor. Why would they target me in particular?

Noting my silence, he continues.

"I hope you've been treated," he pauses, emphasizing the next word, "appropriately on your journey back to your new home." He smiles sadistically and I notice Trident's shoulders bounce in a silent chuckle.

I'm not sure if it is fear or anger pulsating through my veins, or maybe both. I find my voice.

"What do you—"

"Ah, ah, ah," Wisecraft interrupts sharply. "You will not speak until you've been cued to do so. You were given much too many freedoms here during you last two stays with us. You will not have those privileges now.

"Miss McRae, you pirated an exceptional acquisition from us and that has caused us some serious complications." Acquisition? I never stole anything. I simply rescued Marcus and Evie. Wisecraft seems to acknowledge the puzzled look I must be carrying.

"Perhaps acquisition was an improper term for you to comprehend. You took our favorite genetic test subject before we had completed our measurements."

Test subject? My mind races back through my memories of all those blood tests they inflicted on Evie. They took so much blood from her she had this semi permanent ghostly complexion and was always tired. Then I remember something Glenn said. *Apparently, Evie's genotype has some unique properties. I don't know exactly what they are, but the scientists are very intent on extracting some portion of her DNA.* Evie is the 'acquisition' they are referring to? We really are all just lab rats to these monsters.

"Evie," I murmur, as the discovery sinks in.

"Bright girl," says Wisecraft. I'm not sure if he's referring to Evie or me. "So what are we to do about this? Marge, perhaps you could shed some light on our dire circumstances."

I glance over to the screen displaying Marge Rosenfritz. She glares directly at me, her position not as rosy as Wisecraft's.

"Miss McRae," she says in a smooth, almost hypnotic, voice that clashes with her haggard image. "Evie's genes are to be an integral portion of the vaccine we are developing. Not only does she have the double mutation for the HDD-374 virus immunity, but we've discovered some other special properties as well, that could be very promising for the long-term health and reproduction of our species. Without her genes, this valuable vaccine can not be made and these properties may be lost forever."

"But you already took her blood," I snap. "More than enough from the look of it."

"Her blood has been through extended trials of testing. We simply do not have enough left for the production of a vaccine. However, your condition may negate the need to recover Evie."

My condition? Is she referring to the pregnancy? I've been in denial about it for so long, despite the overt ballooning beneath my gown. All those times I said I didn't want this baby, that I wished it would just go away, dissolve as my maternal protective instincts take over. *I do want this baby.* They will not take him from me. They will not hurt him.

"Yes, Miss McRae. We had initially intended to bring you back to make an example of you. But this is much more convenient. You share some of Evie's genetic code. And with this being the first post-virus pregnancy we are interested in seeing what other unique properties this child's genetic map have in store for us. You will undergo an amniocentesis to determine whether your child's genes have the same unique properties as Evie's. If so, we won't need her after all."

"No, I won't cooperate," I growl through my gritted teeth.

All three faces smirk. "Your cooperation won't be necessary, Miss McRae," Wisecraft snickers. "As you can see, you are in no position to deny us access." I writhe my arms and legs, trying fruitlessly to escape my bonds.

The heavy door to the round chamber opens and a scarlet-haired woman wearing a white lab coat enters, pushing a cart full of medical instruments and a blank monitor. My breathing quickens. *They're going to do this now?* My pulse accelerates and the thumping in my head drowns out the words that Wisecraft continues to speak.

The vertical table I'm restrained to shifts backward, tilting back to the horizontal position I woke up in, while the woman in the lab coat prepares a long empty syringe. The needle is exceptionally long and sharp. I wouldn't say I've ever been afraid of needles, not since I was a child anyway, but the sheer size of that thing causes a hot wave of nausea to blanket me. I close my eyes to try and erase the image. I imagine the hill just inside the training arena, where Marcus and Evie met Timber and me for a picnic all those months ago. I remember the happiness, the serenity, I felt being there with them. Then I see a redheaded lady with a big-ass needle. *No!* I attempt to shake my head from side to side, trying to escape the vision.

Next thing I know I feel the gown open over my belly. A warm gel and the familiar pressure of an ultrasound wand glide across my abdomen. Then, without warning, a puncture in my abdomen and the needle is thrust deeply into my uterus. I shriek, unable to contain the pain internally. The shrill sound echoes back to me. *Don't they even use an anesthetic? No. Not for me anyway.* I imagine the vainglorious looks on the faces of the Trinity. They're loving this.

"Hold still," the redhead says firmly as I writhe beneath her. "Hold still and it won't hurt as much." Somehow the words eventually reach my brain and I try to control myself, taking deep unrestrained breaths, but my muscles are still tensed up in knots. My fingernails dig into my palms as I curl my fingers into tight fists. Even my toes curl under, forcing a charley horse that might be agonizing if I weren't so distracted by the pain in my belly.

After an eternity that probably only lasted a minute and a half, the needle glides out. I still feel the aftershocks of the sting it left behind. The redhead drops the syringe filled with clear yellowish liquid onto the tray and wipes my belly with a dry cloth, putting a bandage roughly over where the needle had been.

And then, as if she were nothing more than a room service attendant, the redhead wheels the cart out of the chamber.

The table zips back up so that I can see the horrifying faces of the Trinity again. I close my eyes. I don't want to give them the satisfaction of seeing the terror in my eyes when I look at their smug faces.

"As you can see Miss McRae," the weasely voice of Wisecraft begins, "we always have the upper h—" The sound cuts out abruptly. I hear the Enforcer behind me pushing buttons frantically. I open my eyes but blackness envelops me as if they are still closed.

Chapter 25

I SHIFT MY EYES in every possible direction but all I see is eigengrau blackness. The exact same shade of black everywhere. Not even a sliver of light filters in from under the door. After about a minute, there's a brief electrical snapping sound, and the yellow emergency lights at the edges of the floor flicker on.

"Yes?" the Enforcer appears to be talking to himself, but I know he's addressing a voice inside his helmet. "I'm with a prisoner right now. I don't think I should—Okay. Yes, sir. Be right there." The Enforcer opens the door to the chamber and glances back at me to make sure I'm secure. The restraints are still locked in place; I'm not going anywhere. Then he disappears into the dark corridor, slamming the door behind him.

I twist my hands around inside the solid steel buckles holding them in place. They've made some drastic improvements to this place since I escaped. The old leather straps that held me in place before would have made it too easy to escape again. Maybe if I scrunch up my fingers tightly I can slide them out. With my hands free I might be able to get out of this thing. I try to slide them out, using slow increasing pressure, scraping the skin around the base of my thumb and the heel of my hand. No dice. The opening is just too narrow and the metal will not give.

Hopelessness creeps into the open sores at my wrists and slithers its way through my veins. *Will I never escape this hell?* This is the third time I've been here, maybe it's just meant to be. No. I can't let myself think like this.

Wait a minute. The blackout. The Enforcer's abrupt disappearance. I wasn't sure before how long I was unconscious, but now I know it has been two days. The attack was planned for Liberation Day. Our soldiers must be here. That means Marcus and Glenn are here somewhere, too. *Maybe they'll find me*, I think optimistically.

What are you, insane, Pollen? Maybe it's the crazy pregnancy brain giving me this false hope. They don't know I'm here. They think I'm safe with Timber and Evie at Ceborec. Why would they even think to look for me here? Glenn will be looking for Drake. I can only hope that he'll stumble upon me on the way.

Time passes. I'm not sure how much. I've already counted the twenty-eight chairs stacked along the walls at least fifty times, more or less. I've tried every way imaginable to writhe my hands out of their cuffs. I've even tried to wriggle my head out of the vise to keep my neck from getting stiff.

My memory keeps shifting back to the amniocentesis and I recount the pain. I can feel a bruise forming under the bandage. I hope the needle didn't hurt the baby—my son. I've got time on my hands now, maybe I should think of a name. No. I can't. What if the Trinity takes him before I even have a chance to hold him? I can't bear the thought of forming a bond with him, then losing him, just like Lex. It would be easier for me to go back to the way it was before and just hope that he's never born. What kind of life does he have to look forward to anyway? No, he can't be born. It's the best way. The only way.

The door squeals as a dark figure slowly slides it open. It abruptly stops, then starts again, and continues like that as if the opener is trying desperately not to be heard. Like the old days when I used to sneak out of my house to meet Glenn. Our back door was squeaky like that, but was the only one I could sneak out of without getting caught.

"Pollen," the figure whispers. The raspy female voice sounds familiar, like someone from my past.

"Help me," I whisper back.

The figure strides in quickly, but silently. It's another Enforcer, dressed in blue, but not wearing a helmet. As she approaches, my eyes widen and a flutter of joy ripples through me.

"Respa," I say, a little too loudly.

"Shh."

"You're one of them now?" I ask, trying to sound curious, rather than repulsed. My eyes focus on the mark of the Trinity, just next to her cinnamon brown iris.

"Shh. I'm getting you out of here." Respa disappears behind me. In a few seconds, the cuffs open up and my body slides down. It feels like ages since I've stood up and my legs buckle under me, throwing my body to the frigid, tiled floor.

Respa grips my under my arms and pulls me up, grasping my arm over her shoulder.

"How did you know I was here?" I ask.

"Quorian. He saw them bring you in. Good god, have you gained weight?" she huffs.

I take her hand from around my waist and stretch it around onto my belly. "I'm pregnant."

"Holy shit! You and Marcus?!" I feel the biting stab of a dagger pierce my heart. I'm grateful that I can't tell her the whole complicated story right now. Even if there were time, I don't think I could handle it without having a nervous breakdown.

"It's a long story."

"Well, we don't have time for it now. Congratulations. Let's go."

"Wait, where are we going?"

"To the Web. All hell has broken loose up top. This is the only way to get you out of here."

I struggle to free myself from Respa's grip, ripping my body from her arms. My legs are strong enough now to hold me up on my own.

"No. I have something to do first."

"Oh no, Pollen. Not again," she warns, shaking her head.

"Respa, my brother is here in solitary. I'm not leaving without him."

"I can't break him out."

"Why not? We're going to that level anyway, right?" Surely if she cares enough to help me escape she must have some compassion for my only brother.

"Yes, but the doors down there are secured, even during a power outage. The only way to open them is to launch a system override. If I do it, they'll know it was me from my handprint."

"So come with us," I plead, searching her eyes for some weakness in her stance. "Glenn did and now he's on our side. In fact he's up there right now, fighting with the others."

"I can't," she says, defeated. "They admitted that Glenn was a mistake. That they handled him wrong. When they gouged his eye out, they also took out the tracker. So when he escaped they couldn't track him down. Pollen. I'm an Enforcer now. If I try to escape, not only with they find me easily, but I'll put your people in danger. I can't do it."

We stand in silence as I try to invoke a plan from the recesses of my vibrant imagination, but there's nothing I can come up with that doesn't put Respa, or my friends, in more danger.

I swiftly throw my dirty clothes back on as we talk and strap the empty holster to my thigh. The gun is missing, of course, but if I can find something to use as a projectile I can convert it to a slingshot.

"Where do you launch the system override?"

"You won't be able—"

"Where?!" I snap.

"In the main security control room. It's two floors down from here. But I don't see how you're planning on doing this. You need handprint identification."

"Okay, just let me go here. I'll find my way down there on my own," I say.

"Pollen, you need me to get you into the Web."

"Just point me in the right direction and I'll figure something out. Like I said, I'm not leaving without Drake."

Respa sighs deeply, agitated, and walks me to the door.

"You know where the rotunda is, on the main level?" I nod, recalling the huge atrium with the domed glass ceiling that I passed through during our last escape. "Right now we are about eight stories below it. You won't be able to use the elevator obviously since the power is out. Go right out this door. Follow the corridor around until you reach the fourth hallway. Follow that and then you'll see another hallway on the right. The stairs are at the end next to the elevator. You won't need to be ID'd to get in, but watch out for other Enforcers. And don't rat me out."

I lean in and drape my arms around her shoulders. "Thank you, Respa. I owe you."

"Damn right you do. Now go."

Respa and I part outside the door, going in opposite directions. I clutch the curved wall as I stumble through the corridor, still slightly imbalanced from all that time on the table. *Was I strapped there for the entire two days?* I count the descending corridors as I pass, following Respa's instructions explicitly. When I reach the fourth one I pause and listen, making sure there are no Enforcers waiting in the distance.

I wonder why it is so empty here. I know that most of the Enforcers are above ground now, defending Crimson from our soldiers, but what about everybody else? The inmates, or "refugees" as they are called here. *Ha. Refugees, indeed.* I shake my head facetiously at the thought. They must be contained on different floors. Even when I was living at Crimson before, they never let us wander around down here in the lower levels. Who knows what interesting things I could find if I snooped around a bit more. It's tempting, but no. I'm on a mission. I cannot defect. Granby's influence on me is certainly taking heed.

I make another right hand turn and soon I am at the stairwell. The door is open. Just like Respa said, the scanner is not working. I crack the door open slightly and listen. It is quiet—the only sound that can be distinguished is my own breathing. Even my footsteps are silent, thanks to my Hemlex shoes. Turns out they were a valuable addition to my wardrobe, after all.

Just as I begin to descend the steps I hear the door open on the floor just below me. In full-blown panic mode, I silently dash up the steps to the next floor, and then the next, as the crashing footsteps continue to climb the stairs. Each level that I scale pilfers more energy from my body. But the footsteps below continue to follow. I wonder briefly if I should just leave the stairwell. But fear of the unknown keeps me in here. I need to get back downstairs to rescue Drake and I can't afford to lose any time getting lost now.

Five stories up, I've reached the top of this stairwell. I can't go any further. It must be the highest level in the underground facility. But the footsteps still follow. With no other options left, I swing the door open and enter the corridor. I slide out along the wall and instantly, I'm paralyzed. Wild flames engulf the corridor radiating insurmountable heat over me. Brilliant orange-yellow tendrils lash out in every direction and I sink down to the floor wrapping my arms tightly around my knees. My breath begins to quicken until I'm hyperventilating into my forearm. The snapping pricks at my eardrums and the thick smoke scratches my throat and lungs. *I can't do this!* Involuntary tears pour down my cheeks as I try to overcome this debilitating nightmare. The fire doesn't touch me, yet I can feel its violent fingers reaching out to grab me. I close my eyes and tell myself that it's not real; that I'm imagining it. But the sweat drenching my shirt tells me otherwise. I've got to get out of here.

The door to the stairwell opens and somebody comes out. But they run down the corridor in the opposite direction. Whoever it was must not have seen me huddled down on the floor. Who would've thought my fear would actually save me? My instincts kick in and I crawl back to the door. My quaking arm reaches up and I pull it open and slither back into the stairwell.

I sit upon the top step catching my breath and allowing my heart rate to slow. I've got a lot to do and I must restore my courage and energy before moving on.

Quickly, I tiptoe down the stairs pausing at each floor to be sure nobody abruptly enters the door and finds me. After I determine it's clear, I glide down the stairs until I am two floors below the one I started at. Again, I crack the door open, peering out and listening. I hear faint echoing of footsteps, but they sound too far away to be in this corridor. Gradually I ease my head out, inch by inch, and find that the immediate hallway is clear.

I sneak down the corridor, the beat of my heart marching double time to each silent step I take. I'm thankful for the darkness. I figure if I'm spotted it won't be so obvious that I'm an escapee, at least not at first. At least I could have time to run.

When I reach the next corridor, I pause at the corner, pressing my back against the wall, and listen. Whispers break up the silence, but I can't tell where they are coming from. I edge my face around the corner. I don't see anything but darkness dimly illuminated by the amber lights. I turn back and it's empty in the other direction as well. As I creep out into the corridor a door busts open at the end and three Enforcers come barreling out. I whip around sinking back into the wall, hoping that my presence went unnoticed. I watch fearfully as the Enforcers sprint past me toward the curved security room at the center of this level.

Something tells me I need to get out of here fast, but I don't know which way to go. And I'm not turning back.

The grunts and yelps coming from the direction where the Enforcers went indicate a struggle of some sort. My reckless curiosity leads me into the corridor, inhaling the scent of trouble.

I peer into the central corridor that surrounds the curved walls of the security control room. Six figures are struggling, but the darkness masks their identities. It must be some of our soldiers. Of course. One of the missions was to retrieve the plans for the shuttle. It makes sense that they would be kept in the security control room. Maybe Glenn is among them.

Surely he would have known he'd need to activate the system override in order to release Drake.

My body itches to pounce into the scuffle and help them, but before I get the chance to get close enough, the Enforcers have their guns drawn and aimed at the three soldiers. I reach down to my thigh and pat the empty holster, forgetting briefly that my gun is missing. I'm sure that bounty hunter filched it while I was out. He wouldn't turn me into Crimson with something as valuable as a firearm. I could still make the slingshot, but I have a major problem—nothing to propel. I'm at a loss.

The Enforcers don't shoot the soldiers, much to my relief. Instead they cuff their hands behind their backs and begin to march them in my direction. *Oh no.* I have nowhere to hide. I quietly twist the latch on the door behind me and, miraculously, it opens. I huddle myself inside, leaving the door slightly ajar, and watch anxiously as the Enforcers march past me, escorting the three men. As their faces pass through the amber lights, I get a glimpse of these three men I know too well: Yoric, Glenn, and Marcus.

Chapter 26

MARCUS. GLENN. AND YORIC. Was that some kind of sadistic joke, grouping Marcus and Glenn together? Or did Granby group them together as some sort of ingenious strategic device. Forcing them to forge an alliance. *Very clever, Granby.*

But now that poses a severe problem. They've all been captured. I try to wrap my head around the idea of my three friends being strapped down and tortured, or worse—executed. Panic is too soft a term to describe my current state. *What can I do?* Should I continue my mission to rescue Drake and find the security room? Or should I put that on hold and follow the guys? I can't bear to live without Marcus. Or Glenn. But this might be my only opportunity to get into the security room to launch the system override.

My body trembles so wildly that when I lean back into a shelf, a box of spherical magnets crashes to the floor in an explosion that rips the silence to shreds. They bounce noisily all over the place, making a racket like marbles tumbling inside a clothes dryer. I glance around as I frantically wave my hands around trying to stop them, realizing I must be in an office supply closet.

While the magnets continue to roll over the tile floor, I overhear the brusque tone of one of the Enforcers that just passed.

"Take them to the X level—I'll check it out."

Oh shit. Someone's coming. I yank my holster off my leg and untwist the band that still holds my hair in place after my two-day coma. Some stray strands get caught in the elastic and I wince at the sharp pain. *Silly Pollen. Your head is beaten, bruised, and pounding as if someone took a jackhammer to it. And here you are wincing at a few snagged hairs?* In one quick motion, I yank it out, along with the caught strands, letting my hair fall limply over my back. Despite my shaky hands I attach the sling quickly and carefully.

I can hear the tentative footsteps approaching the door. Without taking my eyes off the door, I paw at the floor until my fingers roll over an escaped magnet. It slips through my fingers, rolling away out of reach.

The door begins to creak as the Enforcer cautiously opens it. Frantically, I grope at the floor. It sounded like a million magnets fell a few seconds ago. Where are they now? Finally, I find one and claw all of my fingers around it so it can't escape. I load it into my sling and draw it back as the man widens the door. It's too dark to see, but I can hear the click of the slide as he prepares to shoot.

I can't knock him out with a marble, I know, especially since the tiny red light indicates he's wearing a helmet to protect his head. But I am at the perfect level and distance to inflict some serious pain to his manhood. I pull back the sling as far as it will go, as if I'm preparing to hit the distant balloon at the outdoor shooting range, aim directly between his legs and release.

"Argh!" he shouts as he collapses to his knees, dropping the gun to the floor with a *clang*. He cups his injury with one hand while probing the floor with the other, trying to locate the gun. But it's too late. The moment it hits the tile I snatch it furiously. While he's still down I tear off his helmet and pummel him with the grip of the gun. Even though he falls to the floor face down, I can't stop myself. All of my rage of the past few months filters down through my arm and into the back of this guy's head. It feels good. Really good.

It takes some serious self-control, but I finally force myself to stop—I've got four grown men to rescue and there's no time to waste. I stand over the Enforcer holding the gun that still has a round in the chamber and aim it at him. My finger trembles on the trigger. As angry and devastated as I am, I can't bring myself to do it. It's one thing to practice shooting people with harmless paint bullets, but actually killing someone, someone completely helpless, is entirely different.

I jam the gun into the back of my pants for safe keeping, while holding on to the slingshot. I search the floor for the rest of the magnets. I grab a handful and cram them into my pocket, before pushing the Enforcer completely into the closet and closing the door.

The silence in the corridor is piercing. All I can hear is the hissing of my own breath and the gentle clinking of the magnets in my pocket as I creep past the corner to the main corridor. Keeping my back against the inner curved wall, I sidestep around the corridor, watching for any sudden movements or shadows in the archways of additional corridors.

Finally, my hand hovers over a dip in the wall—a doorway. The door is closed. My hand trembles over the doorknob, hesitating. Someone will surely be in the room. Perhaps more than one body. They would never leave a place like this unmanned, especially in an emergency situation such as an incursion. Should I prepare the gun or make do with the slingshot? I really don't want to kill anybody if I can avoid it. I decide the gun will be a last minute plan B if it comes to that. I lower my hand onto the knob and turn slowly as not to draw attention to it, but it doesn't budge. They must be using old-fashioned locks in lieu of the scanners. Makes sense.

I pluck the gun from my pants and prepare to shoot the door open. As my finger tightens on the trigger, I hear the rattling of the magnets in my pocket and think back to all the noise those they made when they dropped in that tiny closet. How loud will a gun blast be? Cramming the gun back into my pants I decide on a more rational approach. I knock.

"Who's there?" a terse male voice calls from the other side of the door. I improvise.

"Wyndham sent me for increased security. The attackers have infiltrated the upper levels." I hope that worked. I vaguely remember the name of the lead Enforcer from my last escape attempt. I hold my breath and ready my slingshot and marble as the clicking signals the door being unlocked.

The door swings open and the blinding white light of a flashlight shines in my face. I manage to avoid looking directly at it and before the Enforcer has a chance to aim his weapon I release the sling, sending the marble into his wrist. Both the gun and the flashlight clink to the floor.

We both clamor for the gun. He falls on me as I drop to my knees and I thrust my elbow back into his chest. The Enforcer rams the heel of his hand into my jaw, knocking me sideways and adding yet another head injury to the list. My slingshot flies out of my hand and slides across the floor of the security control room.

The lump in my back reminds me that I have an unfair advantage. Ripping the gun out, I hold it under his jaw and flip his helmet off.

"Stand," I say firmly, lifting his gun off the floor and pointing it at his chest. I rise alongside him, never moving either of my weapons. With of flick of my ankle, the door shuts behind me and I force the Enforcer further inside the room.

"Activate the system override for the solitary level," I say in a smooth but firm tone.

"Hey, I know you," he says in a smooth, raspy voice. "You're that girl who escaped twice. Pollen, right?"

"The system override," I remind him.

"You'll never get out again, you know. There's a huge bounty on your head darlin' and you'd be every bounty hunter's favorite prey."

Huge bounty? Me? After my rendezvous with the Trinity I shouldn't be surprised. They made it perfectly clear they want my baby. But they won't get him. I shake my head to clear my thoughts. I've had enough of his babbling.

"The system override. Now!" I shout. The Enforcer tenses as I jam the gun into his throat.

"I can't, they'll—"

"Do it!"

I loosen the guns to allow the Enforcer to move freely in the room. The flashlight on the floor illuminates part of the room in a ghostly manner, casting large, intense shadows over the floor and up the busy wall, which is covered with small monitors, all blank of course due to the power outage. I imagine if the room was empty of all the electronic equipment it would look similar to the one I woke up in, strapped to that table. A ring of instrument panels circles the walls of the room and at the far end is a large, two-door cabinet, which uses another handprint and retinal scanner to access it. The scanner screen has a strange luminescence to it and some of the panels are lit, suggesting the use of some reserve energy source.

I keep a vigilant eye on the Enforcer, making sure he doesn't make any suspicious moves. He picks up the flashlight and walks to one of the instrument panels on the left side of the circular room. He looks back at me nervously, then places his hand on the instrument panel, where the scanner flashes green briefly, giving the huge room an eerie glow. Then he lowers his face to the panel and scans his eye. A few more pushes of buttons and he looks back at me.

"Done," the Enforcer declares.

"Prove it," I demand. I have no clue what he did at that panel. For all I know he could have alerted the other Enforcers to what was happening down here. How could I possibly trust that this guy did what I demanded?

"Prove it?" he asks incredulously.

"Yes. Prove to me that you launched the system override," I say, still pointing both guns at his chest.

The Enforcer's shoulders slump as he shuffles over to the secured cabinet across the room. It's only then that I realize that the screen is completely black. The luminescence I noticed before has disappeared. He glances back at me over his shoulder and opens the cabinet doors, then shuts them again.

"There," he says. "If I hadn't activated the override I wouldn't be able to open this." I nod, satisfied.

"Shuttle plans. Hand them over," I command.

"What? I don't know what you're talking about." Even though the darkness shrouds his face I can feel his lie in the air.

"Cut the crap. Give me the plans."

He turns back to the cabinet sluggishly. The cabinet doors pop open and he flashes the light inside. I become aware that I haven't moved a muscle since I stepped into this room. Remaining close to the exit, I step to the side and peer around the Enforcer's svelte body to try and get a peek at what is in the cabinet.

The Enforcer turns holding something in his hand that I can't quite make out, because the light of the flashlight blinds me. I squint and raise my left arm over my eyes to shield them from the piercing light. My instincts only kick in after I hear the *POP* of a gunshot. I react immediately, firing both my guns until the Enforcer lies in a bloody heap at the foot of the cabinet.

The sharp resonance of the ear-splitting gunshots echo inside my head for a few seconds. Then it all goes quiet. The creepy drone of the flashlight slowly rolling across the floor is the only sound to break the stark silence following the explosive blasts.

Suddenly, a shooting pain in the left side of my belly drives me to my knees. I drop both the guns and grasp the source of pain with my left hand, while leaning forward with my right. My shirt is wet and warm.

I've been shot.

Chapter 27

A VISION OF Lex's tiny, chubby, smiling face seduces me before the image distorts into his cold, lifeless body dangling from my arms like the limbs of a weeping willow. *Have I done it again? Have I just killed my son?*

I scrub away all the previous desire for this baby to go away, for him to not exist. I want him. I *need* him. I need him so desperately I will continue to fight for him to live. The bullet entered the left side of my stomach, but it may have hit too high to puncture my uterus. It's too soon to know for sure, but I have to hope. I can't give up now.

I slide hand up and down my shorts, wiping the blood off, and pick up the gun, tucking it into the back of my shorts while rising unsteadily to my feet. Those gunshots were massively loud. Someone could burst through that door at any moment.

I stumble across the room to the gaping security cabinet, stepping over the bloody body of the Enforcer I just killed. I don't know why, but it disturbs me—the fact that I killed him. It's the first time I directly killed anybody and despite what he did to me, and possibly my son, it doesn't feel satisfying. It feels awful, like something dark and rotten has just crept into my soul.

I bend over to pick up the glowing flashlight, but that sends a shooting pain deep into my gut, so I adjust my position and squat instead. Shining the light into the cabinet, I'm baffled. There are stacks of flash drives on the shelf, but they are labeled with a series of numbers and letters, nothing to indicate easily what is on each one. On the lower shelves are other types of equipment that I would have no idea what to do with. I assume the plans are on a flash drive. But how do I choose which one to take? I have to take them all.

I peer around the room, looking for a bag of some sort. The flashlight focuses in on a small trash bin. Limping a few steps, I dump out the few candy wrappers and tissues onto the floor and yank out the bag. While holding the bag up to the edge of the shelf I slide my arm across, pouring the entire collection of flash drives into the bag. That ought to do it.

Warm liquid continues to ooze down my shirt and into my shorts. I need to stop the bleeding before I lose too much blood and pass out. Having chronic low blood pressure is not in my best interest now. I doubt they keep any medical equipment in here.

I hurriedly unbuckle the Enforcer's belt and wrap it loosely around my extended waist, checking the size. It looks like it will fit over my bloated belly. I try to rip his jumpsuit, but I can't. I don't know how Marcus managed to do it when he was splinting my injured ankle in the Web all those months ago. Perhaps I'm weakening from the wound. I'll have to find something else. I remove one of my shoes and slide my sock off. It's dirty, but it'll have to do. I wrap it snugly around the belt three times then fasten the belt tightly to my waist. The shocking pain shoots lightning bolts into my abdomen as I pull the belt over it, but I exhale deeply and accept the pain, forcing the belt tight enough to dig ravines into my skin. That should hold off the blood loss for a while I hope.

Time to get out of here. I replace my shoe and turn off the flashlight to preserve the battery, sliding it into an empty notch in the belt. On the way out I snatch up my slingshot and keep it ready to use at a moment's notice

I crack the door and check the corridor—still no sound. All of the Enforcers must be too preoccupied in the upper levels to investigate the noise. Before I leave, I fold up my slingshot and reattach the holster to my leg. One of the guns I held is empty, so I leave it behind. I hold on to the other gun and place the gun from the cabinet that he shot me with in my holster so I can carry the bag more comfortably. Now I've got to find Drake.

I creep through the corridor a bit faster this time not knowing if or when I might pass out due to blood loss. I feel a little woozy, but still very much lucid. Hopefully the wound was superficial. At least I keep telling myself that.

I count the descending corridors as I pass trying to remember how many I passed to get here. Did I pass two or three? *Wake up Pollen. This is important.* If I take the wrong stairwell, I may not make it down to the solitary level. How do I know which is the right one? The corridor I was in had the closet with the office supplies where I left the unconscious Enforcer. That's the only way I'll know for sure.

When I come to the next hallway I crack the first door on the left and peek in. The dim yellow light reflects off a shiny black boot and I know I'm on the right path. Quietly, I shut the door as not to disturb him. The morbid thought occurs to me again. I wonder if I should just shoot him so he can't come after me if he wakes. Waves of nausea wash over me. I feel so disgusted after killing the other guy, I'm not sure I could stomach doing it again. No, he's passed out. By the time he wakes I'll be long gone. Or dead.

I continue to retrace my path to the stairwell in near silence apart from my raspy, labored breath, and listen intently before reentering. My body has the irresistible urge lean on the railing as I descend the first few steps, since the pain from the gunshot wound is beginning to radiate down into my hip. I want to move faster—I'm almost there. But I don't want to risk stumbling and falling, which will probably worsen my injury since the bullet is still lodged in there somewhere. The throbbing in my head and the bruise from the amnio are barely noticeably now next to the gaping wound on my waist.

I descend two more floors before finally reaching the bottom. I open the door just a sliver. I'm sure there must be a few Enforcers on patrol down here. But all is eerily quiet. I slip out of the door, closing it gingerly behind me. The odor of mold and excrement nearly knocks me over and I'm reminded of my not-so-pleasant holiday here so many months ago.

I turn my head looking both ways down the corridor and to the one in front of me. No matter which direction I turn, it looks like an airport runway. Yellow lights line the edges of the floors so far in the distance that they just seem to fade away. I wonder briefly how I am ever going to find Drake's cell in this endless labyrinth.

Approaching the first door, I slide the gun into the back of the belt and switch on the flashlight to check the number briefly—D702. I quickly switch off the light. I can't afford to risk to announcing my presence to any Enforcers that may be stationed down here. Now, I need to find D320. I walk around the corner and check the door number there—D219. I step down to the next door—D221.

Hmm. The numbers are going up. I'll keep going this way. I creep past the next corridor, carefully checking to see if there are any dark figures lurking behind. As I expected, it's clear, so I move forward and switch on the light again to check the number—D225. At this rate it's going to take awhile.

Moving swiftly on my toes I pass five more corridors, then pause briefly to check the number—E225. *What?* I turn back and descend the intersecting corridor, checking the number on the first door—E902. Hopelessness and panic threaten to take control of me as I lean on the scratchy stone wall, but I suppress it the best I can. *Can't give up now.*

I keep to the left and check around the corner of the next intersection, flashing the light quickly on the first door I find—E424. Somehow I'm in the wrong place. At least the first few doors I found began with the letter D. There must be some sort of pattern here. I decide to follow the corridor back in the direction I came from, or at least I think that's where I'm going.

I count five corridors that I pass and check the number—D424. Okay, I'm closer. I continue down the corridor until I check again and find that I am again in a different section of the maze.

I'm about to turn back, when I hear a peep. I'm not entirely sure I didn't imagine it, but I'm not about to take any chances. I slip into the intersecting corridor and creep along the wall, keeping my ears cocked for any clues to the whereabouts of the noise. I don't hear anything, but until my heartbeat calms down, I can't be sure.

Convinced it was probably just one of the prisoners making noise, I continue on. In my confusion, I've lost my internal map. I continue down the corridor and stop to check the number on the door—I514. *I?* I spin around the intersection looking each way. In three directions the corridors seem endless. But the fourth seems to end at a wall in the distance. I follow that one, in an effort to avoid getting lost.

I turn left and check the number—C207. I follow the corridor until I find myself back to where I started at the stairwell and elevator. This is good. I can start all over with the little knowledge I've gained.

The maze seems to be sectioned off in blocks marked by individual letters. The horizontal rows I was in were the 200s and 400s. The vertical rows were the 700s, 900s, and 500s. Perhaps the vertical rows are all odds and the horizontal rows are evens?

I check the door in the first vertical row—D702. The same one I saw when I first arrived down here. I walk to the next descending row to the right and check the first door there—D901. I go back, skipping the first corridor and proceeding to the next. D502. I can feel myself getting close. I ignore the throbbing pain in my side as I lightly jog to the next corridor and flash the light—D302. This is it. I continue to follow the corridor checking the numbers every time I pass an intersection, three in all. Finally I shine my light up to see D319. My body weakens at the memory of my time in this cell. All that time spent recalling my lost memories and preparing for escape. And all that time I was living right next to my presumed-dead brother and didn't even know it. A lone tear escapes my eye, but I wipe it away before it has the chance to reach my cheek.

I shuffle to the next door, D321, clawing the scratchy stone wall for support. I take a deep breath, hoping that the system override is activated down here. If so, the only thing keeping me from my long lost brother is the archaic manual latch. Using the weight of my body, I push aside the heavy steel latch. The shrill shriek of the latch drives piercing needles into my ears, but that won't stop me.

I tug the door using more strength than I really needed because it creaks open quite easily. Inside is a void of blackness; no emergency lights. Nothing.

A fleeting thought crosses my mind—what if Drake is not here? What if Glenn told me the wrong number, or if they moved him and put someone else in this cell? Someone dangerous . . .

"Drake?" I call, clicking on the flashlight.

Chapter 28

THE HUDDLED CHUNK OF FLESH on the floor of the cell that casts a ghostly shadow against the wall is not my brother as I remember. My brother was tall, exceptionally handsome, and built like an ox. This man's clothes are in rags, his skin pale and sallow, his hair long and stringy and matching the grimy beard that has grown from his jaw. His once muscular frame sinks in atrophy. This man is a skeleton. Not the Drake I knew. Not Evie's father.

"Drake?" I call out, still unsure if it is some version of my brother that I am seeing.

"Pollen? Is that you?" he croaks. It's his voice—not the normal healthy Drake, but the Drake who stayed out of school for two weeks with mono when he was seventeen. His throat sounds weak and parched.

"It's me, Drake. Let's get you out of here." I stand at the door, leaning on the frame as my weakness begins to claw at my limbs, too afraid to enter. I know I'm alone on this level, but I still hold on to the idea that someone might have seen me and is waiting for the opportunity to shut the door, trapping me in here. Drake crawls toward me, climbing to his feet. He still towers over me like he used to; but now he's all skin and bones, skinnier than me—even when I wasn't pregnant.

"My god, Pollen, it is you," Drake moans as he cups my face in his hands. He pulls me in tighter; moving his arms around my shoulders and squeezing me so hard I wince in pain. Finally, my emotions catapult me into a tumultuous wilderness. My brother is alive. He's been alive all this time. I cough into Drake's shoulder, trying to stifle the sobs. He pulls away abruptly.

"Are you okay, Pollen?"

"No," I say, but I'm not ready to give him the gory details now about my bleeding wound or the funeral we gave him last summer. "We need to go now."

"How do we get out of here?" he asks looking down the corridor to the left, then right.

"We need to do something first." I grasp his face with my palms, and stare sharply into his hollow eyes. "Drake, do you remember where they took you when they . . ." My voice drifts off. I can't bring myself to say it. Luckily, there aren't many places they took him to outside of the torture chambers.

"You know about that?" I continue to stare into his eyes and nod. He shakes his head, trying to remove the thought so we can proceed. "Yes."

"I need you to take me there. You aren't the only one who needs to be rescued right now."

In the dim light of the corridors I could see the apprehension in his eyes. His lips tightened into a firm line. "No. Pollen, you need to get out of here now." The authority in his voice is the only remnant left of his military stature.

"Drake. You don't know what's happening right now. There is a battle going on above ground. The power is out because we, the COPS, have attacked. Most of the Enforcers are up there, leaving the lower levels insecure. Here," I say, pulling the surplus gun from the back of my waistband and handing it to him.

"How did—"

"There's no time, Drake. We have to go. Follow me."

I lightly jog down the corridor the way I came, turning my head now and then to be sure Drake is keeping up. His energy seems to be increasing with his newfound freedom, while mine is dwindling. I turn left at the end of the corridor and stop to lean against the wall when we reach the door to the stairwell.

"How many floors up?" I ask.

"Just one, I think. It was always a short ride up the elevator."

I open the door and listen. There's some commotion a ways up, but since we are only going one floor I think we can manage to get by unnoticed.

I stumble at the first step, nearly falling on my face, but Drake catches me.

"You okay?" he whispers.

I nod, lying. I can't let him know I'm hurt—he'll never let me continue on my brazen mission. The pain has deepened and I picture a bullet lodged inside my flesh, pinching nerves with every breath I take, every step, even the tiniest fraction of a movement. We continue up the stairs and pause at the door to the next floor.

I crack the door, but I can hear some men talking nearby. Enforcers.

"It's not clear," I whisper to Drake.

"How many?"

"Three, I think. Maybe four."

Drake pulls out the magazine in his gun checking his rounds.

"Enough?" I ask. He nods. "Which way are we going?"

"Left, once we've offed these guys." I wince at the comment. I've forgotten that my beloved brother has not only seen war but was an active participant. My brother, who used to play backyard games with me, who used to tease me about my first kiss, who got married and became a single father to Evie, is a killing machine. And I learned something vital about myself today—I don't like killing people, even the bad guys. *Can I do it again?* I have to try. For Marcus and Glenn. And Yoric, of course.

Drake pulls my arm, tugging me backward, and squeezes between the door and me so he can go first. I would object, but given his experience, he'd be better suited for this role. Plus I'm hoping he'll finish off the Enforcers so I don't have to.

"Stay back," he whispers, even though I already have my pistol ready in my quaking hands. He presses his ear to the door for a few seconds before he bursts through and starts shooting. My body freezes. Although the shots ring out violently, he seems to carry it off with a touch of grace, the way a ballerina can pull of a pirouette with such ease.

I shake myself out of my trance when I hear the oncoming steps of several people trampling down the steps on the floor above us. I jump through the door, shutting it quickly behind me. Four bodies lie on the floor. One of them is gasping, hanging on to life, while the others are still as rocks. My big brother just took out four men on his own. I'm strangely proud of him.

I stand behind the door, the gun still glued to my fingers as I peer through the tiny rectangular window. In the darkness I see three bodies fly past the door, unstopping. As relief sinks in, an amber light shines on the forearm of one of the men. His sleeve has been torn away, revealing an intricate double helix tattoo. I lose my breath for a second before I swing the door open and stumble back into the stairwell. Drake follows.

"Harrison!" I shout in a whisper. He's already turned the corner, descending into the lower level, but stops abruptly when he hears me.

"Guys, hold up!" he calls out to his fellow soldiers. Harrison's dark, shadowy figure climbs back up to meet me. If I hadn't seen the tattoo I wouldn't have recognized him. His onyx hair is cropped super short and no trace remains of his trademark golden stripes.

"Pollen? What the hell? Why are you here?" he shouts, still in a whisper.

"Harrison, it's a long story. Where's Granby?"

"He stayed above ground with the troops. We just released the infinity fly in their greenhouse. Come with us—we're getting out of here."

"Marcus, Glenn and Yoric have been captured."

"Marcus and Yoric, you said?" says the shadowy figure behind Harrison. I lean over to study him, but all I can make out are the whites of his eyes, reflecting the yellow light. It can only be Nicron.

"And Glenn," I correct. I know he's probably the least popular person among this crowd, but I refuse to leave without him.

I'm not sure who the other person is in their group, but he's remaining silent in the back.

"Damn," mumbles Nicron. The three soldiers look at each other and seem to make some sort of silent agreement.

"Harrison, take Kharma and get out of here. I'm going with them." Harrison nods and glances back at me sweetly before he and Kharma shuffle back down the stairs.

"Where are they?" Nicron asks.

Drake steps forward. "This level holds several torture chambers. I'll lead you to the ones I'm familiar with and we'll go from there. You armed?"

Nicron nods and lifts up his semiautomatic rifle.

"Let's go," Drake commands.

I follow Drake to the heap of flesh and watch as he kicks off the still breathing Enforcer's helmet and hammers one more bullet through the eye. My memory flashes back to the attack in the woods, when Glenn did the same thing to the bounty hunter. I shake my head slightly to wipe the vision from my mind.

"Lead the way," I say, as we leap over the newborn corpses. Drake turns back and takes a gun from one of the bodies.

"We'll need more," I say, thinking of the imprisoned men.

"How many?"

"All of them."

Drake takes two, and I slip one into my waistband and hand the other to Nicron. He shakes his head.

"You take it," he whispers.

It's extremely uncomfortable—the hard metal digs into my skin, but I can handle it. It takes my mind off the aching in my belly and it won't be much longer until we find Marcus and the others.

We pass through a series of corridors before Drake begins to slow down and twist around in confusion.

"I can't tell which doors they are. It's too dark."

"Here," I say, handing him the flashlight. My energy is quickly deteriorating, and I know I must leave Crimson soon, before I pass out.

Drake switches on the light, flashing it on the door in front of us. He moves down the corridor to the next door down and then the next, where he halts.

"This is one of them," he says, shining the light on me. His eyes widen and his jaw drops suddenly. "Pollen, you're pregnant? Is that blood?"

I'm slumped against the wall now, almost too weak to stand on my feet. I gaze down at my belly to see the once white sock saturated with blood so dark it could be confused with byrchberry syrup.

"I've got to get you out of here," he cries, bending down to lift me. I dodge out of his grasp, still holding tight to the wall so I don't fall.

"No! We have to get Marcus and Glenn first." Our voices are no longer tiny whispers, but borderline shouting.

"Glenn? You've got to be *fucking* kidding me. Do you know what he did to me?" Drake flashes the light on his bare arms revealing hundreds of round burns like the ones Marcus has. "These are butterfly kisses compared to the other shit he inflicted on me."

"I know what he did, Drake," I mutter. "He told me. Please, just trust me. He's one of us now. We need to rescue him."

Drake shakes his head. "I'll have no part in it. Who's this other guy we're getting? Was he one of them too?"

"No. Marcus is my life. I won't leave without him." Drake studies me skeptically.

"Drake, if it were Ivy in one of these chambers, what would you do?"

Drake looks down deeply in thought. "Okay, let's do this. But if he's not in here I'm not wasting my time or yours looking for him. I'm getting you out of here."

I nod reluctantly.

Drake turns the latch and the door opens. The room appears empty at first. Drake flashes the light in the center of the room, where a metal table, like the one I was strapped on stands upright. Nobody is on it.

Drake pulls me into the room further, but I pause. There's nobody here to rescue. He keeps moving forward without me, and I wonder what is drawing him into the room. He crosses behind the table and shines is light on it, signaling me with his hand to join him.

As I approach, I realize what he was seeing. Somebody is on the table after all. But it is tilted backwards so that his feet are in the air.

"Yoric?"

"Who is that?" he mumbles as if he's just been woken up from a deep sleep.

"Yoric, it's Pollen," I say. Then I turn to Drake. "How do we get him out of this?"

"The controls are over there. I'll see what I can do," Drake says. I try to think back to what Respa did when she released me, but I couldn't see since she was behind me. I hope Drake can figure it out promptly.

After about a minute passes, the restraints pop open and Yoric tumbles on top of me. I try to help him to his feet, but I just don't have the strength.

"Where are Marcus and Glenn?" I ask.

"We got separated," Yoric says, crawling up unsteadily. Drake has returned and grips Yoric under the arms, lifting him up. "Glenn is across the hall, but I don't know where Marcus is." Drake stiffens at Glenn's name.

"Ow, man. Watch it," Yoric gripes, yanking his arm away from Drake. Even in the darkness I can see his face is bruised and bloody. I'm almost too scared to see what Glenn and Marcus look like.

"Let's get them." I weakly stumble toward the door. Drake hooks my arm, stopping me.

"Pollen, no."

I try unsuccessfully to loosen my arm from his grip. "I'm not leaving without them, Drake." He continues to glare down at me. "Are you coming or not?"

"Fine," he says. "But I swear Glenn will not last long after we leave here."

I hold tight to Drake's arm as we cross the corridor. I'm glad I have him to hold on to now—the pain in my belly is sinking into my core, making the simple task of standing as difficult as balancing a high wire.

Yoric opens the door, but Drake just stands there motionless. I seize the flashlight from his other hand and stagger into the chamber. There's no table in this one. In fact, it looks rather medieval. On the wall are various primitive torture devices: whips, canes, and other instruments I can't even begin to identify. Glenn is hanging by his wrists, tied to a thick rope in the center of the room. His toes dangle, just barely scratching the floor. His shirt has been ripped off and lies in shreds circling his feet.

I find it odd that there were no Enforcers in either room. I suppose the guys Drake just killed were meant to be stationed here.

"Glenn," I try to run to him, but my legs turn to liquid and I end up tumbling over, skinning my knee on the cragged surface of the floor.

"Pollen! What the hell are you doing here?" he scolds. The anger in his voice stings. Before I can clamor to my knees, Drake is already hoisting me off the floor.

Yoric circles Glenn, looking at the rope. "Some help here guys?"

"Yeah, right," says Drake. "You're on your own, man. He can rot in here for all I care."

"Drake!" I snap.

"Turn the knob on the panel," Glenn instructs.

Drake shakes his head. "Damn." Drake hangs on to me as he walks to the control panel and turns a large, smooth knob. I watch curiously as the rope lowers, setting Glenn's feet back on the surface. Yoric reaches up, carefully untying the knots.

"Ahh!" Glenn shouts. "Watch the back!"

"Sorry, dude," Yoric responds.

I start to walk toward Glenn, but Drake stops me once again. This time I find the strength to rip my arm away, but I don't have far to go. Glenn runs to me and embraces me before my body begins to plummet once again. He presses his body against me and I wince.

"What's the matter?" he asks, crouching down so that his eyes are level with mine.

"I've been shot."

"What?"

"I'm okay. Let's get Marcus."

"Pollen you're not okay. It's not too dark to see how pale you are. You've got to get out of here."

"Not without Marcus," I cry.

"Yoric and I will get him. You and Drake get out of here. Now."

"No!" I rip myself away from Glenn, finding some reserve energy to keep me upright, albeit staggering. "Nobody is leaving my sight." I pull the guns out of my waistband and shove one into Glenn's hands. I turn to Yoric and hand him the other. "We all stay together!" I demand.

The tone of authority in my voice surprises even myself. Nobody argues with me. My stubbornness becomes me.

The only way to find Marcus now is to check each room. I'm still holding the flashlight but my body is so weak that I can't move fast enough.

"Hey guys," Nicron calls out from the corridor. "We've got company."

As we leave the room, a commotion stirs our attention down the corridor from where we came. Enforcers are pouring down the hall, too many to count in the darkness.

Drake and Nicron toss some metal chairs, carts and tables out into the corridor, creating a makeshift barricade. Glenn pushes me back into the room just before the bullets begin to fly. But I'm not about to give up now. With Drake's expert aim, I trust that I am in safe hands.

Drake, Nicron, Glenn, and Yoric duck behind the barricade, shooting between the empty gaps. I dart out into the corridor behind the guys, crouching down to avoid any stray bullets. I hold on to the wall as I descend further down the corridor. When I reach the next room I open the door and duck inside. I scan the room thoroughly with my flashlight, but it is empty.

I dash across the corridor, collapsing on to the door as I open it and slink inside. The shootout has wound down and I'm scared to look back for fear that someone didn't make it. Or to see if Drake turned his gun on Glenn. *Oh, please, no.* My breath is heavy and uneven. The room starts to spin and I feel like I could pass out at any second. I switch on the flashlight.

There, in the center of the room is Marcus, lying flat on an examination table. I can't tell if he is awake or not because his head is in a vise and he's not moving.

"Marcus?"

Chapter 29

"POLLEN?" His whisper floats through the air, sounding like a serenade to my ears.

I shuffle to him, grasping my wound, imagining that my holding it will make it stop hurting. It doesn't.

As I approach, I tilt the flashlight up toward the ceiling, away from his face so I don't blind him, and so he can see me.

"Marcus!" I gasp, falling onto him. But it's not just my happiness to see him that draws me to him—my legs have given out under me. If the table hadn't been here, I'd have fallen flat on my face again.

My cheek rests against Marcus's bare chest; his shirt has also been removed. Warm moisture glides between our touching skin and I realize I'm crying.

"What are you doing here?" he asks, agitated.

"She's in here!" Yoric cries out behind me. I hear a shuffle of footsteps, but can't bring myself to pull away from Marcus.

"Pollen!" A wave of relief washes over me when I hear Glenn's voice. Drake hasn't killed him. . . yet.

"I need the light," Drake calls out. Glenn takes the flashlight from my hand and flashes it over Marcus and me.

"Damn, Marcus," Glenn whispers. I pull my head back to see what he is looking at. The warm liquid I felt wasn't my tears. It was blood. A pattern of red slices decorates Marcus's abdomen and chest. On the other side of the table is a tray with an assortment of sharp instruments: scalpels, pokers, wire cutters, and a vast collection of knives.

Tears gush out of my eyes at the sight of him.

"Don't," he says. "I'm fine."

Nicron joins us across the table, straining to open Marcus's impenetrable restraints.

"Hold on, Marcus, we're gonna get you out of here," Nicron says.

"Light!" Drake yells, exasperated. Glenn tosses the flashlight across the room, where I assume Drake catches it quietly. A few seconds later, Marcus's restraints are released.

I push myself off of Marcus to allow him get up, but my legs still aren't quite working and I slide down. Glenn catches me just before I hit the floor and lifts me into his arms.

The tension in the room has multiplied tenfold—a triangle of anger and jealousy with me in the center. Just like the mark of the Trinity. For once, I'm glad it's Glenn who is carrying me, and not Marcus. While I want nothing more than to be in Marcus's arms, to assure me everything is okay between us, Glenn's holding me ensures his safety. Drake won't attack Glenn while I'm so close to him. Not yet anyway.

"She's shot," Glenn announces when Marcus raises his eyebrows.

"Give her to me," Drake shouts, pushing his way to us.

"No!" I object, glaring at Drake, and he stops in his tracks.

"Who's this?" Marcus demands.

"Drake," Glenn responds tersely.

"I'm her brother," Drake barks.

"Her dead brother?" My eyes meet Marcus's confused expression and I nod gently.

"Drake, lead us back down to solitary. We need to get to the Web," I mumble.

"We can't," Glenn interrupts. "The reserve power keeps the door activated. We can't get out without an Enforcer's ID."

"I launched the system override. We can get out. We have to hurry." Glenn gazes down into my eyes with an appreciation I've never before seen from him. I'm not the completely helpless waif he's always viewed me as. The corners of his lips curve up.

Before we leave, Glenn circles the table and sets me down on it while he swipes two knives: a large serrated one and a small scalpel. He crams them into his pocket and lifts me again.

"What are those for?" I ask.

"Just in case," he answers.

Drake tosses his spare gun to Marcus and leads us down the dark corridors, dodging the heaps of dead bodies, back to the stairwell. Glenn continues to carry me and I don't argue. I can feel myself on the verge of losing consciousness.

Suddenly, we are back in the gloomy grid of the solitary level. Glenn and I lead the way through the labyrinth since he is the only one who knows how to navigate it.

As I drift in and out of consciousness I feel the shuffle of footsteps beneath me. I can't tell how fast we're going, but it seems to last an eternity. My arms tighten around Glenn's neck and I nuzzle his sweat-laced chest with my cheek. But when I look up at him again I see Marcus. *Who is carrying me?* I must be hallucinating. I inhale the scent, which is salty and musky like Glenn. But his muscled frame is carved and sculpted like Marcus. Glenn or Marcus. That is the ultimate question. Which do I love? Can I love both of them equally? *Do I have a choice?*

I can hear faint whispers of a conversation going on behind us.

"What is she doing here?"

"She wasn't with you guys?".

"No, of course not!"

"Where're the others?"

"I don't know. We completed our objective and were on our way out when she found us."

Suddenly the overhead lights buzz on and I'm jolted into consciousness. Glenn stops dead in his tracks. I glance up at his bruised face. His eyes widen in terrifying awareness. But he doesn't need to tell me anything. I know exactly what he is thinking. The power is back on, which means the door to the Web is secure. We can't get out this way.

Glenn turns back to the others, and for the first time I can really see Drake. His skin is paler than mine, his cheeks and occipital cavities are deeply sunk. Put a set of fangs in his mouth and he'd pass for a classic horror film vampire. The sight of Marcus, with his broken, bloody chest, continues to scratch at my broken heart. At least they left his face alone, I think, trying to placate myself.

Marcus's eyes meet mine and neither of us can seem to pull them apart. The connection is too deep. I can see it now. The love is still there. He can't fight it much longer. But the pain is just as deep. It's killing him to see me in Glenn's arms.

"Glenn, can we still get out?" Yoric asks, breathless.

"Not without an Enforcer's handprint and retinal ID. We'll have to find another way."

"How did you guys get in?" Drake cuts in. "We'll go that way."

"Impossible," Glenn says, deep in thought.

"We came in through a secret adjacent facility—where they are building the shuttle. They've already sent a battalion there to cover the location."

Drake looks confused at the discussion of a shuttle, but doesn't waste time asking unnecessary questions.

"So how do we get out?"

"We'll have to go above ground and fight our way out—"

An echo of heavy stomping and angry voices interrupts the discussion. Glenn dashes with me to the next intersection and we duck behind the corner with Drake following us. Yoric, Nicron, and Marcus settle in the opposite corner across the corridor. A twinge of pain vibrates through me as Glenn gently sets me down on the icy stone floor, pinned between him and Drake.

"Don't move," he says, then he stands up with his back against the wall, in deep concentration. His head nods almost imperceptibly in a steady rhythm and then I realize he's counting. He looks over to others across the corridor, holding up ten of his fingers, and then two. They nod and ready their guns.

I pull my own gun from my holster. The magazine still has three bullets left. I know they won't let me fight, but I keep it in hand, just in case.

The commotion draws nearer and Glenn's eye bulges out of its socket.

"They're spreading," he whispers to Drake. Drake nods and takes his place, standing against the wall on the other side of me. The Enforcers will be coming at us from all directions. This is bad. Yoric and Marcus watch Glenn intently as he points down each corridor. Yoric positions himself as Drake does, turning his back to us and staring down the corridor. Nicron stands against the opposite wall, ready for an attack from behind.

Glenn turns and carefully inches his face out, peering down the corridor. The first shots ring out and he pulls back violently. Taking a deep breath he swings his gun out into the corridor, shoots quickly, and draws back in one swift move. Marcus does the same across the corridor, staying low to the ground as he does.

I'm startled when I hear the shot ring out right by my ear and I turn around to see the body of an Enforcer that Drake just shot lying in a pool of blood.

Shots continue to resonate behind me and I turn back toward Marcus. He was right to deny me the opportunity to join the militia. I never could have done this. Not because I'm scared for myself; I can handle the idea of dying. And I've already been shot so that can't scare me anymore either. No, I can't bear the thought of watching my love die. It's too much. My fear of losing Marcus or Glenn incapacitates me and I'd be useless on the battlefield.

Beyond Yoric and Marcus, in the next intersection, an Enforcer pulls out and fires his weapon. I flinch. He misses and Yoric returns fire, missing as well. Marcus looks down at his gun angrily, pulling out the empty magazine.

"Marcus!" I shout. As he looks up at me I slide my gun across the floor to him. His lip draws up slightly at the corner and he nods to me. Yoric turns back toward me, distracted.

A shot rings out again and I gasp in horror as Yoric falls to the floor. Marcus is oblivious, his attention still turned toward the main corridor, shooting at some unseen Enforcer. Behind me, Drake is shooting again at someone else.

A yelp turns my frightened attention back toward the opposite corridor and I see Nicron fall, grasping his thigh, his face wrinkled in pain.

The Enforcer who shot Yoric and Nicron steps out into the corridor with a clear shot to Marcus.

"Marcus! Get down!" I shout. A spark has ignited inside me. My fear of losing Marcus has strengthened some unknown part of me and my protective instincts kick in. My weakness dissipates, as a second wind takes over.

I one nimble move, I rip my holster from my leg, load two magnets from my pocket into the sling and release it. The magnets fly over Marcus's head, striking the Enforcer in the kneecap. He drops to the floor. Marcus turns to shoot, but he's out of bullets again. I reload my sling and shoot again, aiming at the arm holding the gun. It drops to the floor with a *clank* and as he leans forward his helmet topples off his head. Once more I aim my shot between his eyes. His head hits the floor with a thud. He's still conscious, but stunned.

The labyrinth is eerily quiet. The shooting has ceased. Glenn steps out into the corridor cautiously checking all directions and counting the bodies on the floor.

"We're clear," he says. Drake and Glenn run over to the fallen Enforcer. Drake aims his gun, but Glenn stops him.

He points his thumb to his eye patch and says sadistically, "An eye for an eye." Glenn slides the two knives from the torture chamber out of his belt. I can't watch the gruesome scene, knowing exactly what he plans to do. I try to block out the high-pitched screams reverberating through the endless maze. The sight of Yoric helps to erase my sympathy for that monster.

Marcus and I hover over Yoric. Blood gushes from the gaping, gurgling wound in his neck. He's conscious, but just barely. His body quivers in an effort to hang on to those last few seconds of his life. I sob quietly as I realize he won't make it. He can't speak, but just before he closes his eyes for the final time, he looks deeply into mine and I know what he's thinking. He's thinking about Timber. He wants me to tell her that he loves her. His eyes close and peace blankets his lifeless body.

I fall into Marcus's waiting arms. He winces as I press against his broken chest, but does not push me away. In fact, he pulls me in tighter. My salty tears drip down his skin, leaking into his wounds, but he is not bothered by the pain. He presses his velvet lips to my ear.

"I'm so sorry, baby," he whispers, squeezing me into his embrace. I feel moisture running down my neck and I realize he is sobbing too. "I love you,

Pollen. I'm so sorry." Suddenly I know. He does still love me. I don't know if it is Yoric's death, his experience in the torture chamber, or seeing me here like this, but something in this moment has touched him, changed him. I haven't lost him after all.

Chapter 30

I WISH THE WORLD around us would just disappear and Marcus and I could remain like this forever, embraced in each other's arms, our hearts beating rhythmically in time. My heart feels like it has outgrown its cavity, stretching the ribs out and swelling through the cracks. Tears of sadness for Yoric intermingle with tears of joy. This is where I belong.

"Don't worry about me, guys. I'll be fine," Nicron says as he leans his back against the opposite wall, staring at us with just a hint of a smile on his full lips. I turn back to Marcus, nuzzling him so deeply I hope my flesh would just sink into his and we would become one being.

"You okay, man?" I hear Marcus's muffled voice through the depth of the skin and muscle in his chest.

"It's just my leg. I'll manage." Nicron huffs as he struggles to his feet.

"We need to go. Now," Glenn announces. I don't want to let go of Marcus, and his grasp on me remains firm.

"I'll get her," Marcus says. I don't know if he was speaking to Glenn or Drake, because I won't even look up. My head is still buried in Marcus's chest when he lifts me off the floor and jogs after the others. Every now and then, it goes dark, and then the light appears again. I'm too incoherent to understand if it's the lighting, or if I'm drifting in and out of consciousness again. I don't care what happens now. I don't even care if I die. At least I'll die happy in Marcus's arms.

We come to a halt, and I look up to see what is going on. The ominous steel door to the Web stands before us. Glenn holds some small glistening object in his left hand. In his right hand is a severed hand, caked with gooey blood. A small chunk of ivory bone protrudes where the wrist should be. He holds it up to the scanner. It flashes green then he holds up the object in his other hand to the retinal scanner. It is the eye of the Enforcer. The Enforcer he chose *not* to kill. His bloodcurdling screams still resonate in my head. I'll be having nightmares for years to come about this day.

Glenn drops the severed body parts and wrenches the door open, allowing us to enter the formidable darkness. I allow my eyelids to fall shut again. I'm so sleepy. My arms dangle loosely around Marcus's neck, but they will fall soon, too. I don't know how much longer I can hang on. I'm so tired. Before I lose total consciousness I feel a strange sensation in my belly—not the deep penetrating pain that has been plaguing me for the last hour. No, something just under my skin, the most exquisite sensation I could possibly feel right now. I think the baby just kicked.

I awaken quietly to the gentle beeping of a heart monitor in a tiny room warmly lit with a large table lamp. It takes me a moment to realize I'm in the medical clinic at Ceborec. I'm so used to the intense overhead lights and brightly colored walls of the examination rooms that my location confuses me. This must be a room reserved for the comatose. It certainly is a welcome atmosphere to wake up to.

I flinch as I attempt to sit up. Pain shoots through the left side of my abdomen and back toward my spine. I lift up the light blue blanket covering my disrobed body and gather the cotton hospital gown in my hand until it pulls up over my belly. The heart monitor attached to my left index finger gets tangled in the gown and I have to use my right hand alone to hold the gown in place. My wound is neatly bandaged and another heart monitor is strapped snuggly to the apex of my belly. I fall back on to the pillow and exhale a sigh of relief, despite the pain. The baby is fine. He made it.

The door opens silently and a nurse, Orla, comes in to check my vitals. She moves around the room silently, checking monitors and taking notes on her clipboard.

"Where's Timber?" I ask. My voice sounds raspy, not quite catching in my throat. There's a long pause and I wonder if she even heard me speak.

"Timber's not working today," the nurse finally replies without looking up.

I assume she's already heard about Yoric. Ugh. I really wanted to be the one to tell her. After all, it was kind of my fault he got shot. If I hadn't shouted at Marcus and distracted him, maybe he'd still be here. Timber must be absolutely devastated. She's had my back so many times and now I can't even be there to comfort her. At least she's got a lot of friends here. I'm sure someone has lent her their shoulder to cry on.

The nurse departs almost as quickly as she came in. A few seconds later, there's a knock at the door.

"Come in," I say. I'm sure it's Glenn, coming to check on me. But I'm surprised to see Marcus step in. I guess over the past few months I'd always associated a knock at the door with Glenn, since he came by so often. I flush as the heart monitor displays my increasingly rapid heart rate.

"How are you feeling?" he asks softly, almost in a whisper. His face looks blank. I can't interpret what he's thinking, and that makes my heart race even faster. His eyes seem to be wearing a mask to hide whatever emotion lies beyond them.

"I'm good," I whisper.

Marcus rolls the doctor's stool over to the bed to sit next to me. My heartbeat feels incredibly thick and pushes hard against my sternum, almost painfully. I can feel it rising into my throat with each pulse.

Marcus exhales deeply as he combs his hands through my hair. I've missed his touch. I want to close my eyes and wallow in this feeling. But I've gone so long without him; I don't want to tear him from my sight. His eyes look tired, and sad.

"Pollen, how did you end up at Crimson?"

I explain everything I remember about my abduction while Marcus listens intently. "I saw them. The Trinity. They took some amniotic fluid to test the baby's DNA." Marcus's eyes light up in shock.

"Wait, they were *there*?"

"Well, no, not really. It was like a videoconference. I think they're still down in the bunkers. Marcus they have it out for me. I don't know if it's because I escaped or because of the baby or Evie, but there's a huge bounty on my head now. They're determined to find and detain me."

"How did you get out?"

"Remember Respa?" Marcus nods. "She's an Enforcer now. She found me and set me free. I was on my way to find Drake when I saw you guys being captured." Marcus looks down painfully.

"You should have just left."

"No," I say squeezing his hand in mine. "I wasn't going to leave without you. I'd rather have died."

"Pollen . . . I've been a jerk," he sighs. "I should never have abandoned you like that, after the wedding. I'm really, really sorry."

"You didn't do anything wrong Marcus. I did. I deserved it."

"What you did was abhorrent," he snaps and I wince at his harsh words. But his face melts almost instantly and my tension eases. "But I could have reacted differently. I should have given you the opportunity to explain. Perhaps I would have if it didn't come out the way it did, and if you hadn't lied to me. We should have talked it out. But, in that moment, I was just so angry, so swept up in what happened with *her*, with Siera, I couldn't see any other resolution than to just cut you out of my life. But now I realize I can't do that.

"I went out of my way to stay away from you. To avoid you at all costs. But every time I saw your face, it was like my ribs were collapsing and the pain was unbearable. Not for what you did to me, but for how I felt for you. I couldn't escape it. When I saw you there, bleeding, losing your life with every second that passed, I realized I couldn't live without you. I don't want to live without you. I want us to have a second chance."

"You're not angry with me anymore?" I ask, not really believing what I'm hearing.

"I forgive you, Pollen. But I won't ever be able to forget what you did. Not with this little one coming." Marcus rests his palm on my belly.

"Glenn will be in our lives. Every day."

"I know." Marcus takes another deep breath. "Glenn and I discussed what happened. He explained everything to me; that you were shaken up, drunk, and didn't even know what was going on. He said that you thought he was me. You were calling him Marcus."

I was? I don't remember that, but then, I've tried so hard to block out all memories from that day. I'm sure Glenn was just trying to make amends. He knows that I'll never feel the intense love for him that I share with Marcus.

"Glenn is a good guy. I can see that now. I want him to be involved with the child—if it is his."

"If?"

"There's still a chance—a one in a million chance—but there's still a chance he could be mine."

I can't hide the smile that creeps into my lips. Marcus bends over and kisses me chastely, barely brushing his velvety lips over mine.

A moment of silence drifts between us. As much as I want to revel in this moment of reconciliation, I'm curious about the events that I missed as we left Crimson.

"Marcus, what happened? After we got out?"

Marcus leans over, crossing his arms on the edge of my hospital bed.

"We traveled the Web for a while. Drake and Glenn got into a scuffle. I'm sure you can imagine what that was about. Drake broke Glenn's nose before I was able to break them up." Marcus pauses for a few seconds. He's deciding whether or not to tell me something.

"What else?" I ask, catching his eyes in mine.

"I kind of got into a fight with Glenn too. But it's not what you think."

"What happened?"

"It doesn't matter."

"It does to me."

Marcus stands up and paces the tiny room, taking only three strides each way before turning.

"No, it's not important."

"Marcus, I can tell it's eating at you. Please just tell me."

He stops and turns away from me. "I wanted to go back—above ground. I wanted the memories gone. I thought it would be easier for me to rekindle things with you if I didn't know what happened. That's when Glenn stopped me and told me everything. He said that I would just make it harder on us if I did it. That the memories would come back anyway and we'd have to start all over."

"I'm glad he stopped you."

"I don't know, Pollen. It's going to be hard. For both of us. Especially with Glenn still in our lives. I don't know if I can trust you like before."

"I'll just have to earn it," I say optimistically. "And I will. I promise. Marcus, I never stopped loving you. And I never will."

"That makes two of us," Marcus smiles. He leans over me, cradling my cheeks in his hands and lowers his lips to mine. The heart monitor picks up the pace as he deepens the kiss with intense fury. He only pulls away when he pushes against my wound, causing me to recoil.

"Sorry," he says.

"Don't be." I smile. The pain is sweet coming from him.

"Where's Drake?" I ask after a minute.

"He's getting settled in. Granby's taken a keen interest in your brother. I think he's going to be an officer."

"He'll be the best," I utter, recalling his expertise at Crimson.

"Speaking of Granby," Marcus says, "I think he'll be coming to pay you a visit soon."

"Why?"

"You'll see soon enough," Marcus says with a sly smile. "I have to go. I'll see you soon." He begins toward the door.

"Please stay. Don't leave me, Marcus."

Marcus returns to sit by me again. He brushes my hair back and kisses me on the forehead. "I'll be right back. Get some rest."

Rest? Ha! Like I haven't gotten enough rest as it is. I lie on the bed bored out of my mind for what feels like hours, although it's probably only been about thirty minutes. I'm ready to get out of here and go home. The thought of restarting my life with

Marcus and Evie again sends pleasant shockwaves up my spine. No, I can't wait any longer. I yank the heart monitor off my belly. That's sure to get someone's attention.

As suspected, the nurse bursts through the door in a panic. I'm already sitting up on the edge the bed with my legs dangling over the side. The nurse gapes at me, looks over at the device on the table, and then sternly looks back, shooting toxic arrows into me.

"Miss McRae, you need to keep that on so we can monitor the baby's heart rate. If you need something the call button is right—"

"My baby's fine. I'm ready to go home now. Where are my clothes?"

"You'll have to wait for Dr. Yipolis to give you his approval to leave."

We both remain in our positions for at least a minute, having a thick-as-sludge stare-off. Finally, the nurse backs up to the door, disgruntled.

"I'll call him and have him see you right away," she says solemnly. "Will you please wear the monitor until he gets here?"

"Okay," I shrug, lying back down. The nurse replaces the monitor, adjusting it by millimeters until it hits the right spot.

And the waiting continues. The imaginary ticking clock in my head counts down the seconds with painstaking clarity. About ten minutes later I'm relieved to hear a gentle knock at the door.

"Come in," I call. Once again, my visitor is not who I expected.

"Hello, Miss McRae. I hope I'm not disturbing you," says General Granby. He closes the door and stands in front of it, reluctant to come much closer to me. Why is everyone treating me like some fragile porcelain doll?

"General Granby," I address.

"I'm happy to see that you and the baby survived and made it back in one piece. But I'm still a little confused about how you ended up at Crimson. Could you fill me in?"

"Of course," I say, "if you sit down. I motion him to the stool that Marcus had pulled to the bed. Granby rolls the stool back a few feet then sits, leaning forward with his elbows resting on his knees.

I explain everything that happened, from the day I went above ground to train and was kidnapped, all the way until the moment I passed out in Marcus's arms. Granby sat like a statue for most of the time, only moving once to rub his brow after I described how I was shot.

"Miss McRae, you astound me. Your courage and tenacity is beyond what I would expect from a woman your age who has never received any military training."

"I was just trying to survive," I murmur humbly.

"But you did more than just survive. You rescued three of our men."

"But only two survived."

Granby lowers his head. "Yes, it's a shame what happened to Yoric. But you did rescue him, nonetheless. And you rescued your own brother from part of the prison I thought impenetrable without a full-scale attack. And not only did you steal the plans for the shuttle, we now have more information on Crimson and the Trinity than we could have ever hoped for. Pollen, you went above and beyond the call of duty for any soldier in our militia. If you'd still like to join, after you've had your baby of course, I'd like to award you an honorary advisory role in the militia."

Advisory role? Me? A twenty-one year old girl from Endmore? This is insane. Are they that hard up for good leadership?

"I don't think I'd qualify for such a prestigious position," I grimace.

"Miss McRae, the vast majority of our soldiers are just like you, with no background in military service. In fact most of them have never even handled a firearm before coming here. Since the virus took out so many people, and most of those with any substantial military experience sided with Crimson, we have had to rebuild our military from the ground up.

"I know it sounds completely absurd, but Pollen, you've escaped Crimson three times. Either you've got some excellent strategic ideas in that hard head of yours or you're extremely lucky. We sure could use that kind of luck on our squads."

He really is serious. There's no way I could, even if I wanted to. I can't handle that kind of responsibility, having such a profound effect on the lives of the others. No I can't do it, not with my little boy on the way. Not after Marcus revealed that he wants to patch things up and be a family again. No. I can't jeopardize that.

"I'm honored, sir. But I don't want to join the militia anymore. Especially after I've become a mother. I've seen more death than I can handle and I want to be with my son and protect him."

"Of course," says Granby despondently. He smiles, but his eyes still show strains of sadness. "Perhaps we could find another way to honor what you've done for us."

"That won't be necessary. But thank you."

Another knock at the door interrupts our conversation. Granby stands up and pushes the stool to the side.

"I'd best be on my way. I pray for your safe recovery."

"Thank you."

Granby opens the door and Marcus is standing there, a very concerned expression blankets his face, but he does not come in. As Granby steps out, Marcus begins to shut the door, but not completely and I can hear them whispering among themselves.

"Did you tell her?"

". . . not the best time."

"She won't . . ."

". . . can't find out yet."

The whispering continues, but I can't make sense of any of it. *Are they talking about me?*

Finally Marcus returns to the room and shuts the door behind him. There's a strange emotion radiating from his eyes. One I don't recall ever seeing before. Fear. Heart-pounding, knee-shaking fear.

"What was all that about?" I ask.

"Nothing. Pollen, I really think you ought to stay here for a little longer."

"No. I want to go home," I demand.

"A few more nights. Just to make sure the baby is okay."

"The baby is fine. I can even feel him kicking now. I'm fine. I just want to sleep in my own bed."

"Please, Pollen?" Marcus squats down, leaning his arms and chin on the bed. There's something deeper in his eyes that terrifies me. Like he's trying to hide some awful truth to protect me.

"Marcus, what's really going on?" My senses scream at me that I'm right. He's holding something back.

"I told you, nothing. I just want you to be well."

"Don't lie to me Marcus. I know something is up. Why won't you tell me?"

"Okay, something happened, but it's nothing you need to worry about right now."

"Tell me!" I shout. My heart monitor starts beeping wildly as my fury increases. Marcus combs both his hands through the shortened hair he cut off weeks ago. He's really nervous. I haven't seen him like this before. It's really scaring me.

"Okay! Okay," he tries to calm me down. But before he can say anything, another knock interrupts us.

"No, don't," I urge as Marcus reaches for the door. He looks relieved at the distraction.

Dr. Yipolis enters, holding a folder, and smiles as he greets me.

"Miss McRae, Orla has informed me that you have a desire to continue your recovery at home?"

"Yes, I'd like to go home."

"But I think she should stay," Marcus interjects. I glower at him, and he stiffens, glaring back.

Dr. Yipolis looks from me to Marcus, Marcus to me, with raised eyebrows. He can evidently feel the taut rope of thickened tension between us.

"Well," he says, glancing down at the chart in his grasp, "it looks like the baby is healthy. Your vitals are within normal range. I don't see any reason you have to stay here if you don't want to. You'll just need to get plenty of rest and follow instructions on changing your dressing daily."

Marcus's shoulders slump and he shakes his head, glaring down at the floor now.

"I'll send Orla in to remove the catheter and IV. Then you're free to go."

"Thank you doctor," I say smugly.

"Take care of yourself Miss McRae," the kind doctor says as he leaves the room.

Marcus turns around and places his hands on the counter against the adjacent wall, leaning in and drooping his head.

"Now will you tell me?" I demand.

Marcus remains silent for a minute while I wait impatiently for his response.

"Pollen, don't freak out, okay?"

This is really not good. The tension has just increased tenfold. I can't find the voice to answer him.

Marcus turns around and approaches me. He lifts my hand and folds it between his.

"It's about Evie."

"What about Evie?" I demand, ripping my hand from his.

"She's gone."

"Gone?" I sit up, ignoring the shooting pain and the fetal jabs. I swing my feet around to face Marcus. He steps back.

"They took her."

"Who?" I'm on my feet now, struggling to hold myself up as my legs are a pair of wet noodles beneath me. As soon as they stiffen enough to hold me up, I yank the monitor off my belly and rip the IV needle from my arm.

"The Trinity."

Epilogue

(Marcus)

Oh god I hope she makes it.

My mind flashes back to that fateful day we finally escaped this wretched purgatory. We were so happy then. We were a team. Now look at us. Broken and mangled and at death's doorstep.

How could I let this happen? *Stay with me, Pollen.* She lies lifelessly in my arms as I chase after Glenn and Drake in the abysmal tunnels of the Web. *Drake?* I thought he was dead. How is he alive? I can't make sense of anything anymore.

I thought I was done with Pollen. What she did drove a stake into my heart that I've spent months trying to rip out, but it won't budge. And yet, I'm still hopelessly in love with her. I can't deny it anymore. Especially now that I am on the verge of losing her.

Just behind me, Glenn is acting as a crutch for Nicron. Damn, I hope his injury is not too bad. He's just the type to play off a fatal blow as simply a flesh wound. Like that time we were in the sparring arena and I used too much force with the staff. He limped out of there, laughing it off as a sprain. He ended up with a greenstick fracture of his tibia and had to sit out for the next three weeks while it healed.

Ahead of me Drake is approaching the first intersection out of Crimson. I want to talk to him, but what the hell do I say? Why the hell aren't you dead? How could you leave your daughter behind while you played superhero? And why the hell didn't you get Pollen out of there sooner? *Yeah, Marcus, can you come up with any more hostile questions to welcome him home after being chained up like a scrappy dog for a year and a half?*

"Where are we going?" Drake asks as he approaches the intersection with heavy footsteps. The look of him freaks me out. He looks nothing like

Pollen, like how I'd imagined him. His face is gaunt and ghost-like. His body is nothing but skin and bones covered in threadbare scraps.

"Go left," I say. My voice sounds stale and fatigued, but the adrenaline rush of having Pollen falling away in my arms keeps me moving. "It's about ten miles to the open bunker we used to get down here." Drake nods and leads the way.

"So, you and my sister…" Drake starts, but his voice trails off.

"We met at Crimson," I say, finishing his sentence with my own words. "We've been together since then. Well mostly, anyway."

"Mostly?"

"We were going to get married. But I found out that she and dickwad here got a little frisky in Granby's office. The baby's his." I nod my head back at Glenn and Drake stops abruptly. He turns around and charges Glenn, taking us all by surprise.

Nicron ducks out of the way when he sees Drake coming and hobbles over by a wall.

The first few punches go by unobstructed. Even though Granby insisted that we work out our grievances, it feels sublime to stand back and watch Glenn take a beating. The only thing that would feel better right now is if I were the one throwing the punches. Even Nicron stands back and smirks at the scene. But after the last punch induces a lurid crunch, Nicron attempts to step in between the two. His efforts have little to show since Drake nudges him out of the way easily and his leg gives out. Finally, I lay Pollen down on the floor, gently as if I'm carrying a tray full of antique glassware, and grab Drake from behind, halting the bashfest.

Glenn stumbles and falls back, resting on the floor. In the dim yellow lights of the Web I can see a goatee of glistening blood dripping down his face.

"You're dead!" Drake shouts at him, as he continues to struggle against my arms.

"Take it easy, man," I say.

"You have no idea what he's capable of," Drake growls.

"Yes, I do."

Drake ruffles up his netlike sleeves and shows me his arms, disfigured and mangled from months of torture. I've got nothing on him. I was only tortured for a few hours. I don't know how Drake could have survived.

"I could shoot him right now, but that wouldn't bring me peace. No. I need to see him suffer. And from the sound of it, you do too."

"Glenn and I are at opposite ends of the spectrum, and yes, I did enjoy watching you beat the shit out of him. But we need to take him back to Ceborec. We'll deal with it there."

Drake glances back at Glenn disdainfully, then begrudgingly nods. Nicron is back on his feet and helps Glenn up. The two hang on to each other as they stumble through the tunnel behind us. Just as gently as I set her down, I retrieve Pollen and continue on our course.

Drake looks nervously at Pollen. I can see he wants to take her himself, but I can't bring myself to hand her over to someone who looks so weak. Or maybe I'm just afraid to let go of her. If she dies, I want to spend every last second with her before she goes.

How do I do this? How can I reconcile what she did to me with the irrevocable love I feel for her. Can I ever forgive her? Can I ever forget?

Forget. *Yes, I can forget.* There is a way—a way to lose these past few months that have tormented my soul. A way to forget the pain she caused me, the ultimate betrayal, so we can move on. Yes, I have to do this.

When we reach the intersection at Holly Springs, we turn left to proceed on our path. At the first bunker door we pass, I stop.

"Drake," I say. He spins around. "Can you take her?" He nods and I painfully relinquish my hold on Pollen, delivering her carefully into his arms.

"Nicron, you still got any explosives?" He eyes me warily as he and Glenn hobble toward us.

"Yeah, man, but we're still way too close to Crimson to go up now."

"You won't be going up," I announce. "I will. You guys keep going until you reach the bunker we used to get here. Don't worry, I'll make it back to Ceborec with the other troops."

"What the hell are you doing, Marcus?" Glenn steps forward into the glow of the yellow emergency light. His nose is puffed up on both sides giving him a slight extraterrestrial appearance. The gushing blood from his nose has slowed to a dripping stream over his upper lip.

"I'm going up."

"No you're not," Glenn says as he snatches the small explosive device from Nicron's hand. I lunge forward to grab it, but he ducks away and shoves it into his back pocket.

"Damnit Glenn! Hand it over." My shouts roar down the walls of the tunnels.

"No."

I lunge forward again, clamping my fists around his neck and hurl him back into the wall.

"Don't do it man," Glenn murmurs. "It won't work." For once, Glenn actually looks human to me. There's actually some semblance of emotion in his eye.

My grip loosens.

"I need to forget."

"Marcus, you'll forget about it for a while. But the memories will come back eventually, like they did before. You know that."

I pull away from Glenn as awareness sinks in. He's right. Sure I'll forget about Pollen's betrayal and all the pain I've been through. But, for how long? And what happens when it comes back? Will the past few months become some washed up summer rerun destined to be relived?

"Marcus, I've loved Pollen more than I've loved anyone else in the world. It kills me to see her with you. But she doesn't feel that way about me. The way she feels about you." *Am I really hearing this?* From that jerk that knocked her up. Is this the same guy that put out cigarettes in my arm and lashed my back making it look like a map of the Web?

"But she slept with you," I grumble.

"Do you really think she would make the conscious decision to sleep with me after all the shit I did?" I remain silent.

"Damn, Marcus. You really are obtuse. She was drunk. She was practically apoplectic after the attack that day. I gave her some liquor to settle her nerves. We both drank way too much. I took advantage of her, yes. But she didn't know what was going on. She thought I was you. She said your name over and over again. In her mind it wasn't me she was sleeping with. It was you."

Deep inside my chest, there's a sensation I can't quite explain. It stings, but in a good way—like the burn of peroxide on a wound and the knowledge that despite the pain, it will clean the wound and expedite the healing process. *I can do this.* I can still love Pollen. I'll find a way to get over what she did. Somehow.

END OF PART 2

Acknowledgments

First of all, I want to thank my family for all the support and advice they've given me, especially Walton Meredith. It was his fruitful belief in my talents that drove me to continue writing. Thank you to all my beta readers for the feedback and encouragement. They all kept my spirits high and my motivational motor running. Finally, I have to thank my wonderful editor, Ayla Page, for finding the errors that evaded me. Her knack for grammar made this book complete.

Fall of Venus series

Part 1: Fall of Venus

Part 2: Crimson Return

Part 3: The Trinity

Autumn 2013

Made in the USA
Las Vegas, NV
28 October 2024